THE KIND
WORTH SAVING

ALSO BY PETER SWANSON

Nine Lives

Every Vow You Break

Eight Perfect Murders

Before She Knew Him

All the Beautiful Lies

Her Every Fear

The Kind Worth Killing

The Girl with a Clock for a Heart

THE KIND WORTH SAVING

A Novel

PETER SWANSON

WILLIAM MORROW
An Imprint of HarperCollins*Publishers*

HarperCollins books may be purchased for educational, business, or sales promotional use. For information, please email the Special Markets Department at SPsales@harpercollins.com.

FIRST EDITION

Designed by Kyle O'Brien
Title Page Art by Mongkolchon Akesin © Shutterstock, Inc.
Section Opener Art by Ana L. Garcia © Shutterstock, Inc.

Library of Congress Cataloging-in-Publication Data has been applied for.

ISBN 978-0-06-320498-0 (Hardcover)
ISBN 978-0-06-330850-3 (International Trade Paperback)

22 23 24 25 26 LBC 5 4 3 2 1

To David Highfill

THE KIND
WORTH SAVING

PART 1

THE TENDER AGE OF MURDERERS

CHAPTER 1

KIMBALL

"Do you remember me?" she asked, after stepping into my office.

"I do," I said, before I could actually place her. But she *was* familiar, and for a terrible moment I wondered if she was a cousin of mine, or a long-ago girlfriend I'd entirely forgotten.

She took a step inside the room. She was short and built like an ex-gymnast, with wide shoulders and strong-looking legs. Her face was a circle, her features—blue eyes, pert nose, round mouth—bunched into the middle. She wore dark jeans and a tweedy brown blazer, which made her look as though she'd just dismounted a horse. Her shoulder-length hair was black and glossy and parted on one side. "Senior honors English," she said.

"Joan," I said, as though the name had just come to me, but of course she'd made this appointment, and given me her name.

"I'm Joan Whalen now, but I was Joan Grieve when you were my teacher."

"Yes, Joan Grieve," I said. "Of course, I remember you."

"And you're Mr. Kimball," she said, smiling for the first time since she'd entered the room, showing a row of tiny teeth, and that was when I truly remembered her. She *had* been a gymnast, a popular, flirtatious, above-average student, who'd always made me vaguely uncomfortable, just by the way she'd said my name, as though she had something on me. She was making me vaguely uncomfortable, now, as well. My time as a teacher at Dartford-Middleham High School was a time I was happy to forget.

"You can call me Henry," I said.

"You don't seem like a Henry to me. You still seem like a Mr. Kimball."

"I don't think anyone has called me Mr. Kimball since the day I left that job. Did you know who I was when you made this appointment?"

"I didn't know, but I guess I assumed. I knew that you'd been a police officer, and then I heard about . . . you know, all that happened . . . and it made sense that you were now a private detective."

"Well, come in. It's nice to see you, Joan, despite the circumstances. Can I get you anything? Coffee or tea? Water?"

"I'm good. Actually, no, I'll have a water, if you're offering."

While I pulled a bottle of water from the mini fridge that sat in the south corner of my two-hundred-square-foot office, Joan wandered over to the one picture I had on my wall, a framed print of a watercolor of Grantchester Meadows near Cambridge in England. I'd bought it on a trip a number of years ago not because I'd particularly liked the artwork but because one of my favorite poems by Sylvia Plath was called "Watercolor of Grantchester Meadows," so I thought it would be a clever thing to own. After I'd rented this office space, I dug out the print because I wanted a calming image on my wall, the way dentists' offices and divorce lawyers' always display soothing art so their clients might forget where they are.

Joan cracked open the bottle of water and took a seat as I moved around my desk. I adjusted the blinds because the late-afternoon sun was slanting into the room, and Joan was squinting as she took a long sip. Before I sat down myself I had a brief but vivid recollection of standing in front of my English students a dozen years ago, my armpits damp with anxiety, their bored, judgmental eyes staring up at me. I could almost smell the chalk dust in the air.

I lowered myself into my leather swivel chair, and asked Joan Whalen what I could help her with.

"Ugh," she said, and rolled her eyes a little. "It's so pedestrian."

I could tell she wanted me to guess why she'd come, but I kept quiet.

"It's about my husband," she said at last.

"Uh-huh."

"Like I said, it's probably something you hear all the time, but I'm pretty sure . . . no, I *know* that he's cheating on me. The thing is, I don't really care all that much—he can do whatever he wants as far as I'm concerned—but even though I know he's doing it, I don't have proof yet. I don't *really* know."

"Are you thinking of filing for divorce once you know for sure?"

She shrugged, and that childish gesture made me smell chalk again. "I don't even know. Probably. What really bothers me is that he's getting away with it, getting away with having an affair, and I tried following him myself, but he knows my car, of course, and I just want to know for sure. I want details. Who he's with. Well, I'm pretty sure I know that, too. Where they go. How often. Like I said, I don't give a shit, except that he's getting away with it." She looked over my shoulder through the office's sole window. When the light hit it in the late afternoon you could see just how dusty it was, and I reminded myself to wipe down the panes when I had some spare time.

I slid my notebook toward me and uncapped a pen. "What's your husband's name, and what does he do?" I said.

"His name is Richard Whalen and he's a real estate broker. He owns a company called Blackburn Properties. They have offices in

Dartford and Concord, but he mainly works out of the Dartford one. Pam O'Neil is the Dartford office manager, and that's who he's sleeping with."

"How do you know it's her?"

She held up a fist and stuck out her thumb. "First, she's the only really pretty employee in his office. Well, pretty *and* young, which is the way Richard likes them. Second, Richard is a liar but he's not great at it, and I accused him of having an affair with Pam and he couldn't even look me in the eye."

"Have you accused him of having affairs in the past?"

"The thing is, I don't think he *has* had an affair in the past, not a real one anyway. He does go to this bullshit conference every year for real estate brokers in Las Vegas, and I'm sure he's hooked up with a stripper there or something, but that's not really the same as an affair. And I'm kind of friends with Pam, that's the thing. When she first got the job at Blackburn I invited her to my book club, which she came to a bunch of times, although none of us thought she really read the books.

"I was nice to her. I even introduced her to the guy who does my husband's investments, and they went out for a while. I took her out for drinks at least three times."

"When do you think the affair started?"

"I think it started around the time Pam stopped texting me, which was about three months ago. They've made it so obvious it's like they want to get caught. You must see this stuff all the time?"

It was the second time she'd mentioned that, and I decided not to tell her that it wasn't something I saw all the time because my only regular clients were a temp agency that employed me to do background checks, and an octogenarian just down the street from my office who was always losing her cats.

"My guess is," I said, "that they are trying to be secretive and failing at it. Which probably means that your husband, and Pam, as well, haven't had affairs before. The people who are good at hiding secrets are the people who have practice at it."

She frowned, thinking about what I'd just said. "You're probably right, but I guess I don't particularly care one way or another if my husband is cheating on me for the first time. I don't know why I feel this way but, honestly, it's Pam that is pissing me off a little more than he is. I don't know what game she thinks she's playing. Hey, did you keep teaching after the seniors graduated early that year? I know you didn't come back the next year."

It was an abrupt change of topic and for that reason it made me answer honestly. "Oh, God, no," I said. "I don't think I could've ever walked back into that school. I felt bad about it, but there was only about two weeks left anyway."

"You never taught again?"

"No, not high school. I do occasionally teach an adult ed class in poetry, but it's not the same thing."

"The basketball player," she said, and her face brightened as though she'd just won a trivia contest.

I must have looked confused because she added, "It's all coming back to me, now. For the last month of classes you had us read poetry because you knew we wouldn't be able to focus on full books."

"Right," I said.

"And we read this poem about a kid who used to be—"

"Oh, right. John Updike. The poem was called 'Ex-Basketball Player.' I haven't thought of that for—"

"And you got in a fight with Ally Eisenkopf because she said you were making up all the symbolism in it."

"I wouldn't call it a fight. More like a spirited intellectual debate." And now I was remembering that day in class, when the lesson plan was to dissect that poem line by line, and I'd drawn a map on the chalkboard that located the gas station described in the poem, and the street it was on. I was trying to show how a relatively simple poem such as "Ex-Basketball Player" by John Updike could be as carefully constructed as a clock, that every word was a deliberate choice for both the text and the subtext of the poem. The students that were paying attention had rebelled, convinced I was reading things into the poem that didn't exist. I'd told them I found it interesting they could believe that someone could go to the moon, or invent computer coding, yet they couldn't quite believe that the described location of the gas station in a poem was a metaphor for the stalled life of a high school basketball champion.

Ally Eisenkopf, one of my more vocal students, had gotten visibly upset, claiming I was just making stuff up, as though I'd told her that the sky wasn't blue. I was very surprised that Joan remembered that particular class. I told her that.

"I have a good memory, and you were a good teacher. You really made an impression on me that year."

"Well," I said. "You and no one else."

"You know that Richard, my cheating husband, went to DM too."

It took me a moment to remember that DM was what the kids called Dartford-Middleham High School. "No, I didn't know that. Did I have him in a class?"

"No, you didn't have him in one of your classes. No way did he do honors English."

I was surprised that Joan had married a high school boyfriend. The towns of Dartford and Middleham might not be as ritzy as some of the other towns around them, like Concord, or Lincoln, but most of the kids from the public high school went on to four-year colleges, and I doubt many of them married their high school sweethearts.

"Were you dating him back then, in high school?"

"Richard? No, hardly. I knew him, of course, because he was a really good soccer player, but it was just random that we got together. We met in Boston, actually. I lived there for a year after college, and he was still at BU and bartending in Allston. That's where I lived."

"Where do you both live now?"

"In Dartford, I'm sorry to say. We actually live in Rich's parents' house. Not with them. They live in Florida now, but they sold us the house and it was such a good deal that we couldn't really pass it up. I suppose you'll need to know our address and everything if you're going to be following Rich?" She pulled her shoulders back a fraction and raised her head. It was a gesture I remembered.

"You sure you want me to do this for you? If you already know that he's cheating—"

"I am definitely sure. He's just going to deny it unless I have proof."

So we talked terms, and I gave her a rate that was slightly less than I should have, but she was a former student, and it wasn't as though I didn't have the time. And she told me the details about Richard's real estate office, and how she was convinced that the affair was only taking place during work hours. "You know it's the easiest profession for having affairs," she said.

"Empty houses," I said.

"Yep. Lots of empty houses, lots of excuses to go visit them. He told me that, a while ago, when two of the agents in his company were sleeping with one another, and he had to put an end to it."

I got more details from her, then let her know I'd work up a contract and email it to her to sign. And as soon as I had her signature and a deposit I would go to work.

"Keep an eye on Pam," she said. "That's who he's with, I know it."

After Joan left my office, I stood at my window with its view of Oxford Street and watched as she plucked fallen ginkgo leaves off her Acura before getting inside. It was a nice day outside, that time of year when half the leaves are still on the trees, and half are blowing around in the wind. I returned to my desk, opened up a Word document, and took notes on my new case. It had been strange to see Joan again, grown up but somehow still the same. I could feel myself starting to go over that period of time when I'd last known her but I tried to focus instead on what she'd told me about her husband. I'd tailed a wife once before, but never a husband. In that previous case, just over a year ago, it turned out the wife wasn't cheating, that she was a secret gambler, driving up to New Hampshire to visit poker rooms. Somehow, this time, I thought that Joan's husband was probably exactly who she thought he was. But I told myself to not make assumptions. Being at the beginning of a case was like beginning a novel or sitting down to watch a movie. It was best to go in with zero expectations.

After locking up my office and leaving the building I was surprised to find it was dusk already. I walked home along the leaf-strewn streets of Cambridge, excited to have a paying job, but feeling just a little haunted by having seen Joan again after so many years.

It was mid-October and every third house or so was bedecked with Halloween decorations: pumpkins, fake cobwebs, plastic tombstones. One of the houses I passed regularly was swarmed with giant fake spiders, and a mother had brought her two children, one still in a stroller, to look at the spectacle. The older of the two kids, a girl, was pointing to one of the spiders with genuine alarm and said to her mother that someone should smush it.

"Not me," the mom said. "We'd need a giant to do that."

"So, let's get a giant," the girl said.

The mother caught my eye as I was passing and smiled at me. "Not me either," I said. "I'm tall, but I'm not a giant."

"Then let's get out of here," the girl said, her voice very serious. I kept walking, thinking ominous thoughts, then disregarding them, the way I'd taught myself to do.

CHAPTER 2

JOAN

Before Joan even realized that Richard was at the Windward Resort, she'd met his cousin Duane. It was her first night at the beachside hotel in Maine, a Saturday in August, buggy and hot, the start of a two-week vacation with her parents and her sister. Joan was fifteen.

Duane had sidled up to her as she was taking a walk along Kennewick Beach, trying to get away from her family. He was a muscular teenager, probably a senior in high school.

"Hey, I saw you at the Windward," he said. "Didja just get here?"

She'd seen him, too. In the lobby, sitting on one of the couches outside of the dining room, his legs spread apart. He had bad posture and a low hairline that made him look a little like a caveman.

"Yeah, we got here today," Joan said, still walking.

"Sorry about that. This place kind of sucks. Full of old people."

"It's not so bad," Joan said, even though she basically agreed. "This beach is pretty."

"Yeah, the beach rocks. I was just talking about the hotel. I mean, once it's nighttime there's like nothing to do. Hey, slow down, you're walking so fast."

Joan stopped and turned.

"I'm Duane," the kid said.

"I'm Joan."

"Look, like I was saying there's nothing to do at night, so I just wanted to tell you that a bunch of us are going to be down at the beach around ten having a little bonfire. It'll be cool if you showed up. Or not."

"Who's going to be there?"

"There's this pretty cool kid named Derek. He's a busboy here but a waiter over at the Sea Grill. He's hooked me up with beer a bunch of times, and some pretty sweet pot. Honestly, there's like no one cool here. I have a cousin but he's practically retarded. Just thought you looked cool and like you might like to party."

"Well, maybe," Joan said. "Is it just going to be you and this guy Derek?"

"Oh, no," Duane said, shaking his head. "There's some girls who are in a rental house down the beach. There'll be there, too."

"Well, maybe," Joan said again.

"Sweet," Duane said. "Like I said, around ten o'clock, and we'll have a fire going."

She hadn't planned on going, but Duane had been right about there being nothing to do at night. After a disgusting dinner in the dining room—baked fish and scalloped potatoes—her parents were sitting in the lobby listening to some old geezer on the piano and her sister, Lizzie, had gone up to their room to read. At ten o'clock her parents had gone up to bed, as well, and Joan was still in the lobby, flipping through a magazine. She decided to walk down to the beach, at least say hi. Maybe Duane wasn't as big a douchebag as he'd seemed.

She left the resort and crossed the sloping lawn that led to Micmac Road, crossing it to get to the beach. Even though the day had been hot, it was pretty cool now, and Joan was glad she was wearing her thickest sweatshirt. The beach was dark and quiet, but Joan saw the flickering light of a bonfire about two hundred yards away and made her way toward it, her feet sinking in the soft sand. When she got close to the fire she could tell it was just two guys there, and she could smell pot on the breeze. She almost turned around right then, but Duane spotted her and leapt up, jogging to where she was.

"Oh, fuck," he said, his voice too loud. "You came." He turned back toward the fire, laughing, and shouted to his friend. "Told you she'd come."

Joan decided to hang out with them for five minutes, nothing more. The bonfire was really just a few pieces of smoldering driftwood, and she could barely make out what Derek even looked like. He was a dark figure crouched on a washed-up log, wearing a baseball hat. Duane offered Joan a seat on a small plastic cooler, then handed her an open can of warm beer. She thanked him and took a sip. Duane snapped a lighter and took a hit of pot from a glass pipe, then offered that to Joan. "No, thanks," she said.

"Don't smoke?"

"No, not really. I'm a gymnast."

Both the boys burst into laughter after she said that, and Joan almost got up and walked away, but something stopped her. Instead she said, "What's so funny?"

"It's not funny. It's hot." This was from Derek, his face still hidden underneath the shadow from the brim of his hat. His words were raspy and slurred.

Duane kicked out, hitting Derek in the shin, then said, "No, you're a good girl. I get it. Is your team any good?"

Joan talked a little bit about her freshman year as a junior varsity gymnast while she finished her beer. At one point she watched as Duane turned and stared intently at his friend Derek, who got up, mumbled something about taking a leak, then disappeared into the darkness. The fire was now almost completely out, one piece of drift-wood pulsing with a little bit of orange light. Duane said, "You look cold," and slid next to her on the cooler, draping an arm around her shoulder.

"I'm actually fine," Joan said, and Duane laughed like she'd just told the world's greatest joke. She knew what was coming next but was still a little jarred when he pulled her in closer to him and pushed his mouth up against hers. For a moment she just went along with it—mostly because it was easier—but then he grabbed her hand and put it in the crotch of his shorts, and Joan said, "Hey," twisting away from him and standing up. The cooler upended, and Duane landed on the sand.

She thought he'd laugh, but instead he said, "What the fuck, Jesus," jumping up and swiping sand off his shorts and legs.

"I gotta go," Joan said, and started walking away. There were dim lights in the distance on the other side of the road, and they were blurring in her vision because she had started to shake.

Duane caught up with her and grabbed her arm. "No, stay awhile," he said. "Don't be a tease."

Joan's heart was now thudding in her chest, and she felt a little distant from herself, the way she sometimes felt right before doing a routine in a competition. A voice inside of her was telling her she should just make out with him some more, maybe jerk him off, and then he'd let her go home, but instead she said, "Let go of me."

"Like this," Duane said, and squeezed her arm, digging his fingers in. She cried out, and he let go of her, and Joan turned and ran, her legs feeling heavy in the soft sand, her eyes filling with tears. She only looked back when she'd reached the road, and Duane hadn't come after her. Still, she ran the rest of the way back to the hotel, heading straight up to the bedroom she was sharing with her sister.

• • •

"Hi, Joan," came the voice, almost obscured by the steady breeze coming off the ocean.

She was prostrate on a large, pink beach towel, and jerked around nervously, expecting to see Duane. But it was a pale, lanky boy looming above her. "It's Richard, from school," he said. "We were in Mrs. Harris's social studies class together."

"Oh, hey, Richard," she said, recognizing him, and shifted onto her back. It was funny he'd identified himself as from that class, since they'd both grown up in Middleham, gone all through elementary and middle school together. Still, she didn't think that they had ever spoken in all those years. It was strange to see him in Maine.

He shifted uncomfortably, wearing a black T-shirt and a pair of worn, green bathing trunks that were cut unfashionably short. The high sun moved behind a wispy cloud and she could see him better, his eyes seeming to rest about one foot above her head. "What are you doing here?" she said.

"My aunt and uncle and my cousin come here every summer for a month, and I'm staying up here this year with them."

"For the whole month?"

"I've already been here two weeks, so two weeks more. Yeah. How about you?"

"I got here yesterday with my parents and my sister. We're here for two weeks. At the Windward."

"Oh, yeah. Me, too," he said. He looked back over his shoulder as though judging the distance from the resort, but didn't say anything. Joan was as far down the beach as she could get, hoping to avoid Duane, even though she knew she'd run into him eventually.

"It's gross there, isn't it?" Joan said.

"Is it?" He looked down at her for what felt like the first time, and Joan felt as though his eyes had landed somewhere around her chin. At least he wasn't staring at her in her bikini, although she did suspect maybe he was working hard not to; she was pretty sure that Richard, known primarily as either Dick or Dickless since the fifth grade, had maybe never even talked to a girl.

"It smells," she said, "and the food is disgusting. The only thing good about it is that it's close to the beach."

"There's a pool," Richard said.

"You go in there?"

"I did once, but there was a bunch of little kids and I thought that maybe they were peeing in it."

Joan laughed, then turned her head because she could see a group of kids coming down the beach. No, not kids, maybe college students. And Duane wasn't one of them. One of the girls was smoking a cigarette, and Joan could smell the smoke on the air.

"I guess I'll see you around," she said to Richard, who seemed to be watching two gulls squawking at each other near the grassy part of the beach that separated the wide expanse of sand from the road.

"Oh, yeah," Richard said, and moved off down the beach. She watched him for a little while, then flipped over onto her stomach, and stared at the corner of her towel, at the few flecks of sand that had crept onto it. She closed her eyes but kept thinking about the sand, finally shifting over enough so that she could swipe them off the towel.

That evening, sunburned and starving, Joan was keeping her eye out for Duane in the large dining room of the resort. The buffet that night was lasagna, either meat or veggie, and salad, and garlic bread. She'd spotted Richard, her awkward classmate, across the room, sitting at a table with a tall, skinny woman with curly hair and a fat, older man who was wearing shorts and white socks pulled up to his knees. What had Richard told her? He was there with his aunt and uncle and a cousin. She wondered for a moment if that cousin might be Duane, and as though she'd conjured him with her thoughts,

Duane suddenly appeared, lumbering between tables and arriving to sit with Richard and the two adults. Even seeing Duane from a distance made Joan feel ill. It was strange to think that skinny, nerdy Richard was related to a meathead like Duane.

"I can't believe how much sun you got, sweet pea," Joan's mom said for the second or third time.

Joan pressed a finger into her forearm, watched her reddened skin turn briefly white then red again. "It's a base," she said. "If I have to be here for two weeks then at least I'm going to get a wicked tan."

"It's so bad for you," Lizzie, her sister, said. Lizzie had just finished her freshman year of college, at Bard—she and Joan were exactly four years apart—and now Lizzie was suddenly a feminist, and a vegetarian, and concerned about things like getting a sunburn.

"You went to Florida last summer, and I didn't even recognize you when you came back you were so black," Joan said, knowing she was talking too loud, but still annoyed when her mother shushed her.

"And now I probably have cancer again," Lizzie said. "You should try to learn from my mistakes, Joan. It'll make you a better person."

Lizzie was smiling now, trying to make up to her sister, but Joan frowned. "Daddy, what do you think? You're a doctor."

Her father, drinking a coffee, blinked rapidly and pulled himself back into the conversation. "I'm a dentist, Joan. Think about what?"

"Think about me getting a good tan this summer."

"Sure," he said.

"Just do me a favor," her mom said. "Slather yourself with aloe tonight and promise to wear at least thirty-something SPF tomorrow, okay? It does look really red."

"It feels fine," Joan lied. Ever since her shower her skin was starting to hum all over, and even though she knew she couldn't, Joan had felt like she could almost sense a burning smell coming off her.

"Did you know there's a library here?" Lizzie said, clearly trying to change the subject, and for that, Joan was thankful.

"Is there?" her mother said.

Joan's parents and her sister all began talking about the books they were planning on reading during their vacation while Joan pushed a hard crust of garlic bread around her plate.

Joan was keeping her eye on the table where both Duane and Richard sat. She wondered if Duane was scared of running into her, if he wondered whether she'd told anyone how he'd acted. But he didn't look nervous from across the room. He was slouched in his chair and kept looking at his watch. After about five minutes he got up and walked out of the dining room. Joan kept watching the table. Richard got up and went back to the buffet to look at the desserts. She found herself standing, then walking over to the buffet, as well.

"What is that?" she said, when she'd gotten close enough to Richard so that he could hear her.

"It's rice pudding," he said. "But there's also chocolate cake."

"Was that your cousin at the table with you?" Joan said.

"He was there a moment ago. That's my aunt and uncle there now."

"What's your cousin like?"

"Who, Duane?"

"Yeah."

"He's maybe the worst human being I've ever met."

"Really?" Joan said, not really bothering to hide her excitement. It was what she'd been hoping to hear. "What makes him so terrible?"

"Pretty much everything. Why are you asking? You want to meet him or something?"

"I already met him. Yesterday."

"You did?"

"Yeah, he invited me down to the beach for a bonfire at night and I stupidly went."

"Did he attack you?" Richard said, as though he were asking her if she'd had dessert yet.

"Oh my God," she said, her voice rising in pitch reflexively, but then, whispering, she said, "He kind of tried, but I got away."

"Yeah, I figured he probably would the way he talks about girls. You're lucky, I guess."

A large, bearded man was now across from them on the other side of the buffet, meticulously touching the rim of each dessert plate before selecting the biggest piece of cake.

"I should go back to my table," Richard said.

"Okay. Maybe I'll see you at the beach tomorrow," she said.

"Oh, yeah," Richard said, almost as though he weren't really listening to her, and then went back to his table with a bowl of rice pudding.

That night, lying in bed, Joan couldn't sleep. Her whole body felt as though tiny pins were being poked through her skin, and she was too warm. Lizzie had spent all night reading a book called *White Teeth* in bed, wearing headphones, while Joan had flipped through channels trying to find something to watch. There were only about twelve channels here, three of them showing baseball games. She ended up watching the Julia Roberts movie where she runs away from her husband. When it was over it just started up again, and now she was wide awake in her bed. Lizzie was asleep.

She kept thinking about the close call the night before with Duane, but also Richard. Even though he'd grown up in the same small town as she had, she probably hadn't thought once about him since that time in middle school when she'd walked into Mr. Barclay's science class and Mr. Barclay was handing Richard a stick of deodorant. It was not a total surprise. Richard basically wore the same shirt to school every day, and he reeked. Joan had run to lunch and told everyone at her table what she'd seen, and for a while everyone called Richard Old Spice, which was probably an improvement on Dickless.

After eighth grade all the Middleham kids went to the Dartford-Middleham High School, and Joan barely saw Richard anymore. He'd grown a ton between middle school and high school and looked less like that scrawny kid with clothes that didn't fit and a home-made haircut. He was still a complete freak, though. It was strange that, right now, he felt like an actual friend in this place. They had stuff in common. Not just that they grew up in the same town and went to the same school, but it turned out that they shared a common enemy. She was hoping to find Richard tomorrow, and get more information about Duane.

CHAPTER 3

KIMBALL

The night after seeing Joan Grieve Whalen again I went online and studied her husband's company's extensive website. Blackburn Properties had photographs and profiles of the brokers, the agents, and the office staff. Richard Whalen's profile picture had been taken outside on a sunny day, some sort of parkland behind him. He had short cropped gray hair and the kind of raw but handsome face that looked as though he spent time on boats. In the short biography that accompanied his picture he mentioned his hobbies were paddleboarding, freshwater fishing, and road biking. There was no mention of a wife.

Pam O'Neil, the woman Joan was convinced was sleeping with her husband, listed her hobbies as horseback riding and boogie boarding. She had long blond hair, and very white teeth, although it was possible the picture had been touched up. She looked as though she was in her mid-twenties, about ten years younger than Richard Whalen or Joan.

I tried to imagine the two of them together, and it wasn't partic- ularly hard. My guess was that if Joan thought they were having an affair, then they were having an affair. Smoke and fire and all that. I tried to form a plan in my mind, the best way to move forward on this case, but found I kept thinking about Joan instead. And not the Joan who had been in my office earlier that day, but the Joan who had been in my classroom fifteen years earlier when I'd been a first-year teacher.

The thing about my year at Dartford-Middleham High School was that I was full of unspecified dread long before James Pursall brought a gun into my classroom. It began during Christmas break, when I'd been prepping furiously to teach my classes the upcoming spring semester. The previous fall I'd been a student teacher, my host a veteran teacher named Larry O'Donnell, who liked to go over lesson plans down at the Bullrun pub when it opened at five p.m. The good thing about Larry was that he didn't seem particularly interested in sitting in on my class, observing me, then hitting me up later with the multiple things I did wrong. But that was also the bad thing about Larry. While I was teaching, he was in the supply closet, napping.

My hardest classes were the two sections of American lit for sophomores. It was a pretty routine curriculum, covering Walt Whitman, Mark Twain, Emily Dickinson, Hemingway, Fitzgerald. The kids were unimpressed, and it turned out I was a less than stellar disciplinarian. I spent most of my time each class trying not to turn my back on them for even a few seconds. My third class was senior honors English, the class that Joan Grieve was taking. The kids were essentially respectful, and there were even a couple of them who seemed to enjoy reading and talking about books. Most of the kids, however, just thought the class would look good on their college applications. They were well behaved but absent.

By early December I was looking forward to the semester being over, counting the days, and wondering if I'd made the correct career choice. Then one afternoon, just after my last class of the day, when

I'd been erasing the chalkboard and mentally replaying the class that had just ended, Larry O'Donnell and Maureen Block, the English department head, came in to see me, shutting the door behind them. They asked me if I'd noticed that Paul Justice, one of the veteran teachers, hadn't been in for a few days. I *had* noticed, but hadn't thought too much about it.

"He's not coming back," Maureen said. "And I'm not sure, but I think we've dodged a major bullet. The girl who made the complaint said she's not going to the police."

"Oh," I said.

"Larry has kindly offered to take over Paul's freshman classes for next semester, but that means someone has to keep going with senior honors, plus Paul's composition classes. We were hoping you might consider helping us out."

"Oh," I said again.

They gave me a night to think about it, and Dagmar, my girl-friend at the time, convinced me that it was too good an opportunity to pass up. "They'll offer you a full-time job at the end of the year," she said. "It's a good school." Dagmar and I had met at the same master's program out in Western Mass and she was teaching middle school in the Hudson school system. I had a sudden vision of the two of us fixing up a farmhouse in Central Massachusetts, and spending our lives complaining about grading papers. I couldn't quite decide how I felt about that.

I took the job, and that December, with Dagmar back in the Midwest with her family, I holed up in my squalid apartment in Cambridge and planned the remainder of the year with my honors class. They'd given me leeway, so I planned a whole unit on poetry, and one on mid-century suburban literature, thinking they might enjoy some Cheever stories, and was considering assigning *Deep Water* by Patricia Highsmith or some Richard Yates. I was reading a lot, and I was trying to write poetry, but I could feel my life unfolding before me, and it felt like a life both quiet and a little bit desperate. And once that thought got into my head, it was like catching a chill from a cold swim—I just couldn't shake it.

I started teaching again in January, and the feeling didn't go away. Entering the classroom each morning, after walking from my unreliable Omega through a dim, freezing dawn, I was consumed with a kind of existential terror at the day ahead. Once the day began, it was okay. There were even moments of joy. John Cheever's "The Swimmer" turned out to be a hit, although the majority of the students were enraged by the ending of the story, by the way it slipped into the surreal. They were literalists, these affluent high school seniors, and they had one foot out of their high school towns and into prestigious colleges, then grad school, then good entry-level jobs in Boston or New York or Washington, DC. They comprehended suburban ennui, but they didn't want to feel it.

I wish I remembered more about James Pursall but mostly what I recall was a quiet loner who sat at the back of the room. He handed in his assignments, and he would comment during class discussions, but only if I called on him. He had very white skin, dusted with acne, and very black hair that always looked unwashed. The classroom was cold, and I remember he never took off his jacket, a bulky winter parka that was either navy or black. I do remember that before the shooting, I had dubbed him "boy most likely to go on a killing spree" in my mind, picturing compact Russian machine guns suddenly emerging from his puffy winter coat. But I never thought it would really happen.

I do, however, remember Joan Grieve. She sat in the first row, made sure to comment at least once a class, and came to me after tests and essays to see if she could get me to raise her A minus to an A, or her B plus to an A minus. I knew she was a gymnast because the gymnastics team was good that year, and people were talking about them. She wore tights to class a lot, and hooded sweatshirts, and there was always a large water bottle on her desk. What I really remember about her was that she was a watcher, one of the students who kept her eyes firmly on me when I was lecturing or trying to lead a class discussion. She wasn't the only student who kept their eyes at the front of the class, but it was still rare, most of my students staring into space or directly at their scarred and doodled-on desktops. She watched me when she wasn't taking notes, and instead of making me feel as though I was making some kind of difference . . . *If you reach just one kid* . . . it made me feel exposed.

There was one odd incident with Joan, right before the Easter break. I had handed back a pop quiz so, unsurprisingly, Joan came up to me after the class had ended. I was sitting at my desk chair and she was standing, but even so, her head was only a little higher than mine as she argued that the quiz wasn't entirely fair because I hadn't been clear that they were supposed to read *all* the Anne Sexton poems I'd assigned them.

As she was talking, there was one other student still gathering her things in the classroom. Madison Brown was also a gymnast, plus a close friend of Joan's, and I assumed she was taking her time in order to wait for Joan to plead her case. But once Madison's giant backpack was zipped up, she slung it over her shoulder and headed for the door. Just before she exited, she turned and said, "Better look out, Mr. K, Joan told me she has the hots for you."

I rolled my eyes dismissively, hoping to alleviate the embarrassment of the moment, but when I looked at Joan her face had gone red. I thought at first it was embarrassment, but her eyes were on the door that had just swung shut, and I remember thinking it was closer to rage that I was seeing. Still, I got up to prop open the door, hearing Maureen Block's voice in my head—*Never be alone with a student behind a closed door*—and when I came back, Joan's face had returned to a more normal color.

"You don't need to worry, Mr. Kimball," she said. "Madison is just being a bitch, pardon my French."

"I thought you two were close."

"Who? Madison and me? I mean, she's on the team, too, but we're not exactly close. And what she said about me . . . I mean you're good-looking for a teacher, but you're not my type."

I laughed. "Don't worry about it," I said, wanting this particular strain of conversation to end. "And just because this has turned awkward, I'll cut you a deal. Write a few sentences tonight about the meaning behind 'The Room of My Life' and I'll up your grade on the pop quiz."

"Thank you, thank you." She bounced a little on her sneakers and left the room.

Two weeks later Madison Brown bled out on the floor of that same classroom while James Pursall stood over her with a gun in his hand. I stood staring at the tableau, about three feet away, and my bones had turned to rubber, and then James lifted the gun, angling it toward his own chest, toward that bulky winter parka, and pulled the trigger.

I think the entire incident—from the moment James pulled the gun from the depths of that coat to the moment he lay next to Madison on the floor—took all of two minutes, maybe even less, but time in those two minutes moved at its own sickening pace. It was hours from the moment the gun emerged to the moment when the entire class, including me, became aware of it. I'd been talking about their upcoming public speaking assignment, where they each had to give a mock valedictorian speech for graduation. I'd been telling them that they should be creative, that I was not interested in hearing the exact same speech twenty-four times. And then James had yelled, "On the ground, everyone," and no one moved. I thought it was some kind of joke, maybe he was demonstrating a very untraditional valedictorian speech, but then he was standing on his desk chair, the gun in his hand, and half the students dropped down below their desks, and a girl named Missy Robertson—I remember it because she's a local weatherperson now—began to loudly sob.

"Everyone," he said, louder this time, and the rest of the students got down on the floor.

I was leaning up against the front of my desk, my usual position when I was teaching, and I remember my hands were out in front of me, and I said something like, "James, let's talk."

It made him look at me from across the room, his eyes wide beneath the shock of greasy, inky hair. I opened my mouth to speak again but didn't. I wanted to live and somehow I knew if I made another attempt to defuse the situation he was going to shoot me. That decision, to not speak, to keep quiet like the students on the floor, altered my body chemistry. I can't think of a better way to describe it. My bones hollowed out, my organs liquefied. My chest was empty, as though I'd pulled my heart out of it and handed it across to James Pursall. I was frozen in place.

He came down off his desk, and walked between the cowering students, swiveling his gun, and saying, "Eenie, meenie, miney, moe," in a shaky, unreal voice, and even at the time, from back within the dusty cave where I was cowering, I remember thinking his heart wasn't in it, that he'd decided in advance to try to terrorize the other students, but that he just wanted to get the whole thing over with.

At the front of the room, when he was only a few feet from me, he turned around and took a few small steps, so that he was standing above Madison Brown, curled into a ball around the bulk of her backpack. He aimed the gun at her, then braced his trembling right hand with his left, and I knew he was about to shoot. I pictured myself springing from the desk I was still leaning against, grabbing him around the chest so his arms would point upward, shaking that gun loose, dropping him to the hard linoleum floor.

Instead, I watched as he put two bullets into Madison Brown. She didn't even move when he did it, like she was already dead.

Then I watched James Pursall make like he was returning the gun into his coat, but he pulled the trigger instead, and dropped to the floor next to Madison.

I've gone over those memories a thousand times since that day, and I no longer entirely trust the details. I realize it might have been worse had I tried to do more, but that doesn't stop me from knowing, deep down, I failed in that particular situation. Yes, it could have been worse. But as it was, it was pretty bad.

So it was a surprise to realize that Joan Whalen, faced with a crisis in her personal life, had sought me out as someone who could solve it. I'd always assumed the kids from that classroom only remembered me as a mediocre teacher, plus the adult who had failed them on the worst day of their lives. But somehow Joan remembered me differently. And I wondered why.

CHAPTER 4

JOAN

After dinner on Monday night—some sort of chicken thing with ham and cheese—Joan wandered the resort, hoping to find Richard, while at the same time hoping to avoid his cousin Duane. She'd seen them both in the dining room, at a far table, but had purposefully made sure to not make eye contact with either of them.

Ever since Saturday night, when he'd attacked her on the beach, she'd been obsessing about getting even with Duane. All through dinner—her parents and her sister planning tomorrow's scenic drive—she'd plotted her revenge, acutely aware of the throbbing bruises he'd left on the inside of her arm when he'd grabbed her. If he ever spoke to her again she'd tell him that he looked like an ape and she found him physically repulsive. She imagined kicking him in the balls as hard as she could, and she even allowed herself images of doing worse things to him, like gouging out one of his eyes with a butter knife. Having that thought was a strange mix of pleasure and disgust. Joan was always happiest when she had an enemy.

She'd looked for Richard, his nerdy cousin, on the front porch of the resort, and in the bar area, where kids were allowed to hang out and drink soft drinks. There was a game room near the dining hall, a long narrow room with a foosball table, two pinball machines, and a couple of old arcade games. No one was in there but two little boys with their father. One of the boys was standing on a stool, whacking at a pinball machine even though it wasn't on.

Joan went back to the lobby, scanning for empty chairs. But some old folk singer had set up in the corner of the lobby, singing a song about margaritas, and the lobby was full. She went over to the small gift shop area and spun the rack that contained paperbacks, then remembered her sister saying that there was a library somewhere in the resort. She thought maybe Richard, if he was anywhere, might be there. She asked the girl at the front desk, who wasn't a whole lot older than her, where the library was. The girl looked confused, then said, "Oh, the free library. It's all the way up on the third floor."

"Is it open?"

"Oh, yeah. I mean, as far as I know it's always open."

Joan climbed the stairs to the third floor of the resort, where the reek of mold and dust was particularly strong. She found the library, its lights on. It was just a room, really, an old handwritten sign calling it UNCLE MURRAY'S BOOK NOOK, and inside the room were floor-to-ceiling bookshelves, plus several freestanding shelves in the middle of the space. In the two corners of the room that she could see were worn leather chairs for reading. She thought she heard a noise, the dry sound of a page being turned maybe, and she said, "Hello," into the room, her voice sounding frail in her own head.

"Uh, hello," came a voice back, and she moved around the center shelves, and there was Richard, sitting in one of the leather chairs, holding a book.

"Oh, hey," she said, trying to act as though she hadn't been looking for him.

"Hey," he said.

"Is this your hangout?" she said.

"What, this library? Yeah, I guess so."

She walked over to a wall of books, touched one of the spines with a finger. "What are you reading?"

He held up a hardcover with a black cover. "*The Bachman Books*," Joan read. "By Stephen King. My mom reads him, I think."

"I actually have this book back at home, but I didn't bring it with me, and now I'm rereading it."

"Is it good?"

"It's four books that he wrote under a different name. Richard Bachman."

"Do you like them because he called himself Richard?"

Richard looked confused, then glanced at the cover himself. "Oh, it never occurred to me that we have the same name."

"Really? I always notice when someone's called Joan because no one is called Joan anymore. It's an old person's name."

"I guess it kind of is," Richard said.

"Thanks a lot."

"Old names are good names. Would you rather be called Madison or something?"

"I'm going to tell Madison you said that," Joan said.

Richard shrugged. Joan could tell that he kind of wanted to get back to reading his book.

"So remember last night when you asked me if your cousin Duane attacked me?" she said.

He shifted in his seat. "Yeah."

"I think he would have done it, if he'd had the chance. I had to run away from him and everything." She thought about showing him the bruises, but they were high up on her inner arm and she'd have to take off her sweatshirt.

Richard put the book down on his lap. "You're lucky he didn't catch you. Like I told you, he's one of the worst human beings I've ever met. I'm sure he's a rapist, too. He talks like one."

"What do you mean?"

"Like he always points out girls and says really disgusting things, like what he wants to do with their ass and stuff."

Joan shivered. "Ugh, gross. Did you like him when you were little kids?"

"No, he was terrible. He used to steal my toys, and he used to beat me up."

"I'm sorry about that," Joan said.

"You're laughing."

"Am I?" Joan said, and laughed some more. "I'm an inappropriate laugher. That's what Madison calls me. I don't mean anything by it."

"I don't care," Richard said.

They were quiet for a moment, and Joan could hear voices somewhere out on the third-floor hall. "Does anyone else ever come in here?"

"This library? Sometimes, but mostly people just come in here and get a book and leave. I come up here to read at night because Duane's probably in our room watching sports and farting into his pillow, and I don't really like to hang out in the lobby with all the old people."

"It's a little creepy in here."

"There's a framed letter over by that shelf with all the photography books. This place was started by some relative of the owners because he wanted to create a free lending library for all the people who came for the summer. It was his life's work or something."

"Is he dead now?"

"Uncle Murray? Yeah, totally dead. Can't you sense him in here?"

Joan laughed, then worried for a moment that Richard was being serious. But he laughed too. "I have a really good sense of smell," she said, "and when I was a kid I thought I could smell ghosts."

"Oh, yeah."

"Yeah. I can tell that Uncle Murray is definitely a ghost in this room."

"What does he smell like?"

"He smells like creepy old man. Like crusty underwear and soup."

"Ugh," Richard said.

Joan crouched to look at the spines of some books that looked familiar. She realized she was standing in front of the young adult shelves, which included about a hundred Nancy Drew novels. It felt weird telling Richard, a boy she would never talk to at high school in a million years, how she thought she could smell ghosts. It wasn't anything she'd told anybody else, not even her parents. Suddenly, she had a panic that when she started sophomore year Richard would always be by her side, trying to talk to her, or something.

"So this is what you're going to do for your summer? Sit in a smelly room and read books?" she said.

"Sure," Richard said, unfazed by what she thought was a pretty condescending tone.

"Okay, well," she said, about to tell him she was going to go back to her room to watch television, but she spotted a cluster of books written by Joan Aiken. "Look, Joan," she said.

He looked where she was crouched, and said, "Joan Aiken. Did you read *Wolves of Willoughby Chase*?"

"It's right here," Joan said. "No, I haven't. Any good?"

"Not bad."

Joan stood up, leaving the book on the shelf. She really did think she needed to go, even though the thought of going back to her room, where her sister would probably be reading or journaling or something, was not that appealing.

"So you'd help me get revenge on your cousin, right, if I wanted to?" she said.

Richard pushed his lips together, as though considering it. "Sure," he finally said. "If I had the guts, I'd murder him, then he wouldn't be anyone's problem."

Joan laughed, and said, "Oh my God."

"What?"

"Are you serious?"

"No, but I've thought a lot about it. I only wouldn't do it because I'd probably get caught and have to spend my life in prison."

"So how would you do it?"

"How would I murder him? I've given this a lot of thought, actually. He's from New Jersey, so if I had to murder him there, I'd probably just hire some Mafia people to bump him off."

"You'd need a lot of money for that, probably."

"Yeah, I hadn't thought about that. I guess I could murder him here. He's actually a really terrible swimmer. I mean, he can swim and all, but he always looks like he's struggling to just stay afloat."

"Drowning him. I like it."

"He's always looking for alcohol, so I'd give him a bottle of whiskey or something, and then push him in the pool when he was too drunk to swim."

"That could work," Joan said, moving to look at a separate shelf of books. There was a large Stephen King selection at eye level and she spotted the empty spot where the book Richard was reading had probably been.

"Nah," Richard said. "There's too many things that could go wrong. He'd have to be pretty drunk to not be able to climb out from the deep end. There's a ladder there."

"You could keep pushing him back into the pool with that long . . . whatever it's called, the net they use to skim the pool."

"It might leave evidence," Richard said. "It would cut open his head or something and then they would know that it wasn't an accidental drowning. When you kill someone it has to look like an accident, or it has to look like someone else killed them, otherwise it's no good."

Joan touched the spine of a book called *It*. "You've given this a lot of thought."

"About killing my cousin? Yeah, I have."

She laughed. "Would you really kill him if you could get away with it?"

"Sure," he said.

Joan looked at him. He was wearing the cargo shorts he always wore and a striped polo shirt that was a little too tight on him. Probably a shirt his mom had bought for him in middle school. His book was still open on his lap, and he was holding a finger at the place where he'd stopped reading. He looked back at her, his expression unchanging. She thought his face was like a blade, with his thin, bony nose. He had some hair on his upper lip, and she wondered if he was hoping to grow a mustache or if he just hadn't bothered to learn how to shave yet.

"You really would kill him?" Joan said, again. For whatever reason, probably because the expression on his face never changed, she didn't really know if he was being serious.

"I'd kill a lot of people if I could get away with it. My cousin Duane, for sure. I'd kill Garrett Blake, and my stepfather. I'd kill lots of people if I could go back in time. Hitler. Richard Nixon."

"What did Garrett Blake ever do to you?"

"What, you like Garrett?"

"No," Joan said. "Not really. As much as you, probably. I just think of Garrett as someone you don't even think about, not someone that you want to kill."

"Garrett was probably my best friend from second grade to fifth grade, and then he stopped hanging around with me when they started calling me Old Spice."

"Oh," Joan said. "Just so you know I never called you that."

"I don't care," Richard said. "All the kids called me that, I guess. It's just that Garrett was pretty spineless about it. He didn't even want to be seen with me."

"So what about Tommy Fusco? You wouldn't want to kill him?" Tommy had been the biggest bully, by far, at Middleham, the type of kid who made the Richards of the world miserable.

"I might kill Tommy if I had the perfect opportunity, like if it just fell in my lap or something. I mean, he's a pretty repulsive person, but I just don't give him that much thought. He's a bully, but he's actually not that good at it. I mean, he's not smart enough to know how to really hurt people."

Joan thought about that. "Yeah, you're probably right. So who's a smart bully, then?"

"Your friend Madison."

"Oh my God, I can't believe you just said that. She's my best friend, you know."

"You asked me who a smart bully was, and I thought of her. Remember what she did to Wendy Cook in eighth grade."

"Wendy tried to steal Madison's boyfriend," Joan said.

"Oh, maybe. I don't know all the details. I just remember that Madison pretty much destroyed her."

That was how Joan remembered it too. Madison had decided to ruin Wendy Cook's life, and then she'd done it by spreading rumors and by convincing other eighth graders to not speak to her. It had been a full-fledged campaign. Joan had done her part, mostly because Madison asked her to, and when Wendy had been pulled from school (the rumor was she tried to kill herself) Joan remembered her parents sitting her down, asking her all about it. She'd lied and told them she felt terrible for Wendy.

"So what you're saying is that you'd probably kill my best friend, if you had a chance?"

"Yeah, probably," Richard said, but he smiled, as though he was joking, which would be the first time she'd seen him making any kind of joke. "I mean, to tell the truth, I don't give her a lot of thought."

"Well, she doesn't give you a lot of thought, either."

"I'm sure."

The fluorescent light above them flickered suddenly, the room darkening then springing back into light.

"Uncle Murray," Joan said.

"Yeah. It does that, the lights."

"Look, aren't you scared I'm going to tell Madison what you said about her, that I'm going to go back to school and say how you want to kill people?"

"I hadn't thought about it. I mean, you can do what you want. I can't stop you."

"She'd probably try to make your life miserable."

"Honestly, my life is already miserable, and it's not like we'll be in school forever."

"It's three more years," Joan said.

"Exactly. Not forever."

There was another slight pause, and Joan said, "Well, I should probably go."

"Okay," Richard said, and he looked back down at his page. She studied him briefly. He had thick, black hair, and the hairline pointed down in the middle of his forehead. There was a word for that, but she couldn't remember it. The truth was Richard was far less of a nerd than he was just two years ago, and even though his eyes were a little too close on either side of his nose, they were an intense shade of blue. In the right clothes he'd probably be borderline cute.

"Hey," she said. "The best way to murder Duane would be to walk out to the end of that jetty on one of the days when the waves are crashing in, then just push him off the edge. He'd never be able to get back up onto the rocks, and you could just say that he slipped."

Richard gently nodded his head, as though he was thinking about it. "Yeah," he finally said. "All I'd have to do is say something like, I bet you can't walk all the way to the end of the jetty in the rain. And then he'd have to do it. And then I could pretend to slip, but I'd actually push him in. Even if he lived he wouldn't know I was trying to kill him. Thanks, Joan," he said.

She held her palms out and shrugged. Richard was still thinking, nodding his head. "It's a perfect plan," he said.

CHAPTER 5

KIMBALL

At ten thirty on the Tuesday morning after I'd met with Joan I was sitting at a chain coffee shop on Colonial Road in downtown Dartford. I had a view, not a great one, of the Blackburn Properties office across the road. It comprised a single brick storefront between a florist and a women's upscale clothing store. From where I sat I could make out Blackburn's plate glass window, an array of property cards adhered to it from the inside. The front door, unfortunately, was obscured by both a red maple and, underneath it, a white SUV with a Tufts bumper sticker.

There hadn't been too much activity at the Blackburn offices since I'd arrived at the coffee shop, and I was now drinking my second latte, and picking at a banana muffin. I had brought a small paperback edition of *Selected Poems of W. H. Auden* with me, thinking that nothing would make me blend into the background more than being a shabby guy in a coffee shop flipping through a slim volume of verse. But now that I was doing it, I realized how much I stood out among the other patrons around me, all of whom stared at open laptops, or conducted conversations through invisible headsets.

I opened my own laptop, logged onto the free Wi-Fi, and looked up W. H. Auden on Wikipedia. What I really wanted to do was go onto the Blackburn website again, and reread the employee profiles, but my computer screen was angled toward the inside of the shop, and I didn't want any random employee picking up their breakfast seeing me scroll through their site. Instead I learned that Auden had been twenty-three years old when he'd published his first book of poems, a fact that would have depressed me at one point in my poetry-writing career, but these days I'd lowered my ambitions so that all I hoped to do was to actually finish a poem that wasn't either complete doggerel or a limerick.

Keeping half an eye on the comings and goings across the street I opened up a Word document on my laptop, and wrote the line, "A putty sky was scuffed and grazed by every livid tree," but couldn't come up with anything to add to it. I hit the return key a number of times, then quickly wrote a limerick:

> *There once was a woman named Joan,*
> *Convinced that her husband did roam.*
> *So she hired a dick*
> *To find out what his dick*
> *Got up to when he wasn't home.*

It was not one of my better limericks—Joan didn't rhyme with home or roam for one thing—but I thought it was probably better than my pretentious line about the putty sky.

The door to the coffee shop swung inward and a blond woman entered who looked a little like the profile picture of Pam O'Neil, the woman Joan had identified as having an affair with her husband. She went up to the counter and ordered a chai tea, her voice flat and nasal. She was wearing a pair of black trousers and a velvet blazer, an outfit that seemed to be the kind of ensemble an office manager of a real estate company might wear. While she waited for her tea she studied her phone, at one point smiling at something she'd just read, and I got a look at her teeth, not remotely white. In fact, for someone so young her teeth were abnormally stained, and that was what made me think she was absolutely the same woman from the Blackburn website with the photoshopped picture.

I must have been right because when she left the coffee shop she crossed the street and disappeared behind the maple and the white SUV. I saw the top of the real estate office's door swing open. Thirty seconds later she came back out onto the sidewalk, held up what must have been her key fob, and pressed the lock button. A blue Toyota on my side of the street beeped, its lights flashing once. Underneath the limerick I wrote down her license number. Detective work. I even knew that at least some of the employees of Blackburn parked on the street, even though Joan had told me yesterday that there was a small parking lot behind the offices, and that her husband drove a silver BMW.

I wondered what to do next. There was no reason why I couldn't sit in this coffee shop all day, except for the fact that it might be a huge waste of time, and a waste of Joan's money. At least I had an eye on Pam O'Neil's car so that if she went anywhere I could follow her. But what if Pam wasn't the woman Richard Whalen was fooling around with? Or what if they were having an affair but only hooked up once every two weeks? Then it was going to be a long, caffeinated week for me. I ate some more of my muffin and considered my options. I could find a way to install spyware onto either Richard's cell phone or Pam's, or I could find a way to get to know Pam. Maybe she'd confide in me. Both of those options were risky. Maybe I'd get lucky and Pam and Richard would come meet for coffee at the next table over from me and loudly confess their love.

The coffee shop was starting to fill up again after a period of quiet, and I realized it was the lunch crowd, buying wrapped sandwiches to go. I stood and walked to the bathroom, my body stiff from spending all morning on a hard chair. When I returned to my table I glanced out the window and saw that the blond woman I believed to be Pam O'Neil was getting into her car. I quickly stowed my laptop back into my backpack, cleared my table, and was back outside as she was pulling away. My own car, a ten-year-old Taurus, was just half a block away but I had to wait for about four slow-moving vehicles to go by before I was able to pull out onto Colonial Road. I'd lost sight of the Toyota, but kept heading east toward Dartford, hoping I'd spot her if and when the road straightened out. Two of the cars in front of me turned left at a major intersection, and I was able to speed up a little, but after a mile I realized I'd lost her.

I pulled over into the parking lot of a strip mall split evenly between a Subway, a consignment shop, and a mom-and-pop liquor store, and booted up the Maps app on my phone. I did a search for nearby restaurants. It was lunchtime and maybe Pam was meeting someone. There were lots of take-out places along this stretch of road, but only one proper sit-down restaurant I could spot, a place called Little Marsh Grill. I drove there and circled their small parking lot. No blue Toyotas. But I parked anyway. I needed to eat lunch.

At five o'clock I was back at the coffee shop, at my same table, laptop open in front of me, same Auden book open on my lap. And the blue Toyota was back in front of Blackburn Properties, this time on the opposite side of the street, but within my view. I never did find out where she'd gone over her lunch hour. I'd eaten a toasted ham and cheese sandwich on pumpernickel at the Little Marsh Grill, and nursed a Guinness, then I'd taken a brisk walk out behind the restaurant along a series of raised wooden pathways that actually did traverse a little marsh. I watched a pair of white egrets come in for a landing along a shallow patch of ruffled water. The air temperature had dropped since the morning, and I could see my breath. I shoved my hands into my pockets and kept walking, telling myself to stretch out my legs in preparation for another stint at the coffee shop.

The white SUV that had been blocking my view of Blackburn Properties' entranceway was no longer there, and I watched a few people exit the office. One was a man who looked about the right age to be Joan's husband, but he was on the heavy side, and was wearing jeans and a sweatshirt, not the outfit a broker would wear. When Pam O'Neil exited the building I grabbed my things and got to my car faster than I had before. I had the engine running as she passed me going west along the road. I pulled out and did a U-turn that caused two cars to stop short, horns blaring, then I was behind her making our way through the rush-hour traffic, heading northwest. She got onto Route 2 briefly, then exited around West Concord, where she pulled into the large driveway of an apartment complex. I parked as far away from her car as I could while still keeping her in view. She got out, and I assumed she would head straight into the building. It was a Tuesday night after all, and I wasn't sure what I had expected from my day shadowing the real estate offices.

But instead of entering through the double glass doors she kept walking across the lot and toward the intersection where we'd turned to get to her apartment building. I got out of my car to see better, and when the lights at the intersection turned red, she crossed the road. In the fading light I watched her cross the parking lot of a Chinese restaurant called the Taste of Hong Kong and enter through the front doors.

I got back into my car and drove the two hundred yards to the Chinese restaurant, parking in its nearly empty lot. The Taste of Hong Kong had a brick exterior and a steep shingled roof; there was an A-frame around its front entrance with a high peak, and on either side of the framing was the name of the restaurant in bright blue ornate script. I sat in my car for about thirty seconds before deciding to head in. Crossing the faded asphalt I could already smell the odor of Chinese food in the crisp fall air. It smelled of seared meat and brown sugar.

The interior of the restaurant was so dark it took a moment for my eyes to adjust. There was an ornate fountain by the empty hostess stand, and I was instantly transported back to a similar Chinese restaurant in a similar town when I was a child. My grandparents would take me there at least once a month and I would beg for pennies to throw into the fountain.

"Just one?" a voice said, and I looked up. A tall woman in black trousers and a white button-down shirt held a menu. She tilted her head to the left, indicating a low-ceilinged dining room with bright fluorescent lighting. To her right was the entrance to a cocktail lounge. I could make out a long bar in its dim interior.

"Just a drink," I said, and she tilted her head in the other direction. I passed her and entered the bar. There was a large fish tank on its far wall that glowed yellow. The long, lacquered bar had a padded rim and swivel stools in red Naugahyde, and Pam, the lone patron, sat at the exact midpoint. The bartender, a young Asian man wearing a Hawaiian shirt, was mixing a drink. I sat at the nearest stool, aware of Pam, her head turned, checking me out.

I was starting to take off my jacket when she spoke. "Don't be a stranger, hon," she said. "You can sit closer if you like."

CHAPTER 6

JOAN

It was the hottest day of the summer vacation so far, and after breakfast, Joan slathered herself in sunscreen, changed into her bikini,
and walked to the beach with her blanket and towel, a large water
bottle, her sister's Discman, and a copy of *Gerald's Game* by Stephen
King she'd taken from the library the night before.

She crossed the road, then walked up and over the worn wooden
ramp that spanned the brief rise of dune that edged the beach. It
was low tide, the sand and the sky almost colorless, the brightness
of the sun rippling the air. Once her blanket was spread out, and
free of all sand, she lay down on her front and tried to stop thinking
about the conversation with Richard from the night before. She'd
gone over and over it while lying in bed, and she'd barely slept, slipping in and out of strange dreams. Now, with one ear pressed into
the blanket, warmed already by the sand, she listened to the gulls
squawking, and the low shushing of the waves, more like a sensation
than a sound. She must have fallen asleep because her neck was all
of a sudden damp with sweat, and she turned herself over onto her
back, confused a little about where she was.

After swallowing half the cold water in her bottle, she propped herself onto her elbows, and looked across the beach through the aqua tint of her sunglasses. Last year at high school, her best friend Madison had developed an almost obsessional crush on a senior named Eric Hall, and for at least half of the year Madison could barely even look you in the eye if she was anywhere near a place where Eric might be. She was always hunting in the distance, down school hallways, and across the cafeteria, for a possible appearance of the mythical lacrosse player. It had annoyed Joan to no end, but now, on the beach, she felt herself doing the same thing. Scanning the shimmery bodies on the wide expanse of the beach, looking for anyone who might be Richard.

And it wasn't a crush. She had zero interest in kissing Richard or doing anything else with him. No, it was something more than that. The things he'd said last night, the matter-of-fact way he'd talked about killing his cousin, had done something entirely different to her, made her feel dangerously alive, almost intoxicated. She'd been drunk a few times in her life, mostly on warm beer snuck to an outdoor party, or else on something gross like the bottle of Frangelico she and three other gymnasts drank during a sleepover at Madison's house.

But those times hadn't compared to the summer before, when her parents had hosted a garden party. Her dad's best friend, an older Canadian man named Angus, who wore white suits and had a white beard, had been making himself a martini in the kitchen when Joan wandered in to look through the kid's cooler for more Sprite.

"You're drinking a martini," she'd said to Angus.

"You have a good eye. Have you had one?"

"No," she said. "I'm not even fifteen yet."

"They're quite delicious. I'd offer to make you one, but then I'd get in trouble when people saw you tottering around the garden with a martini in your hand. What's in your glass there?"

Joan's glass was mostly ice at this point, plus a wedge of lime and two cherry stems. "It's just ice," she said.

"Well, here you go, then," Angus said, stepping carefully toward her and tipping the full contents of his martini glass into hers. "Drink it very slowly. And know that I will deny this interaction ever happened."

She'd returned to the garden and began to sip her martini. It was so incredibly strong it made her eyes water, but there was also something so pure and adult about the way it tasted. It burned her tongue, but in a good way. It was gone too soon, and when she got up from her patio seat and walked across the party, everything was heightened. The smell of the flowers, the snippets of adult conversations, the sun on her hair. She felt as though she could levitate if she'd wanted to, that she was weightless.

"What shows do you watch, if any?"

She turned, and three of her mother's friends were looking in her direction. They'd been talking about TV shows—she'd heard them earlier—and she stepped into their circle, still holding the ice-cold glass, and joined the conversation. At first, she'd wondered if they could tell she was drunk, but they didn't seem to be able to. They were all talking about *ER*, and then *Friends*, and Joan was telling them how Joey and Phoebe were secretly the smartest ones on the show, and they were all laughing.

Later, she thought about how easy it was to be an adult, how easy it was to make other people like you. She was no longer drunk, but she felt powerful, like she'd gotten away with something. It had been an electrifying day, and there had been a moment, lost now, where she remembered knowing something that no one else in the world knew. It had both thrilled her and filled her with a kind of righteous anger. But now she couldn't remember exactly what it was she had known.

And that was oddly how she'd felt the night before in the library at the Windward Resort, listening to Richard talk about killing his cousin, and offering up suggestions. Being free to say those words had felt like drinking a martini in front of a gardenful of adults, all who had no idea how the world actually worked.

Because if Richard had been saying those things to an adult, they would think he was kidding. But down deep Joan knew Richard had been serious, and it hadn't bothered her at all.

A greenhead was biting her thigh and she slapped at it. It lay dazed on her blanket and she flicked it away. She watched it struggling in the sand for a while, then lost interest. She stood up, then walked down to the water. A woman in a black skirted bathing suit stood hip high in the ocean, gently splashing herself with water, girding herself to go all the way in.

Joan waded in, annoyed to find the water really was that cold, numbing her ankle bones. She took a few steps out to where there was a dip in the sand then sank in past her hips. She made a tiny gasp, and the woman in the one-piece laughed and said something about how cold it was. Joan shrugged and dove under the approaching wave, then swam out to where the waves weren't breaking, the water starting to numb her skin all over. She swam back and forth for a while until her lungs hurt then tipped her head back and floated on the surface, closing her eyes. She could hear kids screaming, but they sounded as though they were far away.

As she stepped out of the surf she scanned the beach, looking for her blanket, and that was when she spotted Richard—she was pretty sure it was him—walking high up along the edge of the dunes. When she reached her belongings, he was about a hundred yards down the beach, but she could still see him. She dried off quickly and began to follow. He must have been walking slowly, since, in just a few minutes, she wasn't that far behind him. Suddenly, she felt self-conscious and slowed down. What was her plan? Was she going to catch up with him, see if he wanted company? Or did it make sense to just bump into him randomly?

He stopped up ahead of her, crouching down to look at something in the sand. She slowed too, but he didn't stay crouched for too long. He got up and kept walking. She reached the place where he'd crouched. It was hard to see at first but there were the bleached bones of a gull, and a few feathers. She placed her feet in his footprints and crouched, as well, studying the exposed spine of the bird, the way it curved to its head, picked of flesh, but with its beak half covered with sand.

"Oh, hey," came the voice, and she looked up at Richard. "Were you following me?" he said.

If anyone else in the world had asked her that question she'd have denied it, but somehow, because it was Richard, she said, "I was swimming, then saw you walk by. Wanted to know what you were up to."

"I'm just walking. Want to come with me?"

They walked down to the end of the beach, to where a pile of black, seaweed-fringed rocks jutted out into the ocean. "Do you like tide pools?" Richard said, peering down into a pool of water, half obscured by one of the black rocks.

"I can't honestly say I've given them that much thought."

He smiled at her. "I only like them because they're filled with things." He crouched down, and Joan stood over him. With Richard crouched, and her standing, they were practically the same size. She looked at his dark neck, one of the few parts of him that was truly tanned. He wore a black T-shirt today, and not one of his striped polo shirts. She watched, fascinated, as he submerged his arm into the water, putting it in the dark crevice formed by the rock. When he pulled his hand out it was cupped and he showed her a small green crab he was holding delicately between his fingers. "See?" he said.

"I don't know how you stick your hand in there."

The crab's small pincers waved angrily, and Richard slid it back into the tide pool, where it darted away. He stood back up, and Joan saw a thin ribbon of blood was coming off his hand.

He looked at it, surprised. "Oh, it got me," he said, washing his hand in the tide pool. Then he looked more closely at the ragged cut between his thumb and index finger. "Do you want to go swimming?"

Joan wasn't particularly interested in getting back in the water, but said, "Yes," anyway, and watched as Richard, after pulling off his T-shirt and leaving it on the sand, bounded out into the waves, spun so that he was facing her, then fell backward into the water. She joined him, the water still shockingly cold, and together they floated for a while.

"I've been thinking about what we talked about last night," she said.

"About Duane?"

"Yeah."

"He told me last night that he fucked you on the beach." Richard made air quotes when saying the word *fucked*.

"What?" Joan said, although it was more like a scream.

"He didn't say your name or anything, but he mentioned you were a gymnast so I figured he was talking about you."

"What did he say?"

"Not much. First he was talking about the girl who works behind the desk, and what he wants to do to her, and then he said he'd already fucked the only other hot girl at the hotel, and how you were a gymnast and everything."

"Why'd he even mention that?"

"What? Being a gymnast? He said gross stuff about it."

"Like what?"

"I don't want to say."

"Just tell me."

"He said you were totally horny, and you did a split on his cock. Something like that."

Joan let out a guttural scream between her clenched teeth. "That's a total lie. He's disgusting."

"Yeah, what did I tell you. I knew he was lying, though. Don't worry."

"Did you tell him you knew me?" Joan said.

"I didn't."

"Why not?"

"I don't know exactly. I figured he'd be weird about it."

Joan, trying to relax, had tipped back and was floating again. The sky was a hard, cloudless blue.

"It's good you didn't tell him we know one another."

"Okay," Richard said.

"I mean, no one knows we know each other," she said. "Maybe we should keep it that way. We could be secret friends, and no one would know about it except for us."

"Sure," Richard said.

A wave lifted them, and they slid down its back side. "You probably think I'm just saying that because I don't want people at school to know we became friends or something," Joan said. "I hope you don't think that."

"Oh," Richard said. "I didn't really think that, at all. But it would be cool to be secret friends and have no one else know."

"Okay," Joan said. "And now that we are friends, I need to tell you that I'm getting out of the water because I'm too cold."

"You should go ahead," he said. "I'm going to swim a little bit longer."

Before leaving him, Joan said, "I hate your fucking cousin."

"Yeah, me too. Join the club."

She took a few strokes toward shore then rode up and over a crashing wave that deposited her hard onto her hip in the shallow water. It hurt a little but she was a gymnast and used to being hurt.

She walked back alone to her towel, tired from all the swimming and from the relentless sun. She toweled off again and lay down on her stomach, closing her eyes, and imagining what she'd do to Duane if she got the chance.

That night, during cocktail hour, Joan got herself a Shirley Temple from the bar, and wandered the lobby. There was live music again, a man on a piano this time, and a woman singing jazzy songs. She saw Richard's aunt and uncle, taking up a sofa that could have easily fit four people. She hadn't seen Richard since earlier that morning on the beach. And she hadn't seen Duane.

By the front desk there was a little gift shop area, with paperbacks and magazines, and snacks and soft drinks. The girl who Joan had talked with the night before was behind the desk, tipped back on a high chair, flipping through a magazine. She looked really young, too young to have a job, Joan thought, and remembered what Richard had said about Duane wanting to fuck her. She had dyed blond hair and a kind of pudgy face, with a heavy lower lip. She wore a lot of makeup around her eyes. Joan wandered over and said hi.

"What can I help you with?" the girl said, sitting up abruptly.

"Just saying hi, actually," Joan said. "What's it like to work here?"

"Oh," the girl said, putting the magazine down on the desk. "It's actually a pretty great job. Last summer I worked as a hostess over at the Kennewick Lodge, and my feet hurt all the time, but here it's really busy on Saturdays because that's when most people check in or check out, but the rest of the time I just sit here and answer questions or sell people Pringles. It's totally easy, and the guy who runs this place is actually pretty nice. You're staying here, right?"

"Yeah, I'm Joan. You had a job last year, too? How old are you?"

"I'm seventeen, but I know that I look fifteen. I'm Jessica. Where are you from?"

Joan told her, and it turned out that Jessica knew someone who went to Dartford-Middleham High School, but Joan didn't know the kid she knew. They talked for a while about that, then Joan asked her about other teenagers at the resort.

"You're basically it, right now," Jessica said. "Well, almost it. It's kind of a resort that's for old people, I think, because there are, like, constant buffets. I don't think it's too exciting for someone our age. The beach is nice."

"Yeah, the beach is nice," Joan said.

Jessica's eyes suddenly looked alarmed. "Hey," she whispered. "Don't look, but have you met some guy named Duane who's around your age? He's been here for two weeks."

"Duane, I don't think so," Joan found herself saying, her back stiffening at the thought that Duane was now in the lobby.

"Okay, you can look now, over your right shoulder. He's the jock-looking guy with the skinny kid. I don't know anything about his brother, or whoever that is, but stay away from Duane. He's kind of a creep."

"Oh," Joan said. And she was about to ask Jessica what had happened, but a woman with a child clinging to her leg was looking for something in the ice-cream freezer and Jessica went to help her.

Joan looked over at Richard and Duane, but only for a moment because Duane was looking toward her, his jaw moving rapidly like he was chewing gum. She went to the paperback rack and spun it, wondering why she hadn't told Jessica about her run-in with Duane. And then she thought: it's a good thing I didn't tell her. Because, and she was just beginning to admit this to herself, she actually thought that Richard might be serious about killing Duane. And if he was really going to do it, she had made a decision that she would help him. The thought of it was terrifying, but also made her feel like she was levitating off the floor.

"Sweetheart, you okay?" It was her mom, appearing out of no-where, and Joan realized her mom had been standing there talking at her for a while.

"Oh, sorry, I'm in a daze."

"You're sun-dazed is what you are. We're going in to dinner now. You coming?"

"God, yes. I'm starving."

CHAPTER 7

KIMBALL

"I didn't mean to be so pushy, but if we're the only two people at the bar then we might as well sit close enough to one another and have a conversation."

I'd moved to within one chair of Pam in the yellow light of the cocktail lounge.

"How's your Tuesday going?" I said.

The bartender was placing a pale, peach-colored drink in a lowball glass in front of her. It was garnished with a generous sprig of mint that she pushed down into her glass. After taking a sip she said, "Well, I'm alone at a bar at just after quitting time, so I guess it was that kind of day."

I ordered a Tsingtao beer and Pam said, "I thought you'd be here for the cocktails. Do you know who this guy is?"

I must have looked confused because she said, "This is Pete Liu. He was named a rising star in . . . what magazine was it, Pete?"

The bartender uncapped my beer and was pouring it into a glass. "It was *Saveur,* and it wasn't 'rising star,' it was 'one to watch.'"

"Pete's going to be modest so I'm going to boast for him. He's only going to be a bartender here for about five more minutes until he gets poached by some high-end hotel bar, so I do recommend you try a cocktail."

"What are you having?"

"I'm having a mai tai, but it's so much better than anything you've ever had that's been called a mai tai before."

After I finished my beer, I ordered one too, and Pam was right. It was the best drink I'd ever had in a Chinese restaurant. She was also pretty good company. We talked food and drink, and it wasn't until we'd decided to split an order of shrimp toast that she got around to asking me what I did.

"I'm a writer," I said.

"Oh, yeah?"

"Aspiring, I guess. I write poetry, mostly, and I teach classes here and there."

"Is that enough to make a living?" she said.

"I live in a cheap apartment, and I don't have health insurance. So, no, it's not really a living, but it's all I've got."

"What are you doing out here?"

I'd been prepared for that question and I told her I'd come out to walk around Walden Pond, then took a drive to look for a place to have a drink and just stumbled upon the Taste of Hong Kong. "How about you?" I said.

"How about me what?"

"What do you do?"

She took a breath that raised her shoulders a little then said, "I'm an office manager at a real estate company."

"You like it?"

"I don't dislike it, and I'm good at it. It's just that . . ." Her phone had buzzed and she apologized and took a look at it. I was halfway through my cocktail and beginning to feel it. Before I had too many drinks I decided I needed a plan. Or maybe my plan should be to get drunk with Pam O'Neil and then get her to confess she'd been having an affair with her boss. Case closed. I hadn't decided yet.

"Sorry about that," she said, putting her phone facedown on the bar. "My friend Janey who was originally supposed to meet me here an hour ago is now saying she'll be here in an hour. I don't know if I believe her or not. Hey, are you looking for a girlfriend?"

"Not particularly," I said, maybe a little too fast.

"Don't panic," she said, laughing. "I just thought that Janey, my friend, who may or may not show up here in about an hour, is free. And she's a very successful real estate agent."

"Well . . . ," I said.

"I won't embarrass you, and I don't even know why I'm trying to set you up with my friend. I don't know you."

"How about you?" I said, hoping to change the subject.

"What about me?"

"Are you in a relationship?"

She pressed her index finger to the bar, rubbing at an invisible stain. "I'm in a complicated and stupid relationship that I need to get out of."

"That sounds interesting."

"Oh, God no," she said, and turned to me. "It's many things, but I don't think interesting is one of them. For one thing it's much more of a threesome than a twosome."

"Well, actually," I said. "That does sound interesting."

She whacked at my arm with the back of her hand. "No, not like that. Not like you're thinking. I'm done talking about it, anyways, because it's depressing." She smiled sadly, and I got my first real look at her teeth, gray in the light of the cocktail lounge. She quickly closed her mouth, and I wondered if she was self-conscious about it. Up close I thought she was less pretty, but more interesting looking, maybe even beautiful, than I'd thought she was when I'd seen her earlier in the coffee shop. She had a face that constantly changed, all her emotions passing across her features. Her chin was a little pointed and she had a short upper lip, but her pale blue eyes were bright and intense. I decided not to push her about her complicated relationship, hoping the subject would naturally return.

"How's the real estate market out here?" I said.

"Competitive," she said, as the shrimp toast arrived.

Pete the bartender asked me if I wanted another drink. "Another beer," I said, deciding to nurse it for a while, maybe order more food. Pam took a sip of her mai tai, tipping the glass back so that the ice rapped against her teeth. "Can I get you another of those?" I said.

"On your poet's salary?" she said, then her face fell, and she immediately said, "God, that was so rude. I'm sorry."

"No, don't be. I'll show you up when I sell a sonnet to Hollywood for a million dollars."

She laughed. "Okay, one drink, but the shrimp toast is on me."

"Okay," I said.

By the time our drinks were in front of us, and we'd ordered more appetizers, I noticed that the bar was starting to fill up. One stool had been taken up by a grubby-looking guy who kept his parka on and ordered a Budweiser, but the rest of the new patrons looked more like swank couples arriving for a big night out. The high-tops in the bar area were all occupied, and Pete was putting cocktails together at a very fast pace.

"He's kind of a cult figure," Pam said. "I'm surprised you just wandered in here."

"I had no idea."

When Pam's friend Janey finally arrived, the lounge was borderline crowded, and Pete had help behind the bar, a young woman with pink hair wearing a gingham dress. I was introduced to Pam's friend, and we both had to lean in in order to talk to one another; she was enveloped in a cloud of perfume, and it took all my will-

THE KIND WORTH SAVING | 59

power to not sneeze. After introductions she arranged herself on the stool on the other side of Pam. She was wearing a light gray suit over a silk blouse. Her hair was stiff from some sort of product, and she had a lot of makeup on. If I'd truly wandered into the Taste of Hong Kong as I'd said I had, and randomly met Pam, then I would most certainly be settling up my bill and leaving. I didn't have a lot of interest in getting to know Pam's friend, and we couldn't hear each other anyway, not with all three of us sitting at the bar. I excused myself to go to the bathroom, trying to figure out what to do next. Pam was getting drunk and talkative. If I stuck around there was a good chance she would eventually tell me the whole story of her affair with Joan's husband. Or else I might find out she wasn't having an affair with Richard Whalen. Or maybe she'd simply talk with her friend Janey the rest of the night, and I would learn nothing.

Walking back across the lounge I decided to stay for at least twenty minutes more, just to see what might happen. When I reached the two women, Pam slid from her stool to the one next to it, and insisted I sit in the middle, so we'd all be able to talk to one another.

"I feel like I'm invading your night," I said, and both women shook their heads.

"All we're doing is gossiping about work," Janey said. "We can do that anytime. Besides, I'm here for one drink, tops, and then I'm going home. It's a Tuesday."

"Where do you both live?" I said.

"Right across the road," Pam said. "Both of us do, actually. We don't live together but in the same apartment building."

"Colonial Estates," Janey said. "It's neither Colonial nor an estate."

They both laughed, and Pam said, "But they have a pool."

"And an exercise room that no one uses."

"Yes."

"So this is your local bar?" I said.

"Yes, we'd probably come here even if Pete wasn't here." The bartender, cleaning a glass during a rare lull, heard Pam say his name and nodded toward us, seeing if we needed anything. "No, we're fine," Pam said. "Or maybe we should all get one more drink then call it a night."

We all agreed, getting one more drink, plus our bills. Pam and I wrangled over who was paying for what drink, and what snacks, then, when we had finally figured it out, we paid up, and the three of us moved with our new drinks to a high-top table where it would be easier to chat.

It was clear that Pam was still imagining Janey and I might be a romantic match, so she kept the conversation going by asking the two of us questions. It got a little awkward when, after explaining again how I was a poet, Janey asked for my full name so she could look me up online and read something I'd written. I gave my name as Henry Dickey and said that I wasn't sure they'd find anything about me online. If I'd given my real name, they'd find nothing about poetry, either, although they might find a listing for my investigative services, and they would almost certainly find out about my involvement as a police officer investigating the deaths of Ted and Miranda Severson two years earlier.

"Henry Dickey, Henry Dickey," Janey said aloud, in order to memorize my name. She finished her drink, then told both of us she needed to go tinkle and then maybe Pam and she could walk across the road back to their apartments. "Unless you two want to stay—"

"No, I'm ready to go," Pam said, and I nodded.

Janey ticked away on heels, and I turned to Pam and said, "This was fun."

"You should come back here. To the Hong Kong. Become a regular like Janey and me."

"When do you guys usually come here?"

"Tonight was unusual, actually. Thursday night we are almost always here, for sure. And sometimes on the weekend if nothing else is going on. But, yeah, Thursday night is a good time. It was nice meeting you, Henry."

Janey came back and the three of us exited into the cold night, the black sky busy with stars. I hugged them both goodbye then watched as they walked together to the intersection, pressing the walk button that stopped the traffic.

Driving back to Cambridge I went over the evening in my mind. I was still wondering what Pam had meant by saying her relationship was more of a threesome than a twosome. Was it her way of telling me she was the other woman coming between a married couple?

When I got back to my apartment, Pyewacket the cat let me know how unhappy he was that I'd been gone all day. He herded me to his food bowl, and I gave him his dinner, then set up my laptop on my desk. I took notes about the day, wanting to put in writing some of the exact phrases that Pam had used in describing her relationship to me. After doing that I leaned back in my chair and thought for a while. Pyewacket, done eating, leapt up into my lap, purring. There are many things I love about cats but one of them is their short memories. After he'd gotten sufficient chin scratches he jumped back down to the floor. I opened the document on my computer where I wrote down ideas for poems. At the top of the page I wrote, "There once was a drinker named Pam."

CHAPTER 8

JOAN

There had been so little to do over the last few days that Joan had read *Gerald's Game* then another Stephen King book called *Dolores Claiborne,* and now she was reading *Pet Semetary.* She'd been to the library several times but hadn't seen Richard, and because of her sunburn, she'd temporarily stopped going to the beach. In the middle of the day she read in her room, propped up on several pillows, drinking cans of Diet Coke. Her mom and dad had developed a sudden interest in going antiquing, driving aimlessly through southern Maine and coming home with lobster buoys, vintage postcards, and other stuff that was going to look ridiculous back at their house in Middleham.

And Lizzie, Joan's sister, was nowhere to be found. She'd made a friend two days earlier, another female college student visiting her parents who were staying at Windward for the entire month. It seemed as though Lizzie and this girl, Denise or something like that, were suddenly joined at the hip (her mother's phrase), and at breakfast that day Joan, reading her book, had overhead her parents whisper something about Lizzie maybe being a lesbian.

Sometimes in the later afternoon, when the sun was lower in the sky, she'd walk down to the beach carrying just a towel and go for a swim. If the afternoon was cool, she'd take a walk first, usually down to the stone jetty then back, just so she'd warm up a little, get sweaty enough so she wanted to run into the cold water. It was on a Friday, when Joan and her family had been at Windward for almost a full week, that she came out of the water, and saw that Duane was watching her clamber up the incline of damp sand that led to the ridge where she'd planted her clothes and her towel.

"I saw you out there swimming," he said.

"Uh-huh," Joan said.

"The water's pretty cold." Duane was wearing a T-shirt that said GEORGETOWN PREP on it.

"It's not that bad, actually." Joan stooped to pick her towel up off the beach, snapping it in the wind to get any sand off it before wrapping it around her torso.

"Yeah, I guess," Duane said, and stared out at the ocean as though he could tell its temperature just by looking at it.

"Hey," he said, and jerked his head back, as though he were trying to get his dog to heel. "Sorry if things were a little weird the other night."

Not wanting to talk about it, Joan said, "Whatever."

"You didn't tell anyone, did you?"

"About what? You being a dick?"

"Look, you were the one—"

"Forget it. Whatever. I don't care."

Duane nodded, as though he were pondering her words, then said, "Well, if you don't care then I thought maybe you'd want to come hang out again. At the beach. I'm going to be there tonight with some friends."

"Yeah, who? You and that creepy busboy?"

"No. There'll be more kids. Derek's inviting a couple of his friends. And there are these girls coming. I don't know their names, but they're not locals or anything. They're staying at one of the big rental houses down the other end of the beach."

"Probably not," Joan said.

"Hey, whatever. I just thought you might be pretty bored of this place."

While he'd been standing there, he'd slipped off one of his flip-flops and had dug his foot into the soft sand. She knew he was trying to be nice, that he was remembering the last time they'd hung out, and was pretending it had never happened. She was almost positive he wanted to say something to her like, "Don't be a baby," or "What, you don't drink?" And part of her really wanted to tell him she'd rather read in her room than be out on a dark beach with him and his gross friends, but, instead, she said, "Yeah, okay. Maybe."

"Cool," he said.

Joan wanted to dry off, but she didn't want to do it in front of Duane, so she kept the towel wrapped around her and slid her own sandals back on her feet, trying to ignore the wet sand trapped between her toes.

"I'm going to head back now. I'm cold."

"Oh, okay," Duane said. "See you tonight." He turned awkwardly, and made his way in the direction of the hotel. Joan, happy that he hadn't waited for her, dried herself off, pulled on her denim shorts, all while watching Duane work his way up the beach pretty slowly. Maybe he was hoping she'd try to catch up with him. She wasn't planning on it, though, and she wasn't planning on meeting him and his townie friends at the beach later, either. What she really wanted to do now was to find Richard and report on this interaction. When Duane was far enough ahead of her, she hung her towel over her neck and made her way back to the Windward.

• • •

Dinner that night was meatloaf, and the only good news about that was there was also mashed potatoes.

Joan's father was napping, so it was Joan and her mother and her sister, and halfway through the meal, Denise, Lizzie's new friend, joined them. She was a senior at NYU and she had a really short haircut, but with one long strand that came down the left side of her head, and that she kept tucking behind her ear, almost like a nervous tic. She wore a tank top and had one of those tattoos all the way around her bicep muscle, a little interlocking pattern, and Joan wondered what it would look like when Denise was old and saggy.

"Have you started to think about college yet?" Denise asked Joan.

She hadn't, but said, "Maybe somewhere in Boston," just to have something to say.

"So you think you might want a city school instead of a country school?"

"I guess so."

Denise then told a long story about the nine different colleges she'd applied to and the ones she'd gotten into and the ones she hadn't, and Lizzie kept smiling at her and nodding along like it was the most fascinating thing she'd ever heard.

While they were talking, Joan saw Richard, who she'd spotted earlier with his aunt and uncle, go up to the buffet. It was relatively quiet up there, so Joan quickly finished all the potatoes on her plate and told her mom she was going back up for more.

"She's got a hollow leg," her mother said, as Joan got up, leaving her dirty plate at the table like you were supposed to.

The buffet had two sides, the trays of food identical on both so it didn't matter which side you went down. Joan cut into the line on the opposite side from Richard, grabbed some more potatoes, then said, "Hey," across the sneeze barriers.

He'd been getting more potatoes, as well, and he looked up.

"Meet me in the library after dinner," Joan said. "I have news."

Richard nodded, and Joan went back to her table, feeling a little stupid and a little excited at the same time. It felt as though they were playacting, being secretive, but it wasn't entirely playacting, was it? When Richard talked about doing something to Duane, he seemed serious.

When Joan got to the library, Richard wasn't there yet, which was fine since there was a woman in a muumuu looking through the fiction shelves. Joan pulled a random Judy Blume book from the kids' section and plopped down on one of the leather chairs. It was *Deenie,* a book she thought her older sister had once read, and she flipped through the pages, not looking at them. The woman, whose hair was dyed and stiff and looked like a helmet, kept talking to herself as she browsed the books, saying things like, "Oh, I think I've read that one," or reading the titles out loud. At last she pulled a book down, a chunky paperback, and was quiet while reading its back cover. "I guess this'll have to do," she said aloud, then glanced in Joan's direction. Joan kept her eyes on her own book. The woman left.

About ten minutes passed, and Joan was pretty sure that Richard wasn't going to show up. She felt angry again, wondering if he was trying to avoid her, but then he was suddenly standing at a nearby shelf. She hadn't heard him come in.

"Oh, hi," she said, as though they were meeting randomly.

"Hi, there," he said.

Joan leaned over in her chair to see around the shelf that was in the middle of the room.

"We're alone here," he said.

"Oh, good. Guess who I talked with today?"

"Duane?"

"Yep. I was swimming right before dinnertime and when I got out of the water he was standing by my clothes and towels waiting for me. Like he hadn't attacked me the other night."

"What did he say?"

"He wanted to know if I'd come down to the beach again tonight and hang out with him and his friends."

"Jesus. What did you say?"

"I was going to tell him off, but then I figured maybe I'd say that I was going to come, at least lead him on a little."

"Uh-huh," Richard said. He seemed to be thinking.

"He said there would be more kids there this time, including two girls who are staying at some rental house. I guess he figured I might come if I knew other girls would be there."

"So are you going to go, or what?" Richard said.

"Where? To Duane's beach party?"

"Yeah."

"I wasn't planning on it."

"Maybe you should go, but just for a little bit, like one beer, then leave."

"Last time I went he was all over me. This time he'll probably kill me, or something."

Richard grinned, exposing his very white teeth. "I don't think Duane is a serial killer. At least not yet."

"Why do you think I should go?"

"It will be like baiting the hook. Remember we talked about how the best way to kill Duane was to get him out to the end of the jetty and then push him in the water?"

"Yeah."

"Well, you've got to get him interested first, make him think he has an actual chance with you. And then it will be easy to lead him out to the jetty."

"Tonight?" Joan said too loud, then whispered, "You want me to lead him out there tonight?"

"No, not tonight. There'll be other people on the beach, and they'll all know you went with him. No, I just think you should show up tonight to keep him interested, and then sometime next week you could ask him to secretly meet you at the end of the jetty."

"You *are* using me as bait?"

"I guess so," Richard said. "Do you feel like a worm?"

"A little bit."

There was a sound in the hallway, like someone knocking on a door, and Richard went to the entryway to the library and looked out. "Nothing," he said when he came back.

"Do you think it will be safe if I go meet Duane and his friends tonight? I mean, do you think there will really be other girls there?"

"I don't know," Richard said. "If you want, I could go down to the beach, too, and spy on the party. It will be dark, and I don't think they'll see me. That way I can make sure that you get there safe and that you're able to leave. Just don't stay long, but act like you don't totally hate Duane. Then later he'll do whatever you ask him to do."

Joan thought about it. Her skin was tingly, like she was about to give a presentation in class.

"Okay, I'll go down and have one beer with them."

"Good," Richard said. "What time did he say?"

"He said around ten o'clock."

"You want me to come to the beach, too?"

"No, I'll be fine."

"Sounds good. And maybe we should meet back here tomorrow night at the same time and talk about what happened."

"Sure," Joan said.

Richard left the library first, then Joan, going back to her room. Lizzie was out. Joan began to imagine what it would be like if she was the one who walked out on the jetty with Duane on the night he died. She imagined the attention she'd get, the pity, the worrying looks. She thought about that time when she was eight years old and went missing for a night. It was the week after Lizzie had gotten the all-clear on yet another cancer scan, and as a celebration present had gotten a Discman. She'd spent every minute listening to grunge music on it, singing along tunelessly. One night when Lizzie was out Joan stole the Discman plus a couple of CDs and went into the deep closet that was located in the spare bedroom of their house. She sometimes went there to be alone, burying herself underneath a bunch of old blankets that were stacked in the far corner. That night, she'd lain in the closet listening to Lizzie's weird music until she must have fallen asleep, not waking up until the following morning. After stumbling out of the closet in the early morning she was surprised to hear adult voices that didn't belong to her parents coming from downstairs. She followed the sounds, walking into the kitchen where her mother and father, both standing, were talking to a uniformed police officer sitting at the kitchen table taking notes. It was her mother who spotted her first, her eyes widening, mouthing Joan's name then racing and pulling her into a tight, smothering hug.

Her parents had thought she'd left the house and gone missing. There was lots of laughter and annoying hugs, and even the police officer had stuck around for a while, enjoying the happy outcome. She remembered thinking at the time how easy it had been to make everyone worry about her, and she also remembered thinking, not for the first time, that grown-ups just weren't as smart as she thought they were. But she'd loved the attention, especially since it meant less attention being directed at Lizzie and her miraculous recovery. Her dad had an expression—he liked to say that when you learned something you should put it in your back pocket for later, and that was what Joan had done, then.

And now, if she and Richard actually did what she thought they were going to do, she was going to be a tragic celebrity for a while, the girl who was with a boy when he drowned. The thought of it was scary and thrilling and even though she wouldn't be leaving to go to the beach party for another few hours she changed into the clothes she planned on wearing, a pair of jeans and her fleece hoodie, then flipped through the channels looking for a movie to watch while she waited.

CHAPTER 9

KIMBALL

I'd parked my car in the lot of a Dunkin' Donuts at a busy intersection about a mile from where Richard and Joan Whalen lived, and I'd angled it in such a way so I could watch the traffic go by. I was looking for Richard's silver BMW, assuming he'd have to pass through this intersection whether he was going to the offices in Dartford or in Concord. But it was just past ten o'clock and my coffee cup was empty, and I'd either missed him, or he'd gone another way, or maybe he was already at one of the offices, even though I'd been stationed in my lot since eight that morning.

I decided to give up, and just as I started the engine, I saw a silver car about four back at the lights going in the right direction. I swung out of the lot, pulling into the traffic of the cross street, timing it so that after I watched the BMW pass through the intersection, my light turned green and I was able to get about three or four cars behind him. Two of those cars veered off to head toward Route 2, and I got closer to Richard. I followed him all the way to the Dartford office, where he parked on the street right in front of Blackburn Properties. I went past him and pulled into an open spot about two hundred yards down the road, worrying that Pam might walk by and spot me. In a feeble attempt at anonymity, I put on one of the baseball caps I kept in the glove compartment while keeping an eye on my side mirror. I was glad I'd waited because I watched as Richard, in a navy suit, came back out of the office with a file folder in one hand and got back into his car. He did a U-turn, and I waited thirty seconds and followed him. He was most likely going to an appointment somewhere, or to view a house, but I figured I'd follow for a little while. If he was sleeping with Pam O'Neil, then they were doing it sometime during the daytime hours.

I followed Richard to Sudbury and into a recent development, big houses on big lots, and every house in a slightly different style. A few Tudors, a few classical Romans, but all of them enormous and most likely made from the cheapest materials available. Richard pulled into the driveway of a house with Tuscan columns and mismatched gables, and I drove past, finding myself at a cul-de-sac. Looping back around I saw that an older couple from the house Richard was visiting had come out to greet him. I left the neighborhood.

Not knowing what to do next and feeling as though I was on a well-paid fool's errand, I drove into Concord center, parking in a free lot next to a cemetery off Main Street. I hadn't been to Concord for two years, and the last time I was here I had nearly died. I had been following Lily Kintner, a person of interest in two connected homicides, the murder of Ted Severson in the South End of Boston, and the subsequent murder of his wife, Miranda, in southern Maine. Lily had come after me with a knife, managing to successfully slide it between two of my ribs, and I'd been rescued only by the presence of my then-partner Roberta James. That day had changed everything for me. Even though I call Lily Kintner a person of interest in the case I was working on, the real person of interest was Brad Daggett, the contractor working on building their summer home in Maine. He'd been having an affair with Miranda Severson, and he had disappeared after Miranda's body was found. He was still missing, and as far as I knew he was presumed to be responsible for both deaths.

The murder of Ted Severson was my final official case as a member of the Boston Police Department. Without telling my partner, I had been trailing Lily Kintner, an archival librarian who lived in Winslow, Massachusetts. She was part of the investigation because she'd recently met Ted Severson on a flight from London to Boston, and afterward they'd met for drinks. She had also gone to college with Miranda, Ted's wife. Most importantly, she'd lied to me when we first met, telling me she hadn't known Ted Severson. I knew she was involved in some capacity but couldn't prove anything, and that was why I'd been following her. According to Lily Kintner she'd become frightened of me, so frightened she'd sought to protect herself by attacking me with a knife. The assault case against Lily Kintner was dropped after it was discovered I'd written multiple unsavory limericks about her, and that I was acting on my own behalf. And that was why I was removed from the Boston Police Department.

The truth was that I *had* become a little obsessed with Lily Kintner during the investigation. It was partly due to the fact that she had withheld information from me, and it was also partly due to the fact I'd fallen in love with her. No, maybe that's not right. Not love, exactly, but total obsession. I couldn't get her out of my mind. The Boston Police Department was right to fire me, and I was lucky, I suppose, that Lily Kintner never filed a civil suit. Not knowing what to do next with my life I'd gotten my private investigator's license.

And I still thought about Lily every day.

I got out of my car, locked it behind me, and strolled down the main drag of Concord. It was a little too early for lunch. Besides, part of me wanted to go look at the place where my life had nearly ended, just curious to know how it would make me feel. I reached the rotary at the end of Main Street and looked up at the hillside cemetery that loomed above the town. The day was windy and dead leaves were piling up against the headstones. I was about to cross over to enter the cemetery through its narrow stone gate but decided against it. The memories from that day were still fresh in my mind, and I didn't need to stand in the exact spot in order to process what had happened. I'd come to accept the reasons that Lily did what she did. I remembered the surprise of seeing her approach me, the almost gentle feel of the knife sliding into me, and Lily's words in my ear. *I'm sorry.*

My phone buzzed in the pocket of my jeans, and I pulled it out to see I'd just missed a call from a number I recognized as Joan Whalen's landline. She told me, toward the end of our meeting in my office on Monday, that the best way to contact her was by calling her on the landline in her home, but only during the daytime hours. She was a freelance interior decorator who worked out of a home office.

I walked to the Concord River Inn, half a block away, and sat on a stone bench just outside of the old inn's front entrance. I called the number back.

"Hello?" Joan said.

"Hi, it's Henry Kimball. Is this Joan?"

"Oh, thanks for calling me back. Richard's out and I wanted to check in."

I gave her the rundown, omitting the time I'd spent with Pam at the cocktail lounge at the Taste of Hong Kong. Instead, I simply told her I'd watched Pam for the majority of the previous day, and I was shadowing Richard today, and he was on what looked like a legitimate work-related call in Sudbury.

"He told me he had a new listing there."

"I will say," I said, "that keeping an eye on your husband or Pam is probably not the most efficient way to confirm your suspicions."

"What do you mean?"

"For one thing, maybe they only get together every two weeks. That means I'll need to have eyes on one of them the majority of every day, and it could be a long time before anything is confirmed."

"Is that a problem?"

A cloud moved over the sun and the air temperature did one of those sudden drops that are commonplace in New England in October.

"It shouldn't be, but I will say that it increases the chances of my being spotted. Unfortunately, there are only so many spots with a view of the Blackburn offices in Dartford."

"I can't really speak for Pam," Joan said. "But my husband wouldn't notice an elephant parked across the street from his office. One weekend I painted his study walls when he was away, and he never noticed."

"That's good to know. I'll primarily be keeping an eye on him. It's time consuming, though."

"Are you telling me it's a lot of money?"

"Well, I am billing by the hour, so yes, I'd say it's adding up."

"I don't care about that. Besides, what other choice is there?"

"Do you know your husband's pin number on his phone?"

"I do."

"We could install spyware on it that would tell us—"

"I've looked at his phone," Joan said, jumping in. "He's not bright, but he's bright enough to not send texts with the woman he's sleeping with. I'm pretty sure all their arrangements are made in person at the office."

"Probably," I said, and briefly thought about how affairs might now be the last human relationships that are not being exclusively conducted via computers and smartphones.

"Definitely," Joan said, a little breathily, and I wondered if she was out for a walk. Then I remembered she was speaking on her landline.

"So I'll continue with what I'm doing," I said, "and keep an eye on Richard's daily movements."

"Yes, please, and thank you. Honestly, I'll be shocked if you find out that he's not secretly meeting Pam. My guess is that they meet on Friday afternoons. Sorry I haven't told you that sooner but it's only a guess on my part."

"Why do you think Fridays?"

"He belongs to a gym that he doesn't go to very often. It's called For Life Fitness in West Dartford. He usually goes in the morning at the beginning of the week, but lately he's been coming home on Friday nights having been to the gym."

"You think he's going there to take a shower?"

"That's exactly what I think. Otherwise I'd smell her on him, which I probably would, because he knows how good my sense of smell is. And the other thing is that on those Friday nights he's just a little too affectionate with me. I mean, he's not super obvious—he doesn't bring me flowers or anything—but I can read him well enough to know he's feeling guilty."

"This is all good to know," I said.

"But don't just wait until then. For all I know they're going to get together tomorrow."

"Right. Okay, will do. I'll get in touch with you the moment I learn anything."

"Thanks, Henry," she said, and then, reading my thoughts, added, "although what I really want to say is 'Thanks, Mr. Kimball.'"

"Please don't."

After ending the call I sat on the bench for a while longer. A bank of clouds had passed by and now there was sun again, lighting up the remaining leaves on all the trees. An older couple, both of them mildly stooped over, went slowly past me and toward the Concord River Inn. If it was lunchtime for them then it might as well be lunchtime for me. I held the door for them then entered myself, following a narrow, wallpapered hallway that led to the tavern area at the back of the inn.

After lunch I swung back through Sudbury to see if Richard's car was still parked at the house he'd gone to earlier. It wasn't, so I returned to the Dartford offices, parking on a residential street that ran parallel to Colonial Road, then walked past the offices, seeing the BMW in the back parking lot. I looked for Pam's Toyota, too, but didn't spot it either in the lot or on the street. It was possible she was working at the other offices today.

I returned to the coffee shop, the woman behind the counter recognizing me when I came in. "Large latte?" she said, and I nodded.

I took up my usual seat close to the window. I'd brought a novel with me this time. *The Riverside Villas Murder* by Kingsley Amis. I read my book but positioned it in such a way I'd be able to detect any cars exiting from the alleyway between the Blackburn Properties building and the florist next door. I drank my coffee as slowly as possible, and picked at a lemon-ginger scone, and sometime around four in the afternoon, wrote a limerick on the inside back cover of the Amis novel:

> *There once was a bored private eye.*
> *Day in and day out he would spy*
> *On people in bars,*
> *Or out driving cars,*
> *Like a voyeur, but not the good kind.*

Just before five o'clock Richard's BMW nosed its way from the alley back onto the road. I was able to catch up with him about a quarter of a mile down the road, heading toward his house. He veered off at one point but it was just to pull into the large parking lot of a discount liquor store. He emerged holding a paper bag close to his torso and returned to his car. I was parked one row over, and angled so that I had a view through the driver's side window. He put the bag down on the passenger side seat then pulled something from it. I wasn't sure what it was until he raised it to his lips, and I saw him drinking from a nip bottle, tipping it back and downing it all at once. Then he reached into the bag again and pulled out another of the same. This one he sipped at slowly while staring through his windshield out toward the darkening sky. He must have turned on his car's engine because he powered his window halfway down and I could hear music coming from inside. I couldn't be a hundred percent sure, but it sounded like "Lyin' Eyes" by the Eagles, which was way too on the nose, I thought.

When he finished his second small bottle, he got out of his car, and walked with a stiff, awkward gait back to the front of the store, where he deposited the two empty nips into a trash container.

Then he got back into his car and drove home, me following at a slight distance. After he pulled into the driveway of his green Colonial I kept driving, all the way back to Cambridge. At a long red light, I got on my smartphone and cued up "Lyin' Eyes."

CHAPTER 10

JOAN

She left the Windward at just past ten, walking across the empty front lawn, then crossing Micmac Road to get to the beach. It was a dark night, no stars in the sky. Stepping onto the beach she had a brief moment of complete displacement, the water and the sand and the sky all equally black, and making Joan feel as though she were a tiny creature marooned in the middle of a vast nothingness.

She saw a yellow flicker toward the jetty side of the beach and made her way in that direction, walking slowly, ready to turn back if it was only Duane by the fire. But soon she could hear multiple voices, and a loud whooping noise. There were about six bodies grouped around the flames. It wasn't until Joan was close enough to hear their words and see their faces that they even saw her approaching. Duane stood up. "Hey, you made it," he said, and all the other firelit faces turned toward her.

He introduced her around, ignoring the fact she'd already met Derek. Besides him, there were three other guys, two of them who seemed like they might be in their twenties, one of them smoking a cigarette. And there were two girls, wearing shorts and sweaters, hunched over near the fire like they were freezing. Their names were Emily and Anne and they said they were sisters, even though one had very blond hair and the other one was a full-on redhead, her face covered with dark freckles. Duane grabbed Joan a can of beer from a plastic cooler, and she popped it open and tasted it. It was both bitter and overly sweet at the same time, and she shuddered a little after taking a sip.

"You like beer?" Duane said.

"Not really. I prefer martinis."

Everyone had been listening, and the boys laughed, one of them saying, "Oh my God," in a loud, slurry voice.

There were two coolers around the fire, and Joan was offered one to sit on. Duane was nearest to her, and he began to tell her about how there was this liquor store a few towns away in Biddeford, and it was run by this guy whose brother was a cop, so pretty much anyone could buy beer there, no matter how old they were. "All you gotta do," said Derek, "is show them any kind of ID when they ask. Like just present your library card or something, and the guy who owns the place looks at it, then rings you up."

"What kind of beer is this?" Joan said, just to have something to say.

"It's Coors Light. You like it? We have other stuff too. We got Jäger."

"The beer is fine," Joan said, and one of the sisters said she'd do a Jäger shot, and then the bottle was being passed around. When it got to Joan she said she'd do one shot, and she tipped the bottle to her lips, but only sipped a tiny bit.

"It's no martini," one of the older boys said.

"No, it's not," Joan said, and looked at him until he looked away. Then she twisted her beer can into the sand so it wouldn't tip over, and said, "I'm going to take off soon, it's kind of cold out here."

"You're wearing jeans and a sweatshirt," Duane said. "Look at me." He stood up to demonstrate he was only wearing cargo shorts and a T-shirt.

"We're pretty cold, too," said one of the other girls, and then one of the older guys said that his place wasn't too far away from here, and they could all go there and smoke some pot.

Joan stood up and said she really did need to get back to the hotel, that her parents would probably be checking on her soon, and if she wasn't in her room they'd have a fit.

"You aren't going to show off your gymnast's moves first?" Duane said.

"Like what?"

"I don't know. You're a gymnast, aren't you? Let's see something."

"Yeah, let's see a split," one of the older guys said, lighting a new cigarette.

The sand was packed hard where they were all sitting so Joan did a quick handstand, holding it for a few seconds. Everyone clapped. "I'm heading back," she said.

"I'll walk you," Duane said, and Joan shrugged. "I'll be back," he said, as the two of them headed in the direction of the hotel.

"Yeah, right," one of the boys shouted, and Joan looked back. The two sisters had stood up, as well, and she could hear the guys begging them to stay a little longer.

"I don't really need to be walked back," Joan said.

"I don't mind taking a break from those guys. Besides, it's pretty dark out." He was acting as though they hadn't been on this beach before, her trying to get away from him, him squeezing her arm and calling her a tease. Maybe he actually had forgotten?

They crossed the road, an oncoming car casting them briefly in yellow light. When they got to the lawn, he pressed his hand against her lower back, and said, "Slow down, will ya?"

"Why?"

"I want to keep hanging out with you. Seriously, you're like the only cool person in this place. Why don't you show me another one of your gymnastics moves?"

"I probably shouldn't, not without stretching. I might hurt myself. Besides, I don't want to be a tease."

"Hey, look, I'm sorry about that. I was just plastered, that's all. I'm not like that, though. I just want to hang out." Joan could feel that he'd grabbed a bunch of her sweatshirt and was tugging her toward him. Looking at his face in the moonlight she saw the same thing in his eyes that she'd seen a few nights before, a wolfish look, like hunger. If they were still on the beach she thought she'd be in trouble. Even here on the lawn she considered running, then made a quick decision and gave him a hug, saying "Let's hang out again this week, okay? Just the two of us."

He hugged back, then let her go. "Sure, anytime." His voice was hoarse and just as she was turning to leave she saw him adjust the material around his crotch.

She walked the rest of the way to the front of the hotel herself. There was cigar smoke in the air, and as she went up the wooden steps to the wide front porch, an older man on one of the rockers said, "It's nice being young, eh?"

Joan pretended she didn't hear him and entered the lobby.

The following day, because she didn't want to have to deal with Duane, she agreed to drive with her parents to Ogunquit. They had lunch at a pretty good restaurant, even though her father kept saying how they were basically paying double for lunch because they could be eating at the Windward. Then they walked on a path that wound along the rocky coast and got ice cream in a place called Perkins Cove, sitting at a picnic table and watching boats come and go on the water.

"You having fun on this trip?" her mother asked. They were sitting on a bench near a cluster of shops while her father browsed in a used bookstore.

"Yeah," Joan said, as brightly as possible, not wanting to have a conversation about her feelings with her mom.

"Oh, okay. Just checking. Sometimes I can't read you at all, not like Lizzie."

"Lizzie is having fun on this trip," Joan said.

"Yes, she certainly is."

"Do you think that girl Denise is her girlfriend?"

"I think your sister is in an experimental phase, if that's what you mean. I'm not sure she knows exactly who she is right now."

Joan, not really caring one way or another about her sister, talked about it with her mother for a while, only to avoid having to answer questions about herself.

"Here's your father, with a stack of books he won't read," her mother said, and they each watched her father step out of the store and squint into the sunlight, trying to find his family. "Let's stop talking about Lizzie for now. I'm not sure your father's handling this new version of her."

That night at dinner, they all ate as a family in the dining room, Lizzie noticeably quiet. Denise was nowhere to be seen. Duane, wearing a baseball cap and a T-shirt with cut-off sleeves, said hi to Joan in the buffet line, asking her why she hadn't been to the beach that day.

"I went with my parents to Ogunquit," she said.

"Oh, cool," Duane said. "Wanna meet up tonight? We could do another fire on the beach, just the two of us."

"I can't tonight," Joan said. "Tomorrow, maybe?" She remembered what Richard had said about baiting the hook.

"Cool," Duane said.

She hadn't seen Richard in the dining room, but when she went to the library around nine o'clock he was there, sitting in his usual chair, reading a paperback called *The Forever War* that looked like science fiction. He immediately closed the book when he saw her.

"I didn't see you at dinner," she said.

"I walked into town and got a pizza," he said. "I don't think I can take another night with my aunt and uncle and with Duane."

"Duane and I are like this now," Joan said, holding up two fingers, pressed together, and smiling.

"Oh, yeah?"

"Yeah. He walked me back to the hotel after I'd hung out at the beach."

"Yeah, I know all about it. I was watching you."

"You serious?"

"I was sitting over on that bench swing. I watched you guys walk across the lawn."

"Did you see us hug?"

"Yeah," Richard said, and Joan thought back to what her mother had said earlier about not being able to read her. She couldn't read Richard, she realized. Not his emotions, anyway. Was he jealous? Or was he simply scheming? "This morning Duane was telling me all the things he was going to do to you."

Joan, even though she wasn't surprised, felt blood rush into her face. "Ugh," she said. "That is so gross."

"He's gross, I told you."

"What did you say when he told you that?"

"I don't say anything, really. I just listen."

"You don't defend my honor, Richard," she said in what she hoped sounded very dramatic and sarcastic, but as soon as she'd said it, she realized she sounded like her mother in one of her moods.

"I want to kill him," Richard said. "That's pretty much defending your honor, don't you think?"

"Yeah, I guess so. What else did he say?"

"He said you made out with him, and that he could tell you were super horny."

"He really said that? I totally didn't make out with him. In fact—you saw it—I had to hug him to keep him from trying to kiss me."

Richard was laughing.

"He's such a liar," Joan said.

"Yeah, he is. So what are we going to do about it?"

Joan, who had been thinking a lot about Duane the past few days, said, "Are you serious when you say you want to kill him?"

Richard thought for a moment, then said, "Sometimes I am and sometimes I'm not. But I am one hundred percent serious that I wouldn't feel bad for a moment if Duane died, whether I had anything to do with it or not. Why? Are you serious about it?"

"I think so," Joan said. "Let's teach him a lesson."

"Okay."

"Let's push him in the ocean."

Richard was very still, but Joan could tell from his eyes that his thoughts were moving fast. "I'm not kidding," she said. "Let's do this. It'll be fun."

"You'd have to be the one to get him to the end of the jetty at night."

"That's not going to be a problem," Joan said.

"But I can push him into the water."

"Okay."

"You're going to have to lie to some people after it happens. You're going to have to act a part."

Joan didn't need to think. She said, "That's not going to a problem, either."

CHAPTER 11

KIMBALL

I was sitting in my car, torrential rain drumming on the metal roof, keeping an eye on the Blackburn Properties in Concord. Something seemed to be happening in the real estate world, because Richard Whalen had driven to the Dartford office in the morning, stayed there an hour, then driven over to Concord. After having lunch at a Thai restaurant with two women whom I recognized from the website as real estate agents, he'd returned briefly to the Dartford office and now he was back in Concord. The rain that had been threatening all day began just as Richard parked in the lot of the smaller office, part of a strip mall halfway between West Concord and Concord center. Richard pulled his suit jacket up over his head and ran from his BMW to the front door just as the sky split open, dumping the remnants of a hurricane that had been slowly climbing the coast for the past week.

The Concord office was harder to watch than the Dartford one. The only vantage point was its rather small front parking lot; there were no coffee shops or bars nearby, no places to park your car and be hidden. It helped, of course, that anyone looking outside from the office at this particular moment would be looking at the rising flood-waters, and not my car. I wasn't particularly worried about Richard, partly because Joan had told me he had his head in the clouds, but I *was* worried about running into Pam again, since we'd already met. But so far, I'd seen very little of her. She parked on the street in front of the Dartford office, and her car stayed there all day. I'd never seen her in the presence of Richard.

Ever since being in Concord the day before I'd been thinking not just about Lily Kintner and my time as a Boston police detective, but about my life in general, and everything that had led me here. I was close to forty and felt as though I'd failed at just about everything that had meant something to me. I had failed as a police officer when I let my obsession with a suspect get the better of me. I'd failed as a poet, not just because I was largely unpublished, but because I hadn't been able to write anything but dirty limericks for what seemed like forever. And I had failed as an English teacher all those years ago, lasting one year in the classroom and then never returning.

I rolled down my window to get some air, and to hopefully clear the condensation that had built up on the inside of my car's windows. I told myself to stop feeling bad for myself. I had been through two bad experiences and I had survived them. I still had a pretty good hairline, a cat who liked me, and my health. And I wasn't forty quite yet.

The rain turned off as fast as it had turned on, and the skies were briefly blue. Richard, folders tucked under an arm, emerged from the office and got back into his car. I followed him, thinking he was heading back to the Dartford office, but he pulled into the driveway of a Ninety Nine Restaurant at a busy intersection. It was almost four o'clock in the afternoon and there were quite a few cars in the parking lot. I watched as Richard, still holding the folders, entered the restaurant. I scanned the other cars in the lot, looking to see if I could spot Pam's Toyota, but I didn't see it. I let twenty minutes pass by.

I was pretty sure I hadn't been seen by Richard since I started tailing him, so I decided to enter the restaurant, maybe grab a quick drink at the bar, see if Richard was meeting a woman there. Just because Pam's car was nowhere to be seen didn't mean he was alone inside. I was wearing my baseball cap and a flannel shirt, not my usual outfit. I decided to keep the cap on, and I entered the restaurant, a wide-open space with a U-shaped bar at its center. Richard was at the bar, his back to the front door, papers spread out in front of him, and his cell phone pressed to an ear.

A hostess appeared, and I told her I was there just for a drink. She waved me in and I sat at one of the high-top tables that ringed the bar, about two car lengths from Richard. I could hear his voice talking into his phone but couldn't make out the words. He had a pint glass with something clear in it, on ice, with two lime wedges. When my waitress appeared, I ordered a ginger ale with lime and asked for it in a lowball glass. I'd skipped lunch, so I also asked what the quickest appetizer from the kitchen would be, and she said the boneless wings were fast, so I ordered those too.

I sipped my drink, and watched Richard finish his, then nod toward the bartender for another. It was a Tito's and either soda water or tonic. The bartender, who had shiny black hair pulled tightly back in a bun, and overly tanned skin, added two limes and put it in front of him. I hadn't found out too much about Richard's love life, but I had found out that his drink of choice was vodka. He made another call, and this time I could hear him saying something about title insurance, his voice loud and agitated.

A pile of chicken wings arrived at my table, and I ordered another ginger ale. Richard was now looking at his phone, scrolling through what looked like texts. I ate quickly, not knowing when Richard might get up and leave. He was only halfway through his second drink, but he'd signaled the bartender for the check and paid it quickly in cash. I was nearly done with my food when I heard a woman's voice shout "Richard," and he turned from the bar as two women, one trailing a happy birthday balloon, descended upon him. I heard their muffled conversation as all three moved to a large table farther from the bar but closer to me.

"I just got here," I heard him saying, then he offered to buy a round. As the two women—one of them, tall and angular, was familiar as an employee at Blackburn—shucked their jackets and picked seats, Richard brought over two glasses of white wine then returned to the bar to get a bottle of beer for himself. The door swung inward again, and a group of three men entered, all talking loudly. They quickly spotted the table where the two women were sitting and made their way there.

I had asked for a bill with my food, and I put down enough cash to cover it. If this was a work party, as it seemed, then Pam was bound to show up soon, and it made sense for me to leave. I could either head home or stay in the area for a while, maybe come back here in an hour and see if Richard left with any female company. I exited the restaurant and crossed the parking lot to my car. With my hand on the door handle, I heard steps behind me, then a voice. "Hey, you."

I turned to see Pam, dressed in a thigh-length beige coat, and with a knotted scarf at her neck. "Henry, right? It's Pam, from the restaurant the other night."

"Right," I said.

"If you didn't look so surprised right now," she said, smiling without showing any teeth, "I would ask you if you're following me."

"I *am* following you a little bit," I said to Pam, my mind calculating the best way to handle the situation.

"Are you?" Pam looked pleased, but wary. Someone called out her name from the entryway to the Ninety Nine, and she looked over her shoulder at them and waved.

"I've been meaning to go back to the Taste of Hong Kong," I said, "and get another one of those mai tais. I was going to go tonight but didn't think they opened until later. I was hoping you'd be there. It was nice hanging out with you. And your friend . . ."

"Janey."

"Right, Janey."

"You should go tonight. I was planning on stopping by but I have this . . ." She gestured toward the restaurant. "It's a birthday party for one of my coworkers, but I don't think it will go on that long."

"Well, maybe I will head over and grab a drink."

"Stick around there, will ya?" she said, and reached out and touched me on the shoulder. "I'll definitely show up."

"Okay," I said.

I got back into my car and watched her enter the restaurant in the reflection of my side mirror. I needed to decide what to do but sitting in that particular parking lot and thinking about it was probably not the smartest move. I pulled out into rush-hour traffic, turning in the direction that would lead me to the Taste of Hong Kong, and the Colonial Estates, where Pam lived. Twenty minutes later I was parking underneath the high blue letters that spelled out the name of the Chinese restaurant. It was early, but the parking lot was already half full.

Inside the lounge, the bar was filling up, but I managed to grab a seat at the far end, positioned so I could keep an eye on the entryway. The crowd was similar to the one on Tuesday night but there were more of them. Young professionals and hip couples that looked like they lived in downtown condominiums. Pete the bartender was rapidly building drinks. He had help behind the bar, the same young woman who'd been there on Tuesday night, plus a skinny twenty-year-old who was clearly a barback, pouring water and washing glasses.

Pete glanced in my direction, and said, "Pam's friend, right? Mai tai?"

"Sure," I said.

After I was handed the drink, plus a food menu, I took a sip and considered my options. I could finish the drink quickly, pay my bill, and drive back to Cambridge. Tomorrow was Friday, and if Joan was right, her husband and Pam would find an empty house for some afternoon delight, and I'd be there to witness it. Case closed. Or I could stick around and wait for Pam to arrive. She'd probably already be a little tipsy from after-work drinks at the Ninety Nine, and she'd probably drink plenty here at the bar, especially since she'd told me she always came here on Thursdays. And if she drank enough then how hard would it be to get her to confess to having an affair with her boss? And that would be enough for Joan, wouldn't it? She just wanted confirmation, not any actual photographic proof. At least that was the impression I'd gotten.

But there were two problems with staying at the Hong Kong cocktail lounge. The first was that spending more time with Pam made it harder to keep an eye on her comings and goings from the Blackburn offices. Even though I was primarily following Richard, if he were to meet up with Pam tomorrow afternoon, then I'd be following both of them. The other problem was that if I didn't get Pam to confess to an affair with Richard, she might become suspicious of my questions. She'd be on guard if she was having a clandestine affair with her married boss. And maybe she'd even let Richard know that some stranger—a man who'd also been outside of the Ninety Nine—was asking questions about her love life.

Pondering what to do next I noticed my drink was finished. Pete raised an eyebrow at me, and I told him I was thinking. Two couples entered together, led by the hostess to a high-top table that had been reserved. The lights were dimmed a little, and the music—1960s exotica—was turned up. A platter was delivered to a foursome at the other end of the bar, a blue flame in the middle of the food. I decided to stay. But I also decided I would not ask Pam any obvious questions about who she was, or was not, sleeping with. If it came naturally, then I'd see if I could get some information.

I called Pete over and asked him if he could make me a nonalcoholic beverage.

"Sure," he said. "I make a virgin piña colada that's better than most ones with alcohol."

"I'll take it," I said. I didn't know how long it would be before Pam showed up, and I needed to pace myself.

As it was, I only had to wait about an hour.

She came in alone, which was surprising, since I figured she'd bring other Blackburn employees with her. I'd even wondered if maybe Richard Whalen would show up, although I suppose I was hoping he wouldn't. Pam stood in the doorway, yellow light from the bar illuminating her pale coat but leaving her face in shadow so that I couldn't tell where she was looking. But then she was waving and moving through the crowded bar area. I swiveled to greet her, and she kissed me on the cheek. She smelled of white wine and French fries.

I stood up to offer her my stool but the couple next to me offered to move down so that we could each have a seat. Pam shucked her jacket and hung it on the hook under the lip of the bar. "Oh, I'm so glad to be here," she said. "Real drinks, real food."

"I thought you'd show up with a huge crew from your office," I said.

"They're all still at the Ninety Nine, but I couldn't take it anymore. My guess is Janey, who you know, plus maybe a couple of the other agents will show up later."

Pete had spotted Pam and come over, reaching out a fist that Pam bumped with her own over the bar. "Make me that thing with all the basil leaves that you made me a week ago, please, Pete?"

"Oh, sure," he said, then looked at me. "Same again?"

"No, I'll have what she's having," I said.

He departed and Pam took a deep breath, said something about Thursdays I couldn't quite make out over the din in the bar, then smiled widely at me. She had fresh lipstick on.

"How's your week been, Henry Dickey?" she said.

"You remembered my name."

"I did. I even googled you, but nothing came up."

"That's good to hear," I said. "I'd just as soon have no online presence."

"Well, you've succeeded. You're a mystery man."

Our drinks arrived, and Pam asked if I wanted to order some food, and together we looked at the menu, deciding on a few appetizers. I was sorely regretting all the chicken wings I'd eaten earlier.

"So were you googling me for your friend?" I said, after we ordered.

She looked confused, and I said, "For Janey. I got the feeling on Tuesday you were trying to set us up."

"Oh, right," Pam said. "No, now that I know you an infinitesimal amount"—she held up her thumb and forefinger so that they were almost touching—"I'm not sure you're a good match for Janey."

"Probably not," I said.

"So who are you a good match for?" Pam said.

I took a tiny sip of my delicious drink. "I don't know," I said. "Maybe no one. My sister says that I fall in love too often to get married, whatever that means."

"Oh, you're one of those," Pam said.

"One of what?"

"A serial monogamist."

"Is that a bad thing?"

"I don't think it's bad, but it is what it is. You have one intense relationship after another but they never quite reach the marriage stage, right?"

"Maybe," I said.

"I think it's fine. Honestly, what do I know? I used to have all sorts of ideas about what kind of relationship I wanted to have when I got married, and I was also really judgmental about other people's relationships. My parents. My friends. Now that I'm older and I've been through the ringer a couple of times I don't judge so much."

"I like that you call yourself older. You're still in your twenties I'm guessing?"

"Thank you but no. I'm actually thirty-two."

"Well, you don't look it."

"Thanks for that, but I feel it. I feel old, and I feel alone."

"If I recall correctly," I said, "you mentioned something about being in a relationship. Last time we were sitting at this bar."

"Oh, did I? I probably also mentioned that it wasn't making anyone happy, so there's that. I'm hoping to extricate myself from that ASAP. Pete, look this way, will you?" She was holding up her empty glass.

"Well, I'm here if you want to unburden yourself of the details."

"I would but then you'd lose all respect for me."

"Okay," I said, and decided to drop it, finishing my own drink.

Pam managed to wave down Pete and we ordered new drinks just as our food arrived. Before we were finished eating, Pam said something too quiet for me to catch, but she was looking at the entrance, so I did, as well. Janey, with three other women, and one man, was standing with the hostess looking around the bar.

"It's your crew," I said.

"I know, and I'm kind of hoping they don't look this way. Is that terrible?"

"We need to protect our food."

"Yes, we do," Pam said, smiling. Janey had spotted her and was skipping toward us.

She awkwardly hugged Pam around the shoulders then said an extended "Hey" to me.

"It's Henry," I said. "We met two nights ago."

"I remember," she said. "Nice to see you. We're just waiting for one of the big booths at the back. You guys will join us, right?"

I started to say I was planning on leaving soon, but Pam jumped in, and said, "We'll never fit, will we?"

"We'll all crowd in. Besides, Marsha won't stay more than ten minutes, at most."

"We'll swing by in a bit," Pam said, as Janey plucked up the second-to-last snapper dumpling from the plate and popped it in her mouth.

"Sorry," Janey said, pointing at her cheek, then maneuvered away.

"I don't expect you to come hang out with my friends from work," Pam said.

"I don't expect to, either."

"Ha. I can sit here for a while. They won't miss me."

"I won't stay long," I said. "I have to drive back to Cambridge, remember? And it's a school night."

"Are you teaching tomorrow?" she said. I knew she was probably wondering about my work status. Writing poetry and teaching adult ed classes was no one's idea of a lucrative living. I told her I was doing some private tutoring tomorrow for a high school student struggling with writing her college essay.

"I do a fair amount of that," I said. "It's probably how I make most of my money."

"Well, you're a writer, so you have to find something."

"I'm shopping a manuscript of my poetry for publication. But even if I find a home for it, it won't get me any money, and, as far as I can tell, it won't change my life, at all. I'll just be able to say I published a book."

"What kind of poems are they?"

I told her, and it was pretty much the truth. How I'd published multiple poems in well-known journals while I was in my twenties, but at some point, I'd just lost the ability to write a poem. And these days I was writing either critical pieces, or else limericks.

"Limericks?" she said.

"You know—'There once was a girl from Nantucket.'"

"Oh, right."

"It's my sole literary output these days, I'm sorry to say. Where are you from?"

"What do you mean?"

"Where are you from? Where did you grow up?"

"Oh. I grew up in Portland, Oregon."

"Ugh," I said.

"It wasn't so bad."

"No, I mean it's terrible for rhyming in a limerick."

"If it helps, I actually grew up in a town outside of Portland called Buckheaven."

"That does help," I said, and took a long sip of my drink. Then I said, "There once was a girl from Buckheaven . . . Thirty-two but she looks twenty-seven . . . She's been drinking so long, at the Taste of Hong Kong . . . Trawling for unmarried men."

"Oh my God," Pam said. "I'm horrified and impressed at the same time."

"It's my only skill."

"I feel like you've reduced me to a limerick, and I'm not sure I like it."

"It's a first draft," I said. "I can change it, if you like. But it always has to be about sex in some way. It's a limerick rule."

"Yeah, I'll bet," she said, then spun the last remaining dumpling on its plate, and added, "I'm having fun talking with you, but pretty soon that table full of idiots are going to insist I join them, and then you'll leave, and I'll end up getting drunk again at the Hong Kong on a Thursday night."

"Okay," I said.

"I live right across the road. Do you want to come over, and we can drink some wine and keep talking?"

I started to answer, but she interrupted me. "I just heard how that sounded, and so I will honestly say that it's no big deal if you turn me down, and also, I really do just want to keep talking. This is fun."

"Sure," I said. "I'd be up for that."

"Okay," she said, her eyes suddenly bright. "And look, let me pay for these drinks because I know there's not a huge demand for limericks. And one more thing, which sounds terrible, but can you leave first, and then maybe meet me across the road in the parking lot of the Colonial Estates? You can't miss it, it's a bunch of ugly town houses. I just don't want to be the topic of gossip tomorrow."

"I totally get it," I said.

Outside, the temperature had dropped, and I could see my breath in the harsh white light of the parking lot. I drove across the road into the lot of the Colonial Estates, finding a spot that had the word VISITOR stenciled on it.

A car I recognized as Pam's Toyota pulled into the lot and made a wide swing to settle into one of the spots that abutted the nearest building. I got out of my car, telling myself I was only here to get information, and walked across the lot to where Pam stood in front of the building's glass doors, keys in hand.

CHAPTER 12

JOAN

"Have you walked to the end of the jetty yet?" Joan said.

"Yeah, a bunch of times." Duane was lying beside her on the beach, on his back, his hands intertwined behind his head. From Joan's position she could see little white balls of deodorant in the hair under his arms.

"Yeah, but have you done it at night?"

"No, have you?"

"Yeah, of course. It's amazing."

"Really?"

Joan had walked the jetty with Richard the night before, the two of them meeting in front of the Windward by the bench swing, then walking across the road to the beach. The night was clear, clusters of stars and a bright moon illuminating the massive blocks of granite that made up the jetty. Even without clouds, they'd had to concentrate; there were gaps between the granite slabs that got progressively wider as you made your way to the end. And the shadows created by the moonlight were tricky to maneuver. At the point of the jetty waves slapped into the rocks, making strange echoey booms and sending spray up into the cool night air.

At the extreme end the jetty began to slope into the sea, and there was a place to clamber down so you were standing on several relatively flat rocks, fringed with seaweed. In one spot, an overhang provided a little bit of protection. "I'll hide here," Richard said, "back in the shadows. You bring him down and tell him it's the best place to be to experience the crashing waves. He'll follow you, and then I can come out and shove him backwards."

"What if he sees you coming?" Joan said.

"I don't think it'll make a difference. He's strong, but I'll be able to push him off the rock. Besides, we'll both be here. If he fights back, then you can help."

"What if he swims to shore?"

"He won't. But if he does we can just say we were trying to teach him a lesson."

Joan stood, trying to imagine what it would be like to be here with Duane, and with Richard hiding, waiting to ambush him. It actually was an amazing spot, both protected and wide open, waves booming in the rocks, the air filled with seawater, and blackness everywhere, like they were at the end of the world. "I don't like it," Joan said, after a moment. "What if you were crouched down closer to the edge. Right there."

Richard looked where she was indicating, a massive block of granite that looked as though it had tumbled from the top of the jetty and landed so that it was leaning diagonally on one end. Being careful on the slick rocks, Richard took a closer look. "I could stand behind it," he said. "There's actually a piece of metal bar that I could hold on to."

Joan looked too. There wasn't a lot of space between the tumbled piece of granite and the edge of the jetty, but there was just enough for Richard to crouch and hide. And it was high tide now—they'd checked just to make sure—so they wouldn't be surprised to find that the end of the jetty was totally submerged when Joan arrived with Duane.

"It's perfect," Joan said. "Look at this rock here, a little higher than the one next to it. I'll stand on the rock and tell Duane to stand right there, and I'll tell him I want to look him in the eye. He'll know that I want him to kiss me. Then his back will be to you, and you can just grab him and hurl him over the edge. Or better yet," she said, now standing on the higher rock, the spray from the waves making her hair damp, "you can crouch behind him and I can push him. He'll fall straight back, and probably hit his head."

Richard studied the area, looking at the rock where Duane would be standing. "No," he said. "I want to be the one to push him off the edge. You just get him here, and I'll do the rest."

"Okay," Joan said. "When do we do this?"

"That's up to you. Tomorrow night, or the night after. Just so long as the weather is clear like it is now and you can see where you're stepping."

"How should I let you know we'll be out here?"

"I'll probably know because Duane will tell me all about it, but just to be sure . . . give me a signal in the dining room if you're planning on going out that night with him."

Joan thought. "Okay, if it's going to be that night then I'll have my hair back in a ponytail. If it's not going to happen then my hair will be down."

"Okay," Richard said.

"You got it?"

"Ponytail is go. I got it."

"And I'll tell Duane that I'll meet him at ten o'clock, so make sure you're already out here waiting."

"That sounds good," Richard said.

She couldn't see his face where he was standing, but his voice sounded calm, as though they were talking about meeting for coffee, or something. She said, "It's a plan, then."

"It's a plan."

Together they'd walked back along the jetty. A few clouds had begun to move across the sky, and there were moments of complete darkness. Richard reached out and took her hand to help her over one of the larger gaps. They held hands until the clouds moved away and the moonlight was back, draping everything in its silver light.

"It's kind of terrifying and amazing at the same time," Joan said to Duane at the beach. He was now on his side, cocked up on one elbow.

"Who did you go with?"

"My sister, and I did it like the first night we were here."

"Could you see where you were stepping?"

"Totally. The moon was out. It was fine. Sounds like you're maybe too scared to go."

"No," Duane said. "I just don't want you to fall into the ocean and then I'd have to jump in and save you."

"Oh, yeah," Joan said. "Is that what's going to happen?" She was on her side now and checked the positioning on her bikini top to make sure she wasn't exposing herself. She'd been catching Duane trying to secretly look at her body the whole time they'd been at the beach together. He'd found her reading *Pet Semetary,* and asked if he could join her. She told him he could if he didn't mind putting some lotion on her back where she couldn't reach.

"Hey, if you want to go to the end of the jetty at night, then let's do it. It sounds pretty cool."

"You have no idea," Joan said. "Trust me."

Joan got up and stood on her towel, looming over Duane, and told him she was going to go back to the hotel, find out what her family was doing for lunch.

"If you want, we could go hang out at the pool at the rental house where Emily and Anne are staying this afternoon. Their parents are sometimes around, but not always."

"No, I'm good," Joan said. "Let's plan on meeting at the jetty at ten tonight. Don't pussy out on me, okay?" It was an expression she'd never said before but had heard many times.

Duane said, "Ha, ha."

"See ya," Joan said, and made her way up over the dune with her towel rolled and tucked under an arm. Back on the grounds of the Windward she stood under the outdoor shower and got all the sand off her legs and from between her toes. Across the sloping lawn she could see her sister, Lizzie, sitting in the gazebo with her new friend Denise. Even at that distance she could tell they were having some kind of intense conversation, Lizzie gesturing with her hands and at one point wiping at one of her eyes. She wondered, not for the first time, what it must be like to be her sister, to feel everything so intensely, to let someone like Denise affect you so much you would cry. She felt a surge of pity and disgust.

Entering the hotel lobby, Joan saw Jessica, normally behind the front desk, setting out chairs in the alcove where the piano was located. Joan walked over and said, "Hey."

"Oh, hi," Jessica said.

"What's going on?"

"'Afternoon Oldies,'" she said. "Every Saturday afternoon in July and August. This old guy, Mac Kierney, comes in and sings Frank Sinatra songs and things like that. He's friends with Frank, the owner, but he draws a serious crowd."

Joan didn't know if Jessica was joking or not, and said, "Really?"

"Oh, yeah. It's a scene. You should save your front-row seat now."

"Maybe I'll pass."

"Your tan's looking pretty good," Jessica said.

"Thanks. My mom is convinced I'll get cancer."

Jessica was looking at the row of chairs she'd just set out, and said, "Does that look straight to you?"

Joan altered a few of them until they lined up properly. "Sorry," Jessica said. "Didn't mean to put you to work."

"It's okay. I have no idea what I'm going to do all afternoon, anyway. I'm sick of the beach. I wish I was working here, like you."

"Really?"

"Yeah. I can't wait to get a job and make some money."

"It's not so bad."

"Hey, I've been meaning to ask you . . . Remember when you pointed out that guy Duane to me, and then you called him a creep?"

"Yeah." Jessica made a face, pulling down one side of her mouth. "Avoid him at all costs."

"What did he do to you?"

"Why? Are you, like, hanging out with him now?"

"No, not really, but I've talked to him a few times, and I had a beer down at the beach with him two nights ago. Him and Derek—"

"Ugh, Derek," Jessica said. Then quickly added, "Actually, Derek's not so bad. He's an asshole, or whatever, but Duane is not a good guy. I'm sorry. You're probably into him or something, but the second night he was here there was a party at Derek's house because his parents were away, and Duane nearly strangled me."

"Seriously?"

"I stupidly went up to Derek's bedroom with him, and he was super drunk and all over me, and when I went to leave he grabbed my throat and squeezed. He also called me a fat slut but that was a little later."

"'Ugh' is right."

"Anyway, there's always someone like him around here. I would avoid him unless that's your kind of thing."

"Hey, you need help putting out the rest of these chairs?" Joan said.

"No, please. I'm not sure how Frank would feel if he saw me enlisting one of the guests to help me." She laughed.

Joan went to her room, happy to see that it had been cleaned and the beds made since she'd left that morning. She put the air conditioner on high and lay back on the bed, running her fingers along the bumps of the chenille spread, staring at the ceiling and imagining what tonight was going to be like. She was nervous and excited at the same time. *I'm going to kill someone,* she thought, and rolled that idea around in her mind. Then she told herself: *No, we're not going to kill Duane. We're just going to teach him a lesson, throw him in the ocean and see if he can swim.* She thought about that for a while and decided she liked the idea of killing him more.

CHAPTER 13

KIMBALL

"Wine okay?"

I was sitting on Pam O'Neil's white couch, feeling that familiar sense of dislocation that happens when you are suddenly in someone else's private space. I knew it was a mistake the moment I followed her into her one-bedroom apartment. I stood there as she turned on the two lamps in the living area, then went to the alcove kitchen, flipping on the recessed lighting, then dimming them. She lit a candle and placed it on the blond-wood bar that separated the living room from the kitchen area. "Have a seat, and then I'll get you a drink," she'd said. "I desperately need to pee, and then I'm going to change out of these work clothes, if you don't mind."

"Of course," I said, and she disappeared into her bedroom, shutting the door behind her.

I looked around. It was immaculate but a little sterile, two of the walls entirely bare. She had a small television on top of a black bureau. Behind the sofa was a desk with a computer, and above the desk was a framed print that I recognized as a Cézanne. There was also one of those framed collages of photographs, plus another framed photograph large enough I could make it out as a graduation picture, Pam in mortarboard with a parent on either side. For no good reason, it all made me sad.

Pam came back into the living room. I was a little nervous she'd be wearing a silk robe and nothing else, but she was wearing a pair of jeans, the denim thin at the knees, and a black T-shirt with the Rolling Stones lips on it. Her hair was pulled back. She went to the kitchen and came back with two glasses of white wine, both filled to the brim, then she flipped on her stereo system, hit a few buttons, and the room filled with music I couldn't identify but had heard on the radio.

She sat down across from me on the sofa and sighed.

"Good to be home?" I said.

"Always. Good to be away from coworkers. I like talking with you." She looked at me over the rim of her glass. I'd predicted she would have put on more makeup when she'd disappeared into her bedroom, but it was the opposite. Her face looked freshly washed, and her eyes looked smaller without the shadow around them.

"Now I feel the pressure is on," I said.

"It is. Say something interesting."

"I could make up more limericks."

She laughed, as though she'd just remembered the one I'd come up with at the bar. "Please do, actually. I could listen to those all night."

"I can't just keep giving away this talent for free, you know. It's the only skill I have."

"I understand." She smiled her wide smile, and I saw that it was only her two front teeth that were slightly grayer than the rest.

The song switched to what I recognized as a John Mayer song. "Bedtime magic," I said, tilting my head toward the stereo.

"Oh, you're making fun of my music now," she said, still laughing.

"Not really."

"And you think that I brought you here to seduce you with white wine and slow music, and now I'm feeling very self-conscious." There was a little alarm on her face, but amusement, as well.

"No," I said. "I mean, I don't know what to think. Did you?"

"I don't know yet. No, I think I just like talking with you, and I'm pretty sure that if I slept with you I would never hear from you again. I'm not fishing to find out if that's true, or maybe just a little bit. Why did you agree to come here?"

A moment of guilt pulsed through me when I thought of the real reason why I'd come. I said, "I came here because you asked me, and now that I'm here I'm feeling like I'm leading you on or something."

"Leading me on because . . ."

I thought for a moment. "Because I guess I'm not looking for a relationship."

Pam smiled, then said, "I guess I'm not either."

"Why did you smile like that?" I said, although I already knew.

"Because it's a line, isn't it? You're making sure you lay some groundwork down for if and when you spend the night and don't call me ever again?"

"I don't know if—"

"I don't mind. It's fine. I didn't invite you back here to become my boyfriend. Just don't tell me that you're secretly in love with some unattainable woman and that's why you can't commit."

Lily rushed into my head, as she often did, and it must have shown on my face because she immediately said, "Oh, you actually were going to tell me that."

"I don't know if I was going to tell you, but there is some truth to what you said, honestly. I know I'm a cliché."

Pam set her wineglass down on the glass coffee table next to the TV remote, and said, "No worries. I'm a cliché, as well."

"Yeah, tell me about that," I said. "How goes it with your complicated relationship?"

"It's not an original story," she said. "He's married. Unhappily, he tells me. That's about it." She tugged at an earlobe, making me think she wasn't giving me the whole story.

"What does he do?" I said.

"He's in the real estate business," she said, picking up her glass again.

"How convenient," I said, and smiled so she would know I was trying to be funny instead of judgmental.

"Like I said earlier, I've decided to end it. Of course, I've made that decision before and it hasn't worked out, but I think it's different this time."

"Why's it different?"

"Because before, when I decided I didn't want to see him I actually really did. But, right now, I know I'm done with him. It just feels different."

I nodded and set my own glass down with what sounded like a deafening clink on the coffee table. I didn't speak, hoping that Pam would need to fill the silence by continuing to talk about her affair with Richard. I was assuming that was who she was talking about, even though she hadn't confirmed it. But so far nothing she had said had made me doubt Joan's suspicions. She was sleeping with a married man from her office. She'd told me as much. I did feel a little guilty sitting on her sofa, drinking her wine, hoping she'd confirm the identity of the man she was having an affair with so I could turn around and tell his wife. But it was my job, for better or worse.

"Anyway," she said. "Let's talk about anything else but this. It's bringing me down."

"Sorry," I said.

"It's not your fault."

"Well, I asked you about him."

"You did, didn't you? So it is your fault."

"Probably." I finished my wine, and she noticed my glass was empty and asked if I wanted some more. "I should probably go," I said.

"Are you okay to drive?"

"I'll be fine," I said. "I think the pound of dumplings I ate is soaking up the alcohol."

She walked me to the door and told me I should come back to the Taste of Hong Kong in a week, and she would definitely be there. "I will," I said. "I need to hear an update on your relationship status."

"Hopefully I'll tell you that the weirdness is entirely over."

"What makes it weird?"

"Maybe I'll tell you that too."

She leaned in and we kissed, a fraction longer than a friendly goodbye between acquaintances. "That was nice," she said. "And by the way, you really shouldn't be driving home."

"Probably not," I said, and we kissed again. Truth was, it felt nice, and I knew I was rationalizing but maybe it would be okay to spend the night. I told myself I wouldn't ask her any more questions about her adulterous affair.

We moved from the living room into her bedroom, and as she slid her jeans down her legs she said, "No expectations, right?"

"Meaning I shouldn't have any or you don't have any?" I said.

"Both."

I left around four a.m., hoping to not wake her, but she sat up as I was getting dressed and sleepily said, "You're leaving?"

"I have a hungry cat at home," I said. "He's been texting me all night."

She nodded, smiling, then lay back down and was asleep again in about five seconds. I thought of leaving her a note, maybe jotting down a limerick. It would have been a nice thing to do, but I decided against it.

CHAPTER 14

JOAN

The night was mostly clear, but it seemed somehow darker than it had been when she'd walked the jetty with Richard. There were intermittent clouds in the sky and a sharp wind. Joan sat on a round rock on the edge of where the jetty began, waiting for Duane to arrive.

It was only a few minutes past ten o'clock, but it bothered her he was late. Maybe he was chickening out, or else he was drunk with his friends somewhere, and he'd forgotten all about it. What would she do then? Would she walk the jetty alone to find Richard and tell him that Duane had never showed up? The more she thought about it, the madder she got.

But then she heard Duane's voice, saying "Yo," and he was in front of her, dressed in shorts and a sweatshirt, his face in shadow.

"I thought you were going to blow me off," she said.

"No way," he said. "I'm psyched." His words were too loud and a little slurry, and she wondered if he was drunk. When she stood up and got closer to him she could smell beer, but also a skunky smell.

"Are you high?" she said.

"I smoked a little bud with Derek earlier but I'm cool. Why, you want some?"

"No, I'm good."

"High on life," he said, and bark-laughed, then coughed a few times.

"You sure you're okay?"

"Yeah, I'm great. Let's do this thing."

Halfway down the jetty she began to wonder if Duane would make it the whole way. He kept stepping on the edges of the granite and nearly falling over, Joan having to steady him. He eventually sat down on a rock, pulled Joan down so that she was sitting next to him, and went in for a kiss. She kissed him back a little bit, and his hand instantly went to her breast. "Hey," she said. "Let's get to the end of the jetty. It's a lot more comfortable there."

"Oh, yeah? Is there a bed?" He laughed at his own joke.

When he got to his feet, Joan took his hand and they kept going. She pointed out where he should put his feet, and he followed her directions, limping a little and groaning every time he put down his right foot. The sky was darkening, purple clouds crossing the moon, and Joan thought she felt a gust of rain, although it could have been spray coming off the ocean. There were sporadic whitecaps on the black water.

When they were nearly at the end, where the jetty sloped down toward the surface of the ocean, there was a brief flash of light in the sky then a distant rumble of thunder. "Jesus," Duane said.

"It's a long way away," Joan said, staring toward the horizon, where another sliver of lightning fluttered. "We're nearly at the end. It will be worth it."

They began to pick their way down the slope just as a large wave slammed into the end of the jetty and sent up a wall of spray that got them both.

"Holy shit," Duane said, and Joan was worried he would want to turn around, but he said, "It *is* pretty cool out here, I guess."

"Come on down to the very end. The rocks are nice and flat."

"Okay," he said, and together they scrambled down to the jetty's terminus. Joan said, "Come back toward here. It's even flatter."

Duane, crouching slightly, like an afraid cat, moved toward where Joan was, her back pressed to a dry rock under a slight over-hang. He leaned against her, and together they watched the black ocean, periodically lit up by pockets of lightning, waves smacking into the rocks all around them. Joan could see the block of granite that Richard should be hiding behind, but she couldn't see Richard. The rock was soaked though, occasionally getting hammered by waves, and Joan wondered if Richard was even able to hang on back there. She turned toward Duane, what little light there was showing her his eyes, wide and jittery, staring out toward the distant storm.

"Told you it was cool," she said.

He turned, rearranging his face so that it looked unfazed. "Yeah, not too shabby. How long do you think we should stay out here with that storm coming in?"

"Wanna make out?"

"Sure," Duane said. He lowered his whole frame awkwardly to reach Joan's mouth. Their teeth bumped, and Duane, tasting of beer, pushed his tongue up against her closed lips.

"Here," Joan said, and took Duane's hand. "You stand here, and I'll stand here. We'll be the same height." She led him toward the two uneven slabs of granite, both slick with seawater. The wind was picking up and one of the gusts ripped at Joan's windbreaker as they positioned themselves, Joan moving Duane so that his back was to the edge of the jetty.

"You sure about this?" Duane said. His legs were slightly bent so that Joan was actually taller than him.

"Of course, I'm sure. I don't think you think this is as cool as I do." She took his jaw in her hands and bent and kissed him, opening her mouth so that their tongues touched. He tasted of salt, now. He gripped her harder around her sides, as though he were trying to hold on to her for safety. As he loosened his grip, and Joan stood to her full height, she saw Richard.

He had come out from behind the fallen rock, and was standing right behind Duane, wearing jeans and a dark, hooded jacket, both soaked by the spray. He had one hand still on the rock to steady himself. Their eyes met and Duane turned to see what she was looking at.

Joan said, "Fucking creep," and shoved Duane as hard as she could, one of her sneakers losing its grip on the slippery rock so that she went down backward, landing on the base of her spine, while Duane only stumbled backward toward Richard. Joan, still sitting, watched Richard grab the reeling Duane from behind and pivot him toward the edge, shoving hard. Duane's feet went out from under him, and he landed hard on his back, his head cracking on the edge of a rock. He made a noise somewhere between a scream and a moan and began to slide off the edge.

Joan got her legs under her and sprang up. Richard seemed frozen, watching Duane cling to the edge of the rock, one of his hands gripping at a fringe of seaweed, the other waving above him. Joan waited for Richard to do something, to kick at Duane and push him over the edge of the rock into the surging water, but a huge wave rolled in, completely covering Duane, knocking Richard back toward Joan, and soaking them both. When the water receded, Duane was gone.

Joan and Richard stood, holding on to one another, and looking at the rock where Duane had been. Joan hunted the surface of the ocean, now roiling as the lightning and thunder was getting closer, expecting to see Duane bobbing out there, or waving at them, but there was nothing.

"He's gone," she said.

"We should get back," Richard said, as rain began to fall in stinging gusts. "It's dangerous out here."

"Okay," Joan said, but neither of them moved for a moment. They stood clinging to one another, the rain coming in waves like the sea. "We did it," she said into Richard's neck, and turned to look at him, hoping that maybe he'd kiss her, but instead he pulled her toward him and they hugged. She pressed her face into his neck. It was damp and tasted of salt water.

CHAPTER 15

KIMBALL

The following day I had borrowed a different vehicle, a Ford pickup, from the upstairs neighbor in my building, and I was sitting half a block from the Blackburn offices in Dartford. I didn't dare visit the coffee shop anymore, knowing that Pam went there. My spot down the street from the offices was not ideal, but I could just see the space between the buildings where Richard's BMW would emerge if he left the offices.

I felt overtired and unprofessional. All morning I'd been telling myself I'd made a mistake by spending the night at Pam's. All I hoped was that somehow she would meet with Richard today at some empty house or by-the-hour motel, and I could report it to my client and quit this job. Of course, it had occurred to me that sleeping with Pam might mean she would cancel her rendezvous with Richard. This was clearly something she was already hoping to do and maybe being with me would be the catalyst to finally make it happen.

If that was the case, if nothing happened today, then I was thinking that the ethical thing to do would be to step down from the case and not bill Joan Whalen. If she asked me why, I would tell her the truth.

My hope, however, was that something would happen today, and that was why I'd been sitting outside with a hat pulled down around my ears ever since following Richard from the intersection near his house. He'd passed by about ten minutes before nine and I'd followed him, at a large distance, to Dartford. After parking the truck as far away as I thought I could while still having a view of the office, I sat for about forty-five minutes. I did wonder if Pam was in the office, as well. I couldn't see her Toyota on the street but knew that she sometimes parked it in the lot behind the building. I considered walking over to take a look, but decided it wasn't worth the risk. I stayed put, slouched down in my seat, pretending that I was taking a nap, but keeping an eye on the street from under the brim of my hat.

At a little after noon Richard's silver BMW nosed its way out from between the buildings and onto Colonial Road, heading away from where I was parked. I started up the truck, and just as I flipped on my turn signal I saw the nose of another vehicle emerging from the Blackburn lot. It was a blue Toyota. I stayed put, and watched as Pam pulled out onto the road, going in the same direction that Richard had. I waited thirty seconds and began to follow her.

There was one car, an impatient maroon Jeep, between us, and when the Jeep peeled away down Pope Road I hung back but didn't worry too much about being spotted. If Pam looked in her rearview mirror she'd see a truck and a man in a bright red baseball cap. Unless we were stopped at a light I doubted she'd recognize my face.

We were headed west, and Pam exited from Colonial Road onto a side street called Barnum. She was driving slowly, and I hung back as much as I could, not happy with how rural and empty the street was. We wound past fields and old farmhouses, then Pam took a sharp left that brought her onto a narrow, rutted lane. There was a street sign, but it was shrouded by an oak tree that still had its leaves. I took my foot off the gas, letting Pam get out of sight, then drove slowly through the heavily wooded neighborhood, peering down dark driveways to look for either silver BMWs or blue Toyotas. I didn't even know what town I was in, but it seemed solidly middle-class. The houses were either split-level ranches or modest Colonials.

I came to a fork and cursed at myself for not following closer. One way seemed to continue through the housing development, and the other way, at least as far as I could see, cut between farmed fields on either side. I turned left, staying in the wooded area, still peering down driveways. I was a quarter of a mile down the road when I saw the FOR SALE sign, emblazoned with the logo for Blackburn Properties. I glided past the sign, turning my head and spotting Pam's car at the end of the long gravel drive, her rear brake lights on as though she'd just stopped. She was parking next to a silver BMW. I kept going and about three hundred yards down the street found a small parking lot abutting some conservation land. I pulled in and parked.

I knew I needed to head back toward the house and try to confirm that Richard and Pam were there for nonwork reasons. It was obvious, to me, that they were, but Joan needed "a hundred percent confirmation," her words when I'd checked in with her the day before. She'd also mentioned that if I got spotted spying on them it wouldn't be the end of the world, that she would certainly let Richard know she'd hired me to find out the truth. I made a plan. I hadn't gotten a great look at the house as I passed it, but it seemed like one of those single-story deck houses that had sprouted up in the 1970s, meaning there would be first-floor windows that looked into every room. I took out my compact digital camera with the telephoto lens from the glove compartment, even though Joan had told me that pictures weren't necessary. If I had a chance to get a good shot, I'd take it. I also grabbed a different hat, a wool one, plus a pair of wire-rimmed glasses without prescriptive glass. It would change my look from a distance, at least.

With the camera in a fanny pack I walked back along the road. My stomach was queasy and my body ached. I didn't relish the thought of spying on a woman whom I'd been in bed with less than twelve hours ago. Part of me kind of hoped that they'd gone to their hideaway just to have a breakup conversation, although I doubted it. The weather was cool, and I pulled the hat down far over my ears. There was a low, gray sky, and a high wind that moved the top of the pine trees. When I reached the FOR SALE sign I took out my camera and snapped a picture of it, before heading down the gravel driveway. If for whatever reason Richard came out to confront me, I could tell him I was interested in the house. If Pam came out that particular story probably wouldn't hold up. When I was about halfway down the driveway, already studying the blank windows, and trying to imagine where the bedroom might be, I heard two sharp pops that sounded as though they came from the house. I froze for a moment, knowing somehow they were gunshots while still trying to imagine they might be something else. When I heard the third popping sound I was on the move, my feet crunching on the gravel. I passed the two cars and went to the front door. It was painted a dark brown like the rest of the house and there were two strips of beveled glass inlaid on either side. I peered through but could see nothing but a short, carpeted stairway and large ornate vase at its base. There was a doorbell and I debated ringing it, but if someone inside had a gun I'd be in trouble. I owned both a license and a .38 revolver, both of which were locked up in a file cabinet at my office in Cambridge.

I touched my cell phone through the front pocket of my jeans and wondered if I should just call 911. Was I absolutely positive I had heard gunshots coming from inside the house? Could I have heard a hunter in the nearby conservation land? No, it had been gunshots. And they had definitely sounded as though they'd happened in the house. I called 911 and reported the address and what I'd heard, and my name. When they asked me where I was in relation to the house, I hung up.

Phone back in my pocket, I tried the handle of the door. It was unlocked and I swung the door inward. There was the acrid tang of a discharged gun hovering just over the smell of a clean and disinfected house. It was silent.

I walked up the five carpeted steps, which brought me to a hallway with a kitchen on my left, and a living room to the right. I saw Pam's body first. She was seated on a beige couch, her head tipped all the way back, blood pooling in her lap, and running down one side of her neck. I was looking at her from over the back of another beige couch, its twin, that was facing toward her. I stepped into the room, still moving quietly, but as I came up behind the other couch I could make out the body of Richard. He'd been sitting across from Pam, but now he was on his side while his feet were still planted on the floor. In his right hand was a gun I recognized as a Smith & Wesson M&P, and on his right temple was a scorched bullet wound. Where his head lay was soaked in bright red blood and there were white flecks of brain and skull across the sofa's armrest.

I wanted to turn around and walk out of the house, wait for the police. But I forced myself to come around to the front of Richard's body, where I very carefully put two fingers underneath his jaw and felt for a pulse that wasn't there. I only kept my fingers there for about a second and a half, but he was obviously dead. The force of the bullet had bulged his right eye from its socket. I turned to Pam. She'd been shot in the middle of the chest, but also in the center of her forehead. Her blond hair lay feathered down her shoulders as though she'd been posed. I couldn't bring myself to feel for a pulse.

Breathing in through my mouth and blowing out through my nose, I retraced my steps and exited the house by the front door. I walked as far as I could into the woods that skirted the property—only about fifty feet—then bent over and was sick on the fallen orange pine needles.

I heard sirens in the distance.

PART 2

THE THIRD PERSON

CHAPTER 16

KIMBALL

One week after I'd walked into a staged deck house and found the corpses of Richard Whalen and Pam O'Neil, I received a check in the mail from Joan Whalen. I had never invoiced her, of course, and the amount in the check was much higher than what she owed me. She also included a short note:

> *Mr. Kimball, I knew you would never ask for money from me, but I want to pay you for your time. I am sorry you had to find the bodies, but at least you were able to tell the police what you saw. I never suspected Richard would be capable of such a thing, and if I had I would never have gone to you. Best regards, Joan Grieve Whalen*

I tried to imagine Joan's state of mind when she'd written that note, and signed the check, and mailed them both to me at my office in Cambridge. I couldn't. I simply didn't know her well enough, and I'd found myself, during the past week, picking through my memories of being a high school English teacher for one year, and having Joan in my senior honors class.

After giving my initial statement to the lead detective—a young, pale redhead named Jimmy Conroy—I had returned to the Bingham police station the following day and given that same statement again. I had tried to parse the questions that were coming at me, this time with a state detective sitting in the back of the interrogation room, her eyes either on me or on the back of her hand. There were more questions the day after about my relationship with Pam O'Neil, and I answered them truthfully. I could feel the disapproval every time I admitted we'd had a sexual relationship.

"Did she ever give you any indication that she was afraid of Richard Whalen, or that she was nervous about ending the relationship with him?" Detective Conroy said. Even with his thinning hair he didn't look a day over twenty-five.

I told them she had never even confirmed to me the identity of the man she was involved with, and that she had never said anything about being scared of him.

"Is it your opinion that she was definitely going to tell him that she wanted to end the relationship?"

I thought for a moment, then said, "My opinion was that she wanted to end the relationship. I have no idea what happened on the Friday when she met him."

I knew what Detective Conroy was doing, that he was trying to build a story that would account for Richard Whalen putting two bullets into Pam O'Neil and then a third bullet into his own head. And, honestly, it wasn't a very complicated story at all. Richard knew Pam was going to stop seeing him, and she had probably even indicated to him she wanted to talk to him that Friday at lunchtime; maybe she'd already told him it was over. So he killed her, and then himself. Of course, why did he have the gun with him, unless he suspected what might happen? I also wondered why Pam had never indicated to me that Richard had become possessive or unhinged. Maybe she didn't know. Maybe she thought they were having a casual fling, while Richard believed they were Romeo and Juliet. People were like that.

"Do you think she was breaking up with Whalen because of you? Because she hoped that the two of you might continue your relationship?"

It was the same question I'd been asking myself since the day I'd discovered the bodies. "I don't think so, only because she told me she wanted to break off the relationship before we slept together, but, who knows, maybe." He looked at me with dead eyes, and I understood his antipathy.

"Mr. Kimball, one more thing, before you go . . ." It was the state police detective, leaning forward now. "Just to reiterate, because I know you answered these questions yesterday, but you saw no other car in the driveway of the house?"

"I saw two cars. The one that belonged to Pam O'Neil and the one that belonged to Richard Whalen. There might have been a car in the garage. I never checked."

"Thank you. And after you heard the gunshots and approached the house, did you hear anything else? Any other noises coming from the property?"

"I didn't," I said. "And I was listening carefully, expecting to hear another shot, maybe, or for someone to come out of the house."

"I'm sure you were."

I hadn't heard from either the Bingham Police Department or the state detective since that second interrogation. The *Boston Globe* had been reporting on the story daily, and it was now regularly being referred to as a murder-suicide.

After reading Joan's note several times, I went into my office closet, the one that was filled with all the parts of my life that I no longer looked at. I pulled everything out until I found an old cardboard box from around the time that I was teaching at Dartford-Middleham. Inside I found the notebooks where I'd written out my lesson plans. At the bottom of the box I found a green folder that contained about thirty sheets of paper, each one with a hand-written paragraph and the student's name on the top. It had been near the end of the semester, which meant it was very near to the day of the shooting, and my seniors had just about lost any interest in anything academic. I remember the windows of the classroom were open, and warm, lilac-scented air was coming in. I'd talked to them about college, and what their expectations were. They were all college-bound, this particular class, and then, just for some-thing to do, I passed out blank sheets of paper and had them all write down where they thought they'd be in ten years. "Maybe I'll find you in ten years and let you know how close your predictions were," I'd said.

There'd only been about ten minutes left in the class so mostly what I got was either overly optimistic responses—"I'll be married to the love of my life. We'll have a boy and girl, and I'll be vice president of a finance company in Boston"—or else they were jokes—"I'll still be in high school trying to pass honors English."

But there were three people I was particularly interested in. The first two were James Pursall, the kid who had brought a gun to my classroom, and Madison Brown, his victim.

Madison Brown, writing about where she'd be in ten years, had written: "Working in the fashion industry in New York City. Or else at a magazine." She'd sprawled the words quickly in lavender ink, capitalizing almost every word in the two brief sentences. Writing her name on the top right of the paper, she'd put a little circle as the dot on the *i* in Madison.

James Pursall's handwriting was cramped, and I could make out where he'd pressed so hard with his pen that he'd almost torn the paper. He'd written, "In ten years it won't matter what I'll be doing because the world will be overrun by either zombies or zoo animals or zombie zoo animals." At the time I'd simply taken it as a joke, which it essentially was, but in hindsight, maybe the crucial part was his assertion that it wouldn't matter. James had been a quiet kid, smart enough to be in the honors class, but not particularly motivated to do well. But he did all the reading assignments, and turned in his homework, even though he never spoke in class unless I specifically called on him.

I remembered the wording of James's prediction, and Madison's, as well, because I'd obsessively reread each of them several times after the incident, during that terrible year when I'd gone over and over all the different steps I could have taken to stop what had happened. But I didn't remember what Joan Grieve had written, until I found it in the green folder, and then it came back to me. At the time I thought it was humorous. She'd written one of the longer predictions: "Dear Mr. Kimball, in ten years I'll be filthy rich because my first husband will have died in mysterious circumstances while boating off Nantucket. The police will suspect me, of course, being his trophy wife, but Richard Gere will provide me with a perfect alibi, since I'll have been on his yacht at the time of the accident." She'd drawn a smiley face at the end of the paragraph, and I remembered how I'd felt when I'd first read this fifteen years earlier. That it struck me as a summing up of what I knew about Joan Grieve. She was funny and confident, and a little bit scary, like she was always making a joke that was rooted in the truth.

Now, reading what she'd written, I was stunned. It wasn't just that her husband had died in strange circumstances, it was also the odd coincidence of the name Richard Gere. Not that I was reading into it, but it was spooky all the same, that she would eventually marry someone named Richard. But Richard Gere was a well-known, handsome actor, especially back when Joan had been a senior in high school. It was a little strange that she'd picked someone so much older than her, but, again, I was probably overanalyzing. Like I said, there had only been about ten minutes left in the class when I gave them this assignment so it's not as though anyone put a lot of thought into what they wrote.

I left the green folder out on my desk, and went and lay back on my sofa, looking at my phone. But there was nothing there that could stop the constant images that kept coming into my head, alternating between my night spent with Pam in the hazy, cozy light of her bedroom and what she looked like the very next day in that empty house that belonged to no one.

I put the phone down, then got up and took Joan Grieve's prediction with me to the sofa. I read it several more times. Then I did what I'd been doing for a couple of days now—going over and over everything that had happened since I took the job of following Richard Whalen. I thought about every conversation with Joan, how she'd sounded, how she'd acted. And I thought about Pam O'Neil, and everything she'd told me about her relationship with Richard. I kept going back to something she'd said that first night I'd met her at the Taste of Hong Kong. She'd told me that the relationship she was in was more of a threesome than a twosome. Those had been her exact words, and then she'd said something to indicate she wasn't involved in a "threesome" in a physical way. So who was the third person? I assumed she meant that it was a threesome because she was involved with a married man, and that his wife, Joan, was the other party. But it still didn't sit entirely right. People who were involved with someone married didn't say they were in a "threesome," at least not that I knew about.

After another sleepless night, and after making arrangements with my upstairs neighbor to feed Pye, I got into the Taurus and drove west out of the city. It was an overcast day, the wind pushing dead leaves across the road. From the turnpike I got onto Route 84 and went through Hartford, stopping for lunch at a diner. Then I drove another hour through farmland and countryside until I reached the town of Shepaug. There were still clouds in the sky, but here and there the sun was breaking through. I drove slowly, using only my memory. I had to double back once but then I found the long driveway that led to Monk's House, the name David Kintner had given to the restored farmhouse where he currently lived with his ex-wife and his daughter.

I parked my car under a willow tree and stepped out onto the driveway. The air smelled of rotting fruit and woodsmoke. The front door swung open and Lily Kintner stepped out onto the porch. She was wearing old jeans and a turtleneck sweater. Her red hair was tied back.

I walked to the steps that led up to the porch, and she came down and met me.

"You're a surprise," she said.

"Well. I didn't want to call, but I wanted to see you. I hope this is okay."

"Of course. I'll always be happy to see you. So will my father. I just . . . is there a reason you're here?"

"I just finished a case that ended with me finding two dead bodies."

"Okay," she said. The sun was pushing its way through the clouds, and she squinted in the sudden light.

"I think I might have been set up. As a witness."

"Who do you think set you up?"

"A woman named Joan Whalen, or Joan Grieve . . . that was her name before she got married. I wanted to get your opinion because I'm pretty sure she murdered her husband and her husband's girlfriend."

"Okay," she said, nodding.

"Or maybe I just want to think that because if she didn't then it was probably my fault that two people are dead. Sorry, I'm not making sense. I just needed to see someone and I thought of you."

"Come in," Lily said, and reached out and touched my shoulder before turning toward the house. I followed her inside.

CHAPTER 17

RICHARD

It had been five years since Richard had heard from Joan Grieve. He thought about her less these days, but still thought about her often. And then, during a Tuesday afternoon shift at Prince Hardware he looked up from behind the checkout desk and saw her looking at batteries. She glanced in his direction and their eyes met, and then she put the pack of nine volts she had in her hand back onto the rack and left the store.

That night, after eating a burrito in his basement apartment, he drove to the Fairview Library, a gothic brick building across from the congregational church in the small town he'd lived in since dropping out of Worcester Polytech after his sophomore year. There, he nodded at the lone librarian, a mannish-looking woman who once told Richard jokingly she was going to report him because he was always taking out the creepiest books they had. Since then he'd added her to his always growing kill list, and he'd imagined multiple times how he'd do it. He even knew where she lived and that she lived alone. It would be less trouble than changing a tire.

He turned right into the main wing of the library and climbed one of the four spiral staircases that led to the extended balcony that wrapped along three sides, and where the hardcover fiction was kept. There were two reading alcoves, one in each of the far corners of the suspended second floor, and Richard, after ducking down the Se–Tu aisle and grabbing a Dan Simmons book he'd read a few times, went and settled onto an upholstered chair. And he waited.

The Fairview Library was open until nine p.m. on Tuesdays, Thursdays, and Saturdays. At eight Richard wondered if Joan was coming at all. It was possible she had just wandered by mistake into the store where he worked. But if that had been the case, then why had she put down what she was looking at and left? Why had she given him that look?

He heard steps on the hardwood floors below, then listened as those same steps climbed one of the spiral staircases with the cast-iron risers. Richard stayed where he was. If it was Joan, she'd find him. The footsteps got closer, and now he was convinced it really was her, and his heart accelerated just a little bit. It had been many years, but meeting Joan Grieve in the library at the Windward Resort, and then at the Dartford town library all through high school, had been the most exciting, the most honest, moments of his life. He held the book in his lap but kept his eyes on the portion of the railed aisle that he could see.

And then she was suddenly there. She looked older, not physically really, but because of the clothes she was wearing and the way she held herself. She was in a charcoal skirt and a white blouse. She held a small leather purse. She smiled, and shook her head a little, almost as though she couldn't believe he'd actually be here waiting for her. There was another chair in this alcove, at right angles to his, and she sat in it, turning her body to face him.

"What are you reading?" she asked.

He held up *Carrion Comfort* and said, "I was just looking at it. I've read it a few times."

"Of course you have."

"How are you?" Richard said.

Joan looked away briefly and Richard studied her pale neck, a blue vein visible in the fluorescent light of the library. Then she turned back to him. "Maybe you know this, but I got married."

"I heard."

"I married another Richard."

"I heard that, too." He smiled. "It was Richie Whalen, right? From school?"

"Unfortunately, yes. Although now he goes by Richard."

"Uh-huh."

Joan was quiet for a moment, and he remembered that they could do that together, be quiet, neither feeling the need to fill the silence. After a moment, Richard said, "So was it his name that attracted you to him? You only marry men named Richard?"

Her eyes got bright, and she pressed her lips together, then laughed out loud. It sounded dangerous in the quiet of the library. "Well," she said. "I can't remember exactly why I decided to marry him, but it was a big mistake."

"Sorry to hear that."

"I have no one to blame but myself. He's a workaholic, which is fine, because he makes a lot of money, but it's not fine because all he does is talk about work. If I have to hear one more thing about how to properly stage a house, or the current market trends, I'm going to kill myself. *And* he's having an affair, not that I care about that, but I guess I care that he thinks he's getting away with it. He's just selfish and boring."

"Yuck," Richard said.

"What about you? How are you doing?"

Richard knew she was really only asking out of politeness, or maybe just to check that nothing terrible was happening in his life. He said, "My mother finally died, which was a good thing. And my stepfather moved to Florida. Another good thing. I'm still at the hardware store, but you know that already, obviously."

"You should have a better job," Joan said. It was just like her to say something like that to him. It didn't upset him because they'd always been honest with one another.

"I like my job because nobody bothers me. Well, sometimes the customers bother me, but my boss never does. He doesn't give a shit so long as I show up on time."

"It sounds good, Richard. Sorry if I . . ."

"No, don't worry about it. I'm doing okay. Sometimes I'm bored, but now that we're meeting here, everything's better. I'm pretty curious why you wanted us to meet."

She moved her chair a little closer to him, and leaned in. "I want to kill my husband, and I know a way that I can do it, but I need your help."

Those were the words that he'd expected to hear as soon as she told him that she was married. "You want me to kill him for you?"

She slid her hand over toward him and squeezed his thigh, then took his hand in hers. Richard felt the surge of electricity, almost a flood of heat, that he'd always felt every time he and Joan touched. She looked him in the eye and said, "I do. But only if you really want to help."

"Of course, I'll help. I remember Richie Whalen, and he was a total creep."

Joan smiled, and said, "Yeah, he was a creep, and he's still a creep."

"I know I already asked you, but why exactly did you marry him?"

Joan thought for a while, then said, unfolding her fingers, "One, he pursued me, and he was a different person then than he is now.

No, that's not true. But he acted like a different person at the time. He took me to great restaurants and paid a ton of attention to me. You know what's funny? He kept telling me how he couldn't believe he was dating the hot girl from his high school, that it was like a fantasy come true. I mean, I never thought of myself that way."

"You did a little bit," Richard said, remembering Joan in high school, how confident she was, how other students, and teachers, even, seemed to watch her. "You were the queen bee."

"I don't know about that. Anyway, those days are long gone. Now I'm married to a man I can't stand who cheats on me with one of my friends."

"You know that for sure?"

Joan paused, and Richard thought she was considering not telling him something. But then she said, "The woman who's sleeping with my husband is named Pam, and she's the office manager at the company he owns. I know Pam pretty well. We became friends when she first started working there, and she used to complain about how lonely she was and how great my husband was, et cetera, so I talked her into it . . ."

"You talked her into sleeping with your husband?" Richard said.

"I did, actually. I told her she'd be doing me a favor, that I would find out if he was a cheater, and that she'd be doing *herself* a favor because believe it or not Richie Whalen might be a creep, but he's pretty good in bed. So it happened. There was even a time when Pam would tell me about the things he'd say to her, and what they did, and then I guess it got a little awkward—a lot awkward—even though I told Pam I was happy to have the asshole off my hands. I'm a little worried, though, right now, because I get the sense that she wants to end it, and I don't want to lose the opportunity."

"You want to kill them both when they're together?"

Joan squeezed Richard's leg again like he'd just told her he'd brought her a present. "It's so perfect. And they're so predictable.

They've been going to the same overpriced house that's for sale on Friday for a while now. You could be there waiting for them, and I've thought of a way to make it look like Richard shoots Pam and then himself. And I've even got a witness, or I'm planning on getting a witness."

"Why do you need a witness?"

"Because I want this to be perfect," Joan said. "I want someone to say that he saw Richard and Pam go into an empty house together. That he heard gunshots, and then he finds the body. I'll have an alibi, and, of course, no one in the world knows that we have ever even spoken together. It'll be perfect, Richard, just like it always is. We do have a track record to protect, don't you think?"

"We do," Richard said. He was only questioning her about the plan because he was excited to hear the details. It had been too long since he'd had a purpose. "A very perfect track record," he said.

"I still think about Maine, about being out on that jetty with you and with Duane . . ."

"I think about it, too," Richard said. "All the time." He wanted to tell her that he was born on that night, out of that storm, that he came alive on the earth, but he didn't want to overdo it. He knew she felt the same way but putting it into words might be too much.

"So you'll help me?" Joan said.

Richard didn't immediately answer because the librarian's voice was echoing through their wing, telling them that the library would close in fifteen minutes.

"I'll help you," he said.

"Oh, good," she said, and bounced a little in the chair. And he could see the high school student again. She *had* been queen bee. And the way she just acted was probably the way she'd acted when she'd talked one of her dimwit friends into helping out with prom decorations. "Do you remember Mr. Kimball, the English teacher?" she said.

"I never had him, but of course I remember him. He was there, in the classroom, during the shooting, right?"

"Yeah. He panicked, you know? I watched him when it was all happening, and you could tell he was frozen, and I remember thinking at the time that that had been a stroke of luck. It was probably a good thing that we didn't have some Arnold Schwarzenegger type who pulled out a gun from his desk. Did you know that he quit teaching after that, and he became a policeman, which he must have done because of what happened?"

"No," Richard said.

"He got fired because of stalking some woman."

"That sounds vaguely familiar," Richard said. "Did she stab him?"

"Yes. He was following a suspect in a murder case, and she became paranoid and stabbed him."

"I remember that, but I never realized it was Mr. Kimball from our school."

"I didn't at first either, but I put it all together, and, the thing is, he's now a private detective. And he's going to be our witness."

"Okay," Richard said, nodding his head. Joan's eyes were bright, and she had sucked her upper lip underneath her lower one, something she only ever did when she was very excited.

Lights were going out in the library, one after another. "Can we meet in a week?" Joan said. "Here. Same place, same time."

"Yes," Richard said, and Joan got up and left.

Richard stayed in his chair for a minute, in the suddenly dim light of the alcove, then got up and left the library too. Once he was outside, he didn't want to go directly to his car. It was late September and there was a cool breeze, so he walked for a while down past the church, then past the small cluster of shops, all closed now, that made up the entirety of Fairview's commercial district. A ragged dog emerged from between a gas station and a house with a mansard roof. It stood on a gravel driveway, and Richard realized it wasn't a dog, but a coyote, its eyes reflecting yellow in the moonlight. He lifted his arms silently to make himself look bigger, and the coyote turned and trotted away. Richard felt a flush of power, and had a sudden urge to do something animalistic, or crazy, like howl at the moon, or get down on all fours. He stopped himself, knowing that even if no one saw him, it would still be a sign of some form of insanity.

CHAPTER 18

KIMBALL

David Kintner, Lily's father, had made me a very stiff whiskey and soda, about twice as dark as the one he was holding, and we were sitting across from each other in the living room, a coffee table stacked with books between us.

"Remind me, Henry," he said. "Last time you were here was right after . . . soon after Lily returned from . . . from . . ."

"From the hospital," I said, at the same time as he said, "from Winslow."

I liked David for a number of reasons, but one of them was that he had never questioned my visits to see Lily. It wasn't entirely clear that he knew the whole story, but he must have known that Lily had attacked me with a knife because she had felt threatened. This was back when I was a police officer, back when I'd become convinced she had a lot more to do with the deaths of Ted and Miranda Severson than she was letting on. After I'd been suspended by the Boston Police Department, and subsequently resigned, one of the department lawyers told me that Lily Kintner had agreed to drop all charges against me and the department. I remembered reminding this particular lawyer—I picture an ill-fitting suit and a goatee—that I was the one who ended up with a knife in my side. He'd said, "About *that*. This is all contingent on you not pressing any charges against Ms. Kintner, of course." I'd agreed, happy to let the whole incident slide into the past. But I couldn't get Lily out of my mind, and on a whim I contacted one of her doctors at the facility she was housed in, and asked if I could visit. Since there was going to be no further legal action, the doctor and Lily both agreed.

I visited her late in the afternoon on a Friday. I didn't know what to expect but I was brought through two sets of doors into a light-filled sitting room that felt more like the common area of a college dorm than a psychiatric ward. There were vinyl couches and a table with a partly finished jigsaw puzzle, and several patients watching television. Lily entered the room from the other side, and smiled across the room at me as though I were her oldest friend. She was wearing sweatpants and a white sweater and her red hair was tied back at the back of her head.

"Where do you want to talk?" she said, after coming across the room to meet me.

"Where *can* we talk?"

"Here. Or in my room. I'm not on restrictions right now."

We ended up finding an alcove and sat across from one another on an uncomfortable couch. "I'm surprised you agreed to see me," I said.

"I was a little surprised, as well, that you wanted to," she said. "But I don't know. Everything in my life is surprising right now."

"Same for me," I said.

"You didn't think you'd ever be stabbed and live to tell the tale?" she said.

"I definitely didn't think I'd ever be stabbed and then want to go and visit the person who stabbed me. Why do you look so happy?"

"I suppose I'm happy because you're not dead. Because I didn't kill you. I know it's not much, but I'm very pleased you're not dead." It was less the words and more the way she was looking at me, but we became friends, I think, in that moment. I told her about my recovery, and she told me about hers. Before leaving the hospital, I said, "You know, now that we've agreed to not testify against one another, or press charges, we are kind of free to tell each other the truth. We can't hurt one another anymore."

She thought for a moment, and said, "I suppose so. You go first. Tell me something truthful."

"Okay," I said. "I was following you partly because I thought you were involved in the deaths of Ted and Miranda Severson, but really, I was following you because I'd fallen for you. The police department was right to fire me."

She smiled, amused, I think, and I said, "Your turn. Something truthful."

"Falling for me is a big mistake," she said. "I'm not a bad person but I've done bad things."

That was the first of three visits I made to Lily in the hospital. On my last visit she told me about a construction project happening next to her childhood home, how it might uncover an old well, a place where bodies were buried, she said, and I realized that for whatever reason she had decided to entirely trust me. She had handed me the means to implicate her in a crime. The fact that I chose not to do that was what truly sealed our bond. Since those trips to the hospital, we have never talked on the phone or sent each other text messages. I don't even know if she has a phone. After being released from the hospital, Lily quit her job as a librarian at Winslow College and moved back to Shepaug, in Connecticut, to her family home, still occupied by her divorced mother and father. She told me once that navigating between them has become her full-time job. Her mother, Sharon Henderson, is a painter who grew up in Pittsburgh, but has lived in Connecticut her entire adult life, while Lily's father, David, is a relatively famous English novelist who met Sharon when he was a visiting professor at Shepaug University. He lived in America throughout most of Lily's childhood, until the divorce sent him back to London and a third marriage. But he was permanently housed in Connecticut now, having fled his homeland after drunkenly crashing his car in the Cotswolds, accidentally killing his wife. He'd agreed to move back to his old house with his estranged wife, who needed his money to hold on to the property.

"Right," I said to David now. We were still talking about Lily. "Does she still have her house up in Winslow, or is she fully moved in down here?"

"Far as I know she still has the house in Winslow. Rents it out, I think. I suspect, and I also suspect she'd agree with me, that owning a home away from here is of enormous symbolic importance to her. Otherwise she might feel she was stuck here at Monk's House forever, dealing with her mother and me. It's not much of a life."

As though on cue, I heard laughter coming from the adjacent kitchen, where Lily and her mother were preparing dinner. I'd been invited to stay over.

"Are you working on anything?" I said to David Kintner, knowing he wasn't, but wanting to turn the topic of conversation to his writing.

"Ah," he said. "No, sadly. The words don't come anymore, at least not the right words and not in the right order. But did you know that Lily and I, more Lily, really, are going through my manuscripts, doing a little pre-archival work before I die?"

"Are all your papers here?" I said.

"Almost all." Those words came from Lily, who had entered the living room quietly, carrying a cheese board that she placed on the most stable-looking stack of books on the coffee table.

"Yes, almost all," David said.

"Dad thinks he has old notebooks at a rental house in France that you used to go to . . . when was it?"

"Before you, Lil. And then for two summers when you were too little to remember. But I'm not a hundred percent sure, and I'm not even a hundred percent sure that the house is still where I say it is."

"I'll go there and find out," Lily said. "It'll be a good excuse to go on a trip. I'm going to get a drink. Can I get anyone anything?"

We both declined. David leaned forward and plucked a grape from the bunch that was decorating the cheese board, and said, "I don't know what I'd do without her. I'm withering on the vine here." He was staring at the grape in his hand that had just provided the metaphor, and he looked as though a tear might suddenly slide down one of his cheeks. He wore corduroys that were thin at the knees, and a cardigan sweater over a checked shirt. The most robust thing about him was his thick white hair, parted the way it had always been so that it stuck up a little on his left side. He was tall and thin, but his shoulders had rounded a little with age, and there was a noticeable tremor in his right arm.

"You're lucky to have her," I said.

His eyes sharpened, and he said, his voice pitched a little lower, "My understanding from Lil is that you might have something to do with that. That's one of the reasons I like you."

"What are the others?"

"Well, if I remember correctly, last time you were here you not only matched me drink for drink, but you regularly complimented me on my novels. Those are two traits I revere in a houseguest."

"I'm happy to compliment your novels if you keep providing me with drinks," I said.

He grinned, showing off his yellow teeth, then asked me if I'd pick a record. I got up from the sofa and went over to the turntable and the large floor speakers. Elaborate shelving had been built around these items, and one of those shelves contained about three hundred records. I picked a Chico Hamilton album because the cover was interesting and dropped the needle on side one.

"Thank you," David said when I settled back in across from him. "It's no picnic having to get up every thirty minutes to play new music but I refuse to have my music choices cataloged and recorded by some Chinese aggregating corporation halfway around the world. What I like to do is sit here and listen to pressed wax and read actual fucking books and be secure in my knowledge that unless the satellites now have x-ray vision no one in the world knows what I'm listening to and reading except for me. It's actually thrilling. Although I do realize that for a whole generation of human beings the thought of anonymity is worse than death."

Lily returned to the room with a glass of wine and sat down next to her father and across from me. "Is Dad giving you his speech about anonymity?" she said to me.

"He's right. Plus, vinyl sounds better," I said at pretty much the same time as David said, "What precisely do you mean, my speech?"

She turned to her father, didn't answer his question, and said, instead, "Mom's making the quinoa salad."

"Good God," he said. "What is that? Like the third time this week?"

Lily turned to me. "Sharon has become a fan of quinoa salad with cranberries and goat cheese. She makes it a lot."

"It's the only fucking thing she makes around here."

"Beggars and choosers, right, Dad?"

"I suppose. Let's talk about something else. Henry was gearing up to praise me, I believe."

"I want to hear more about what you're doing with the manuscripts," I said, looking at Lily, who was still wearing the jeans and the sweater she'd been wearing earlier that afternoon. She took a tiny sip of her wine and put the glass down on the hardwood floor by her feet.

"What I'm doing is mostly just collecting everything there is and trying to get it into chronological order. Dad was a saver, so there's a lot."

"Do you know where it will all be going eventually?" I said.

"We have an offer in from a college in Arizona and a potential offer from Emory in Atlanta, although"—she turned and looked at her father—"I think they're wavering a little."

"I've lived long enough to become a pariah," David said. "Most of that is my own behavior, and some of that is the changing of the tide. I'm a white man who wrote about white men chasing women."

"Someone's got to do it, I suppose," I said.

"Just not me," he said. "Not any longer, thank God."

"Dad does have a complete unpublished manuscript that he wrote between *Left Over Right* and *We Met at the End of the Party*."

"Really?" I said. "Between my favorite David Kintner novel and my second favorite one."

"Oh, you suck-up," Lily said.

"Don't listen to her, Henry. Tell me again about your favorite novels of mine, and be specific about what you liked about them."

Four hours later the three of us were in the same places in the living room, although in the interim we'd all gotten up to eat quinoa salad and roast lamb in the dining room, then, after dinner, gone to Lily's office, where she showed the piles of notes from her father's career, along with newspaper clippings, foreign editions of his books, magazines that contained his stories, and even a stack of videotapes of the lecture series he gave at Shepaug University when he first visited the United States.

Lily was drinking tea, and David had allowed himself a small glass of undiluted single malt. Sharon came into the living room for a while with a large glass of red wine, and stood behind the oldest sofa in the room, its fabric worn thin by time and cocktail parties. She stared at the ceiling and told us all twice about the ants that were now permanently taking up residence in the pantry.

"We'll worry about that tomorrow, Mom," Lily said. "Why don't you sit and we can all talk about something else?"

"Oh, no. If I sit, I might never get up. I'll just take myself off to bed. Lil, where's Henry sleeping—not in the maroon room, is he?"

"I set up the room on the third floor, Mom."

After Sharon left, Lily suggested to David he take his drink with him to his room and finish it there. "Good advice," he said, and came up surprisingly easily off the sunken sofa. Lily stood too, but he waved her off, saying he'd be fine and left the room, turning at the door and saying, "Good show tonight. Good show."

"He always says that," Lily said. "One night, Sharon threw a trivet at him and he bled all over the table and afterward he said it had been a good show."

"Title of his biography," I said.

"Ha," Lily said, then was quiet, her eyes unfocused, her tea mug in her hand. "Are you ready to tell me about what happened? I looked it up on my phone while we were getting dinner ready. It's being declared a murder-slash-suicide."

"Whoever did it did a good job," I said. "I was first on the scene. It looked like Richard Whalen and Pam O'Neil sat across from one another, like we are right now. He shot her twice, then shot himself with the same gun."

"So why do you think that isn't what happened?"

I took a breath and said, "The night before the murder I slept with Pam O'Neil. I'd gotten to know her because I was following her. She was very sweet. I should never have slept with her, obviously. Now I can't stop thinking that because of that she tried to end her relationship with Richard, which led him to shoot her and then himself."

Lily paused, thinking, then said, "So the reason you think they were murdered by someone else is because if they weren't then you are to blame."

"Yes, that's one reason. I already don't particularly like myself, and if I caused Pam's death I'm going to like myself a whole lot less."

I thought Lily might say something to try and comfort me, and I was glad when she kept silent.

"But," I said. "I do have a deep suspicion, or maybe just a gut feeling, that Richard didn't do it. I didn't know him at all, but I watched him and followed him. He was a cheating suburbanite with a good job, but he doesn't make sense as a murderer."

"You can't really know that," Lily said.

"I know," I said. "Here's the truth. Nothing that I saw over the past week makes me think I was somehow set up. Except for maybe this weird remark that Pam made about being in a threesome, but I'll get to that. The reason I think I've been set up is because of what happened fifteen years ago in my classroom with Joan Grieve. That's what I keep thinking about."

"What happened there?"

"You don't know about it?"

"I know a little. I know that you were an English teacher at Dartford-Middleham High School and that a student in one of your classes shot a girl and then himself."

"He held us hostage for a while before he did it."

"Oh, I didn't know that."

"And Joan was in my class, as well. The girl who was killed was one of her friends."

"Joan who hired you Joan?"

"Uh-huh."

"And what about the boy with the gun? Who was he?"

"Kind of a loner. Like if you were making a movie and wanted your school shooter to be a total cliché you would cast him. Not many friends, crappy home life, into violent video games and comic books."

"But not friends with Joan Grieve?"

"Joan Grieve was a star gymnast and super popular. She didn't hang out with kids like James Pursall. But she was there in the room when it happened, and I think she might have had something to do with it. And then, fifteen years later . . ."

"She comes back to you and the same thing happens again."

"Exactly. And there's one other thing, but I'm almost embarrassed to tell you about it."

Lily shrugged, and I said, "It's actually in my car, in my overnight bag that I packed out of pure hope you'd ask me to spend the night."

"Go get it," she said.

I walked across the driveway to my car to get my bag. The night sky was inky black and dense with stars. The only sign of nearby human habitation was a brand-new house on the far edge of an adjacent meadow, its enormous front door lit by overhead lighting. Before going back into Monk's House I stood for a moment on the front stoop, watching my breath condense and trying to figure out why I was so happy to be here.

Back inside I showed Lily the three pages I'd brought with me, the responses from Madison Brown, James Pursall, and Joan Grieve to the question of what they'd be doing in ten years' time. Lily read all three, then looked at me. She had pale red eyebrows, almost undetectable against her milky skin, but I saw that she had raised them slightly.

CHAPTER 19

RICHARD

For as long as he could remember Richard had narrated his own life. Sometimes it was simply that he recounted his day-to-day existence in a series of interior monologues. Sometimes he imagined he was subject to an extensive experiment, where an alien species had selected him from all the other humans on the planet as a subject to analyze, and he was being watched every moment of his life. He often had these fantasies—the alien ones—when his life was at the most tedious, when a day was defined by nothing more than one elitist comment from a customer at the store, or by an entire evening and night playing *Assassin's Creed* until his eyes stung. When his life was interesting—and his life was seldom interesting—then the narrative would take the form of a future bestselling book, written about him after he had wreaked havoc on the world then left it all behind.

In the weeks after Joan had walked into the store and met him at the library to ask him to murder her husband, he found himself imagining the book version of his life. The author would have to theorize about the facts, of course, and fill in the details. *We'll never know for sure, but it is clear that at some point in time Richard Seddon and Joan Grieve, now known as Joan Whalen, met again. Maybe it was an accident, and maybe it was arranged, but either way, the moment they met a death sentence for Joan's husband was now firmly in place.*

Richard had met Joan a second time in the library late on the following Tuesday night. She had explained to him exactly what she wanted him to do. She knew the house that her husband and his girlfriend went to on Fridays during lunch. She had scouted the location and knew he could park his car on the parallel street in the small parking lot of a neighborhood playground. There were hiking trails nearby, so it made sense that he should dress as though he was a hiker, and then he could make his way through the woods to the back side of the deck house that was for sale. According to Joan, the door that led to the back porch could be opened with a credit card, and the door that led from the porch into the interior of the house was never locked. He should get there before they did, and make it look as though Richard shot Pam then himself.

"That's not easy to do," Richard said.

"Shooting them, or making it look like my husband shot himself?"

"Shooting them won't be hard. The other thing will."

"I know. But if you can pull it off, then we'll have committed a perfect crime. It will be amazing. And if you can't pull it off, if the police suspect that someone else was in the house, they will never in a million years suspect it was you. They'll probably suspect it was me, but I'll be having coffee with one of my clients, so I'll have an alibi. And there is nothing in this world that connects us. Only our own memories. Trust me, it will be perfect, even if the killing doesn't go exactly as planned."

"Okay," Richard said, relieved to know she didn't expect him to be perfect. It wasn't a surprise; it was the way she'd always acted. When she'd helped him to kill his cousin Duane she'd known that things might go wrong. And when Richard had gotten James Pursall to kill Madison Brown for Joan during their senior year of high school there was no guarantee that it would have worked. But the important thing, the only thing, was that Joan and Richard were strangers to one another, that no one knew how close they were, and that would always protect them. It was their superpower.

They'd agreed to meet again in another week. Joan was going to go to Henry Kimball, the ex-cop who used to teach at Dartford, and have him follow Richard and Pam.

"What if he sees me?" Richard said.

"He won't. Just so long as you kill Richard and Pam right after they get in the house, then leave right away through the back. He won't see you, I promise. And just to be safe you should wear some kind of disguise or mask when you're in the house, so even if he sees you, he won't be able to identify you."

"Okay," Richard said.

And then he had to wait another week to see Joan again, to make the final plan. The excitement had been almost unbearable, his days at the store starting to crawl, and his nights at home not a whole lot better. He studied satellite maps of the deck house, and the lot lines around it, planning where he'd park, and where he'd make his way to the house. He wanted to go scout the area but didn't want to take an unnecessary risk. If someone saw him there more than once they might remember him.

Even though the waiting was unbearable, it was only because he was so excited to have Joan back in his life. And to have purpose. No, it wasn't all about purpose, because his life did have purpose, even without Joan in it. He'd spent the past two years drawing up an elaborate plan where he'd use four carefully placed fertilizer bombs to drop all three stories of the Winslow Oaks Convention Center onto their largest hall during a packed event. He'd been considering the best time to enact this plan, at one point flirting with the idea of doing it during the annual New England Concrete Professionals Convention, the one his stepfather used to attend every year until he'd retired and moved down to Florida. That would be very satisfying, except for the fact that Don Seddon himself wouldn't wind up crushed to death under a ton of his own product when Richard brought down the building. No, the real problem with killing a bunch of smug, witless concrete experts was that who the fuck would even care. Richard had a better plan. The Winslow Oaks Convention Center hosted at least two huge proms every spring, one for a regional tech high school, and the other for Chilton High School, one of the ritzier schools west of Route 495. The type of kids who went there were probably a lot like the type of kids who went to Dartford-Middleham, and Richard could only imagine the news headlines if he killed every single graduating senior in that particular town. All those kids in their bad tuxedos and all the girls in their glitzy dresses, acting like they'd accomplished something by graduating from high school and finding someone to have sex with.

If Richard could pull it off, and he really believed he could, his name would be remembered forever.

But for right now, now that Joan was back, he'd put the prom night planning on the back burner. Joan had work for him to do, and she would always come first. She was the one, after all, who had shown him his true world, back when they'd been fifteen years old in Kennewick, Maine. She'd shown him that you didn't need to accept your reality, that you could change it. She'd shown him colors he'd never known existed.

On their third meeting at the Fairview Library Joan confirmed that she'd hired Henry Kimball, the teacher she knew who was now a private investigator, and he would be following either her husband or her husband's girlfriend all week. Richard wasn't too nuts about bringing in the private detective. It seemed unnecessarily complex, but Joan really believed that having a witness, someone who confirmed that an affair was taking place, and someone who would likely find the bodies, added an element of believability. Richard suspected she just wanted to bring in this man from her past, this man who was in the room when all their work paid off and Madison Brown got what she deserved. There was a theatrical element to Joan. Maybe it came from being a gymnast. She wanted things to be beautiful, and she wanted them to be perfect.

On their last meeting together at the library, Joan brought Richard her husband's Smith & Wesson handgun, fully loaded, taking it out of her leather purse and casually handing it across to him.

"He won't miss it this week?" Richard said.

"Highly doubtful. We keep it in our safe, and there's no reason for him to go there. If he does, I'll tell him that I got rid of it. I've told him many times that I hate having it in the house. Do you know how to use it?"

"Point and shoot," Richard said.

Joan pressed her lips together, shrugged a little. She hadn't changed much since he'd first gotten to know her, in Maine. She still acted the same, half amused at everything, at ease in her own skin. Her gestures and her facial expressions seemed the same to him too, and he wondered if she really hadn't changed, or if she acted differently when she was with him, if somehow just being with him caused her to revert to the person she was when they'd first had that incredible experience at the Windward Resort.

"How do you feel about this?" she said, whispering a little because there were actually library customers on the first floor, two teenage girls who kept breaking into fits of giggling.

"You know how I feel," Richard said.

"Do I?"

"I think so."

"You feel good about it, and a little excited, and, most importantly, you are happy to have me back in your life." Joan tilted her chin at him, mugging a little.

"All those things," Richard said. "How do you feel about it?"

"Like I'm going to get my life back. That I'm ridding the world of two insignificant people. And sometimes I even feel like I'm back on the jetty at night. Do you remember that? What it felt like?"

Richard just nodded, and Joan stared at him. He stared back, her eyes hard and blue and looking right into him.

On Friday Richard called in sick to work. It wasn't the best timing because Fridays could be busy, but Richard also knew that George Koestler, who owned the store, could recruit his son, back from college for a long weekend, to help out if he needed him. Richard left his cell phone behind in his apartment. He wore hiking shoes, his oldest jeans, and a fleece top that had been sent to the store by a company that specialized in ripsaws. Their logo was on the front right of the fleece, but it was pretty small and unreadable from more than ten feet away. The Smith & Wesson was in a small backpack along with gloves, a nylon balaclava, and plastic bags that he could wrap around his shoes with rubber bands.

He had considered seeing if he could steal one of his neighbor's cars and return it without them noticing, but decided he was being overly careful. As Joan had said many times, there was absolutely nothing to connect him with her husband, or with her. So he took his own car and drove to Bingham, then down the heavily wooded street to the playground, slowing down to turn into its parking lot, but then driving past because there was another car parked there already, and he'd caught a glimpse of a mother pushing a child on a swing set. He decided to pull his Altima along the shoulder of the road near where the trailhead started. His car jutted a little onto the road, but it was better than having an anxious mother decide to memorize his license plate because he was a sole man parking in a playground lot.

Even though he'd studied the satellite maps about a hundred times he still got a little bit lost on the overgrown trails through the pine forest. But he eventually found the deck house, hard to see in the darkness of the woods because of its exterior stain. Kona Brown, Richard thought, a popular seller at the store. He was early—it was creeping up on eleven a.m.—but he decided to wait inside the house. He got out the laminated lockpick card but the back-porch door was open. He sat on a plastic Adirondack chair and pulled bags over his shoes, securing them with rubber bands, then entered the dim interior of the house, standing for a moment to allow his eyes to adjust.

Richard had grown up in a deck house with a similar layout, the short stairway that led from the front door up to the main floor of the house or led down to a finished basement level. But that was where the similarities ended. His house had been tainted by the arrival of Don, and the ways in which Don made his mother change. It had smelled of garbage and sex, and even thinking of it now made Richard almost throb with rage. This house felt as though no one had ever lived there, devoid of personality, of any vestige of human life. The art on the walls was generic, the living room empty except for two oatmeal-colored sofas facing one another. Through the living room was a master bedroom with a king-sized bed. The blinds were drawn, and the room had that fuzzy surreal look of a dark room in the middle of the day.

After exploring a little more Richard decided he'd wait in the second bedroom, this one completely unfurnished, on the north side of the house. There would be no reason for them to come into that room, and he wouldn't even bother to shut the door. He assumed that they would go straight to the bedroom; he'd follow them inside, shooting the woman first while positioned near the man, then shooting the man on the side of his temple. He thought if he moved quickly there wouldn't be time for either of them to react, to fight back. Still, he felt a tightness in his chest, part uncomfortable and part pleasurable, the way he felt whenever he was on the cusp of violence.

He opened his backpack, removed the balaclava and put it on his head, then took out the gun, sliding the safety off. He waited.

Sometime after twelve he heard the distant sound of a car on a gravel driveway, followed by the sound of the front door opening, then muffled voices. He stood rigid against the wall, listening intently.

It was the woman's voice that he first heard clearly, her saying, "No, no. Let's sit for a moment. I want to have a talk with you."

Then Joan's husband's voice: "We can talk in the bedroom, as well, you know?" And even through the walls Richard could tell he'd said it with a smirk on his face, like he'd just uttered the world's most original joke.

"I'm serious," said the woman.

"Okay. Hearing you loud and clear." And then there was a brief pause and Richard thought that they'd probably sat down on one, or both, of the sofas. He took a deep breath, relaxed his grip on the gun, and emerged from the spare room, crossing the short hall into the main living area. They were on opposite sofas, the woman sitting facing him, and the man facing toward her, so that Richard could just see the back of his head. The woman looked up, her face instantly draining of color, her mouth opening and closing without making a sound.

Richard aimed at the very middle of her and pulled the trigger, hitting her somewhere between her chest and her stomach. Then he inched the barrel of the gun up just a little, aimed, and shot her in the forehead, her head whipping backward, a spray of blood hitting the picture window behind her.

Moving quickly, Richard took two steps forward and pressed the gun against the side of Richie Whalen's head. He was just about to pull the trigger, but Richie was speaking in an almost inaudible voice, saying the word *please* over and over. Richard leaned over him and the man had his eyes squeezed shut, like a child thinking he'd be invisible.

Richard, who'd already imagined this possible scenario, said, "Richie, I'll let you live, but I need you to do something for me, okay?"

"Yes, anything."

"I just need your prints on this gun, okay, so hold out your hand and I'm going to put the gun in it, okay?"

Richie held out a shaking hand and muttered something that sounded like a yes to Richard.

"No sudden movements, okay, Richie, or else I kill you. I'm just going to get your prints here on the handle . . . that's good, and on the trigger. You're doing great."

Later, Richard went over in his mind how easy it had been to simply lift Richie's hand with the gun in it and press it to his head and pull the trigger, his finger over Richie's. The man had not fought back, maybe simply hoping that the bad moment would just go away, maybe simply hoping that if he did what he was told he'd be allowed to live.

As Richie lay dead on the couch, the gun in his hand, Richard moved fast, backtracking out of the house, then through the woods to his car. Driving home a light rain began to fall, peppering the car. Richard flipped through radio stations, and landed on "Beautiful Day" by U2, a song that until this moment had never meant anything to him. A song that assholes sang when their team won a championship. It was still playing when he pulled into the driveway of his house, and he sat there, listening, even mouthing along with the words.

CHAPTER 20

KIMBALL

I told Lily, in what felt like extraneous detail, the entire story of the shooting in my classroom. I told her how I'd frozen up while it had unfolded, paralyzed with fear, and how I'd never really forgiven myself for that.

"You could have made it worse," Lily said. "If you'd tried to wrestle the gun away he might have shot everyone in that classroom."

"Sure," I said. "That's a possibility."

"Or you'd have been shot, yourself."

"A much greater possibility."

"I know you've probably thought a lot about this, but ultimately there's no way of knowing what would have happened if you rushed him. Could have made it better, could have made it worse. I'm just telling you things you already know, right?"

"Yes, I have gone over this a few times in my head over the years." I smiled.

"I'm sure you have. I'm sorry. It sounds scary," Lily said, leaning back farther into her sofa. A nearby lamp allowed me to see only half of her face.

"It's not really the choices I made that I've kept going over for years," I said. "It was the fact that I froze. At the time, even if I thought the right thing to do was to charge James Pursall there was no way I could have done it. I couldn't have done anything, really."

"So you became a cop," Lily said. It wasn't a question.

"Yes. I couldn't go back into the classroom. And I couldn't make a living writing poetry. Plus, I hated therapy."

"And you had a secret fantasy that if you were able to save someone when you were a police officer then that would even the score."

"Probably," I said. "I'm not sure I ever put it that way exactly in my own mind, but, yeah."

"And then I came along and ruined being a police detective for you."

"We don't need to talk about that tonight," I said. "It's late."

"It *is* late," she said.

"Before we go to sleep, tell me what you think about my story, about Joan Grieve."

Lily touched an earlobe and was quiet for a moment. "What I think is that Joan Grieve absolutely had someone kill her husband and her husband's lover. Just like she absolutely had James Pursall kill Madison Brown for her. I don't know how she did it, but she did. There's a reason she came back to you and asked you to follow her husband. It was nostalgia, I think. She has good memories of what happened in your classroom, and she wanted to replicate the experience."

"She did replicate the experience. At least for me. Two bodies dead by gunshot wounds. Something I never thought I'd see again."

"So here's the thing about Joan," Lily said, and she moved forward on the couch in preparation for getting up and going to bed. "She doesn't do these things on her own. Somehow, back in high school, she got James Pursall to do her dirty work. Last week, she got someone else to murder her husband. All we need to do is find that person."

"Okay. How do we do that?"

"I can help you. We need to find out everything about Joan's life. My guess is that some other people in her orbit might have come to bad ends. We'll find something. I just don't know how we're going to do it, but we will."

"So you'll help me?"

Her face was below the lamp now, and I could see both her eyes, pale and green. "Of course I will," she said, "I'll always help you, no matter what."

I woke up in Shepaug, confused for a moment about where I was. The house was quiet, and after walking carefully down the hall to the bathroom, I returned to the attic room, got out my computer, and continued my online search of Joan Grieve.

It was strange, but her name did not come up in any stories relating to the shooting that had taken place in my classroom. My name was mentioned, obviously, as were the names of the deceased. And a few other members of that class had been quoted by the papers. Ultimately, though, the story didn't really have any legs, probably because James Pursall killed only one other person before taking his own life. We live in an age of mass murder, and two dead bodies, even young ones, just don't cut it, anymore.

I stared past my computer screen for a few minutes, my mind still back in that classroom, especially since telling Lily the entire story the night before. One day in the future everyone who was there would be dead and there would be zero memory of the event. And even right now, I knew that my memories were faded and falsified by the passage of time. I opened a blank document, thinking for a moment of a poem, ideas streaming through me just out of reach. I have believed for a while that all poetry is saying the same thing—*I am here*—although what the poet really means is, *I was there,* because all poetry is just a letter to some future reader. Everything boils down to that one sentiment. *I was there.* I was there, and I felt things and saw things and sometimes I understood them, but most of the time I did not. I started to jot down a few lines, along this line, erased them, and wrote:

> *There once was a poet in permanent dread*
> *Over the fact that we all wind up dead,*
> *So he scribbled out verse,*
> *Which just made it worse,*
> *And decided to get laid more instead.*

Then I erased that too and went back to thinking about what I might learn about Joan through online searches. Despite not being named as a school-shooting survivor, Joan Grieve Whalen did have an online presence because of her job as an interior decorator. She had a website, a page on LinkedIn, an Instagram account (all pictures of house interiors, either her designs, or ones she admired), a Twitter account, and a Facebook page that she didn't seem to use anymore. I searched her friends on Facebook, looking for any names I recognized from my year as a teacher. There was one. A girl named Kristin Hunter that I remembered from that honors English class, one of the best students if you went by her essays and exams. I remember the only conversation I had with her was when she'd approached me to see if she could get out of giving her mock-valedictorian speech in front of the room, saying she had an anxiety disorder. I'd told her I'd be happy to work with her in advance to go over some strategies for public speaking. I wonder if there had been a small part of her that felt relieved she never had to give that speech because of what James Pursall did just a few days later. As someone who'd had my own fair share of public speaking phobia, I knew there were times I would have welcomed a mass shooting to get out of giving a poetry reading.

Kristin's Facebook page was private, so I didn't learn anything there, although I doubt there would have been anything of interest. Kristin and Joan had probably not been friends in real life and had just found each other on social media the way that old classmates did. I did find two Grieves in Joan's list of friends. One was a Dorothy Grieve, who turned out to be Joan's mother, a woman who posted pictures of either her cats or her Candy Crush scores. Then there was Elizabeth Grieve, clearly an older sister of Joan, and a creative writing teacher at Emerson College, plus a published poet. She had her own website, a picture of herself on it, and it was as though all of Joan's facial features had been plucked off Joan's face and rearranged on someone else's in a less successful way. The same eyes but too close together, the same beautiful mouth but marooned by a square chin. Elizabeth Grieve's black glossy hair was cut short and turning gray in places. I read the few poems that were on the website, free verse mostly, and confessional. There were several about being a childhood leukemia survivor and one about her father's funeral, and how afterward she'd touched herself in her childhood bedroom looking at the cover of a Nancy Drew novel and dreaming of Bess. There was no mention of a sister. On a whim, I looked Elizabeth Grieve up on Amazon, found her two books—the first was called *Variations on a Theme* and the second *Sea Oat Soup*—and ordered them both to arrive the following day.

I put my computer away, packing it in the backpack I'd brought with me. It was seven in the morning and I couldn't sleep anymore, despite staying up late the night before telling Lily Kintner about recent and past events.

I was in a small bedroom with a slanted ceiling on one side, and a view across a misty field that ended in a line of trees. The walls were painted a ghoulish yellow color, and one of the windowpanes was cracked. I'd slept on a thin mattress on a wooden cot and was now sitting at a child-sized desk trying to figure out if it was too early to go downstairs and see if anyone had made coffee. I could hear a scratching sound at the door and opened it up, letting in a slate-gray cat who stopped to look at me like I was the ghost of a man who'd drowned her kittens. We stared at one another until she decided I was a mere mortal, then she circled the room, eventually coming over and rubbing against my ankle. I thought of Pyewacket, who hated to be left alone overnight at home, and I suddenly longed to be back in Cambridge. In the light of day it seemed strange I'd come here in the first place. Maybe Richard Whalen had really fallen in love with Pam O'Neil, so much so that when he knew she was going to break up with him, he did the only logical thing he could think of. He shot her and then himself, ensuring that neither of them would ever be free to love anyone else ever again. It was certainly the way that it looked. Why was I so suspicious of Joan Grieve Whalen? Was it because if she wasn't involved, then I was, in some part? By sleeping with a woman I shouldn't have slept with, had I brought about her violent death? I pushed the thought out of my head.

The collarless cat leapt onto the small blond-wood desk, and I jumped a little. I scratched her under the chin, then got my backpack and went down the backstairs toward the first floor of Monk's House.

In the kitchen I found Lily's mother, Sharon, wearing a loose lavender dress and frying bacon at the stove, while Lily was putting last night's dishes away. Both turned to look at me, and Lily said, "Coffee's next to the fridge. Help yourself."

"Thank you," I said. "I won't stay long, but I will drink a cup of coffee."

"You won't stay for breakfast?"

"Of course, he will," Sharon said. "I've made double."

After agreeing to stay I sat down at the wooden kitchen table. "I met your cat," I said into the room.

"I don't think so," Sharon said loudly, as Lily nodded only at me, then said, "That's April. She's not really our cat, but she likes to come into our house."

"I'm very allergic, you know," Sharon said. "Lily knows that better than anyone, so I really doubt we have a cat."

Lily said, "She likes the room you stayed in last night, and we think she gets in through the greenhouse at the back, but we haven't figured out how she does it. I've always had a cat here. They just arrive somehow."

Sharon kept putting platters on the table, one of bacon, one of scrambled eggs, one of fruit. David Kintner came down, wearing the same clothes he'd had on the night before, but he'd added a tie, tucked into his buttoned-up cardigan. He sat next to me without saying anything and Lily put a boiled egg in a cup in front of him, plus coffee in a bowl. He proceeded to tap on his egg with the edge of a spoon.

After eating, David said his first words of the day, which were to me. "How long are you here? Do you propose to spend your time rambling the countryside, or drinking, or a little bit of both?" It sounded a little rehearsed.

"I'm leaving, unfortunately, right after breakfast."

"He'll be back, Dad," Lily said. "He promised me."

"Ah, good," David said, rubbing at a stain on his tie.

Lily showed me her garden before I got back into my car. It was dying, of course, but there was still color in places, bronze mums in pots, withering sunflowers, a shrub with tiny leaves that had turned various shades of purple. April, the cat, appeared, skirting quietly along an old stone wall, and looking back at me, trying to figure out if I was the same ghost that had been up in her room.

"I did some research on Joan this morning, just googling her and looking at her social media," I said.

"And?"

"And I began to feel stupid. Maybe her husband just snapped. Maybe she's just one of those unlucky people who find themselves near violent death at different times in their life."

"It's a possibility."

"But you don't think so."

"I don't know what to think until I learn more, but my feeling is that your feeling is correct. She's smart and she makes things happen."

I nodded. It was turning into a pretty day, dark clouds being pushed east, and the early morning sun now warming everything up. "We'll both see what we can find out, then?"

"Let's stick to the plan. If there's nothing, then it was nice to have you come down to visit. It cheers my father up."

"You don't have a lot of visitors?"

"Not ones that he likes. My mother's friends, mostly. Dad's friends seem to be either dead or done with traveling."

"Or both," I said, hoping to make Lily smile.

"Or both," she said.

"Are you going to stay here with them?"

"I have to. Well, that's not true. I need to. And I don't mind it so much. I couldn't have gone back to work at Winslow College, even if they'd have had me. Too many interested stares."

She bent and pulled a weed from the damp soil, her hair falling off her shoulder. Lily Kintner had tried to kill me and almost succeeded, and I suspected she'd killed two other people and gotten away with it. Despite this, spending time with her made me feel a level of peace I'd never really felt before. It was like being with a dangerous animal, but knowing that the animal would never hurt you, would never really hurt anyone unless provoked to do it. It wasn't just peace I felt, but I felt special. Lily had let me in.

And there was another feeling I had about Lily, one that was harder for me to understand, but what I felt for her was a kind of unconditional love, but more importantly, it was a love that didn't require a return of love from her. It was simply enough to be the one who did the loving. I was sure that if I thought about that too long, I might conclude I was simply commitment-phobic, only attracted to Lily because she was unattainable, but I thought it was somehow more than that. It was a deeper love, protective and elemental, and maybe it only existed because of what had transpired between us in that cemetery. Or maybe I was simply blinded by an obsessive relationship, like half the people in this world.

"How should we get in touch?" I said.

"Why don't you come back down here in a week and we'll compare notes. We could call each other, I suppose, but then there'd be a record."

"I'll come down," I said. "One week."

CHAPTER 21

RICHARD

After murdering Richie Whalen and Pam O'Neil, Richard's euphoria was short-lived. Not because of guilt, or worry that he'd be found out, but because going back to the hardware store, to taking orders from George, his boss, or Marie, the store manager, was almost un-bearable. They had no idea who he was, what he was capable of, what he'd done. He'd changed since the killing, just as he was always changing, and they, people who never changed at all, had no idea. They just needed him to unpack the new shipment from Craftsman, or to help Mrs. Conroy find the Gorilla Glue.

They didn't know that one day everyone would know the name Richard Seddon.

They didn't know that they'd be asked to give interviews, where they'd say things like, *I had absolutely no idea. He was a good worker. He was quiet, but I never even thought he was all that smart. I mean, if I'd only ever known what was going on in his head.*

And every time the bell above the front door rang, he'd look to see if it was Joan coming to see him. He knew she wouldn't. It would be foolish of her after their plan had gone so well, but, still, he kept thinking she might come into the store, pick up some batteries, look at him, and leave.

Then he'd meet her at the library. Maybe she would just want to know what it had been like, how Richie had acted when Pam had been shot, when the end of his own life was imminent. Had he fought back? Had he mentioned Joan? Had he begged?

Richard would tell her the truth, like he always did to Joan. He'd tell her how he placed the gun in her husband's hand, closed his own fingers over his, and made him pull the trigger that ended his life, that Richie had been putty in his hands, as docile as a trusting child. Yes, he'd love to be able to tell Joan all this, but he knew it was better that she never knew. They really had committed a perfect crime together, not for the first time but for the third, and the less she knew about the details, the better.

He'd been thinking a lot about the Windward Resort since Joan came back into his life. Thinking about what they had done to Duane out on that jetty, but also about meeting in the library that one last time before they parted ways. He'd been waiting for her, anxious she'd maybe fallen apart during questioning, even though she'd seemed fine immediately after Duane had gone into the ocean.

That next day in Kennewick had been thrilling and terrifying at the same time. His aunt and uncle had been frantic all night, then, when Duane's body had been found early in the morning, they had been almost disbelieving. Duane's mother had turned hysterical, and Richard wondered if it was genuine grief or if she was just shocked that something bad had happened in her life. According to Richard's mother, his aunt Evelyn, the baby of that dysfunctional family, had always been a spoiled brat, wanting someone else to take care of everything, wanting everything brought to her on a silver platter. She'd found the perfect man with Pat Wozniak, a fat bully, but one who revered his wife, and who had inherited his father's successful contracting business. He bought Evelyn everything she wanted, and together they'd created a son with all of their worst traits. Laziness, arrogance, cruelty. On the day after their son was found washed up on Kennewick beach, Evelyn Wozniak had been given sedatives and gone back to bed in her room at the resort, while Pat had spent the day raging at either the investigating officers or the resort staff, unable to believe that there wasn't someone he could blame, and maybe even sue, for his son's drowning.

Richard spent most of that day in his room, assuming they'd leave the resort that afternoon, or that one of his parents would come and pick him up, but also hoping they'd stay long enough for him to go to the library at night. He could wait there and see if Joan came to see him. He wanted to relive the previous night with her, but he also wanted to find out how she was doing, if she was holding up to the pressure of being questioned by the police. He thought she would be but wasn't a hundred percent sure.

Later in the day Richard's uncle pulled him aside to tell him that they'd all be leaving the following morning, that he wanted to get the hell out of this cut-rate hotel but Evelyn was not up for traveling yet. He also asked Richard what he knew about that girl Joan who'd been hanging around Duane, and Richard told him he knew nothing.

After dinner Richard went to the library, found a book to re-read, and waited. He'd grabbed an old beat-up copy of *The Sword in the Stone,* a book he'd loved a few years ago. His eyes went over the words, but he kept thinking of Joan, beginning to worry more and more that she might tell someone everything they had done together. At one point someone came into the library, someone older who grunted a little with every step and breathed heavily. Whoever it was left five minutes later and turned off the lights. Richard stayed where he was, in the dark, still waiting.

It must have been an hour later when he heard the door open again, and the lights turn on. When Joan came around the shelf in the middle of the room, she gasped a little and pressed a hand to her chest. She was smiling, and so was he, and he knew that all was right with the world. She came to him and took both his hands and pulled him up so that they were hugging, tightly, his hands around the small of her back, her face against his neck. They were like that for a moment.

Before they parted that night they'd made an agreement. They told each other that when they got back to high school they would pretend they didn't know each other any better than they ever had. They would be strangers. That was the most important rule.

But they also agreed that if they ever needed something, or maybe just needed to talk, they could simply make eye contact with the other one. In a hallway or the cafeteria. That would be their signal. And if that happened then they'd meet that night, at the town library, an hour before closing time. Richard knew he would never make eye contact with Joan after they returned to school, but the thought that she might initiate contact with him—just the thought of it—would be enough, he knew, to get him through the next three years.

A little over a month later he started his sophomore year. There was a gaming club that Richard joined because it was better than going home immediately after school let out. They met in Mr. Kaufman's science room and played either *Dungeons & Dragons* or *World of Darkness,* but one kid, James Pursall, introduced them to an RPG called *Violence* that wasn't a particularly good game, but it was pretty funny. He became friends with James, an even bigger outcast than him, and got to know the other gamers. There were bullies in the high school, but Richard had continued to grow and was now over six feet tall, and they pretty much left him alone.

He saw Joan all the time, in the hallway, and for half the year they had the same lunch schedule, so he'd see her sitting with her gymnast friends in the cafeteria. They never made eye contact, never acknowledged one another at all. Richard could feel the reality of what had happened over the summer slipping away, becoming more and more dreamlike, even though he knew it hadn't been a dream.

By junior year Richard was made the president of the gaming club, and he and James were best friends, or at least James seemed to consider Richard his best friend. James told him everything, all his fantasies about killing the biggest assholes in the school, and how he had access to a handgun. Richard listened to James's stupid rants and never once told him that he had actually killed someone. He could only imagine the look on James's ugly face if he gave him details of that night in Maine, him partnering up with Joan Grieve, one of the hottest girls in their class, to kill his jock cousin. He doubted James would even believe him, and it didn't matter. He wasn't going to tell him, anyway. He wasn't ever going to tell anyone.

Joan was in his European history class their senior year, sitting up in the front row so that he could watch the back of her head during lectures, her glossy black hair, her hand rapidly taking notes in green ink across her notebook page. Some days, the days she was wearing sweatpants or tights, her hair was pulled back and he could see the white flesh of her neck and the curve of her ear.

They never spoke. They never made eye contact.

Then in mid-December after an essay test, Richard had walked to the front of the room to hand Mrs. Mathur his exam, and on the way back Joan's eyes had flicked up suddenly and caught his. By the time he got back to his seat, his heart was racing. He kept his eyes on Joan, hunched over her paper, writing furiously. Occasionally her head was angled so he could see her profile, the tip of her tongue poking through her teeth as she concentrated. When she'd finished the test she got up from her desk and delivered it to the teacher, then she turned around briefly, and this time stared directly at Richard. He stared back.

They met at Middleham library that night, one hour before closing time. Joan was there first, and he found her in one of the narrow aisles in the basement, where nonfiction was kept. When they were face to face she put a finger to her lips, then quickly checked the aisles on either side of them.

"No one else is down here, I think," Richard said.

"I've missed you."

He smiled, and started to say something back, but it didn't come out. She laughed, in that way he remembered, but also that way he'd seen a hundred times at school in hallways and the cafeteria, her mouth wide open, head tossed back.

"Look," she said. "I want to make this quick, but I have a question."

"Okay."

"Do you remember back in Maine when we were talking about the people who would be on your list . . . you know . . ." He was nodding, and she continued. "Do you remember you mentioned Madison Brown?"

"I don't really remember," Richard said. "But I'm not surprised I named her. Are you and her still best friends?"

"Oh, no," Joan said, shaking her head a little. "Not since the summer. It turns out—no big surprise—that she is a terrible person."

Richard shrugged and raised his eyebrows.

"Right," Joan said. "Go ahead and say it: No duh."

"You said it, not me." Richard thought it was like no time had passed at all since they had last talked, in another library, in another state. "What did she do to you?"

"I thought she was my best friend, but now all she cares about is popularity. She's been talking behind my back." Richard must not have responded properly, because she added, "No, really. She is awful. I realize that now."

Richard nodded, then said, "No duh."

Joan smiled. "So what I was thinking," she said. "Is that you and I could team up again and do something about it."

CHAPTER 22

KIMBALL

The following day, back in Cambridge, I received Elizabeth Grieve's two books of poetry. Her debut was called *Variations on a Theme*. She had won a first-book contest from a small university press, and there was a glowing blurb on the back by the judge of the contest, saying that the book "heralded a stunning new voice that will challenge readers' notions of how a poem is even created."

I did my best to erase that sentence from my mind as I read the poems, some of which I quite liked, and some of which read to me like products of poetry workshops—free verse, present tense, the speaker of the poem obviously the poet herself—and if that sounds like bitter criticism coming from an unpublished poet such as myself, I imagine it is. My favorite poem in the collection was the title poem, which was quite funny, a long list of lines all playing on the famous quote, "Men don't make passes at girls who wear glasses." There was also a rather touching poem called "Wild Hospital Nights," about her bout with cancer, and how a nurse had given her a book of poems by Emily Dickinson.

Sea Oat Soup was a chapbook printed by a letterpress printer, the image on the cover a line drawing of a dissected horseshoe crab. These poems were slightly different from the ones in her debut. They were more surreal, none of them were about cancer, and they seemed to coalesce around a theme, although all I could tell you of that theme was that it was the intersection between the ocean and a lot of sexual imagery. The penultimate poem was the one that interested me the most. I read it three straight times.

Tides

Kennewick, 1999

I came because I was told to,
to wind-combed knolls and marshy views,
to tidepools crammed with crabs
as brittle as the dollparts

clicking in my mind.
You came here too . . .
LUCKY LUCKY ME . . .
a blue-lipped daughter of a blue-lipped man

who took my hand
and showed it to the briny stench
and sea-salt of a slack tide.
I left some knucklebones

behind—they must be white as scallop shells
by now. My parents left behind
an ovulating daughter,
all rotten beachplums on the vine,

and my sister, just turned
the tender age of murderers,

went swimming past the breakers with a boy,
and came back all alone,

while seabirds circled overhead
for what's been killed
and left between the ocean
and its edge.

Kennewick was in southern Maine, a vacation spot split up into several sections. Kennewick Harbor. Kennewick Beach. Kennewick Center. I was familiar with it because, as a child, my family would go on vacations at the nearby town of Wells. I was also familiar with Kennewick because it was where Ted Severson and his wife, Miranda, had been building a summer house when Ted was killed in the South End of Boston.

But what really interested me about the poem was the stanza devoted to the speaker's sister. And by speaker, I meant Elizabeth Grieve because this was clearly a confessional poem that had re-imagined an actual event. It had even been dated. I assumed that calling her sister a murderer and mentioning a boy who drowned was all metaphorical, but I jumped onto my computer anyway, began to research drownings in Kennewick during the year 1999. I didn't find anything, but I did find a drowning that had happened in the year 2000. A teenage boy named Duane Wozniak had gone swimming late at night from the Kennewick jetty and drowned. The article mentioned the girl he'd been swimming with had alerted the hotel staff at the Windward Resort, where he'd been staying. The name of the girl hadn't been stated. It bothered me a little bit that the drowning had happened in the year 2000 when the poem had specified 1999, but I wrote poetry myself, and my guess was that Elizabeth Grieve changed the date because 1999 looked better on the page than 2000, which still sounded to me, and maybe to her as well, like a science-fiction date.

I found one follow-up article on the drowning and it said that Duane had been staying for a month at the resort with his parents, Pat and Evelyn Wozniak, of West Hartford, Connecticut, and his cousin, Richard Seddon, from Middleham, Massachusetts. I searched for a Richard Seddon from Middleham but didn't find anything else besides that one mention. But the name was familiar to me, and on a whim I went to my closet and got out the cardboard box again where I'd stored that part of my life. There was a pristine copy of the Middleham-Dartford yearbook from 2003 that had been sent to me by Maureen, my department head. I flipped through the graduating seniors and there he was, Richard Seddon, in three-quarters profile. Thick black hair and a face like a blade. He was borderline handsome, but I knew he'd been a bit of an outcast, an odd kid, tall and skinny, who kept to himself.

I knew I hadn't had him in one of my classes, so I was trying to remember how I knew him, when it came to me. He'd been friends with James Pursall, the shooter who had killed Madison Brown and then himself in my classroom. In fact I remembered that Richard Seddon was pretty much James Pursall's only friend.

I stared at Richard Seddon's picture, tapping my finger on the glossy yearbook page, wondering where he was now, and how I could find him.

CHAPTER 23

RICHARD

Richard loved to think about that summer in the year 2000 when he'd first met Joan, and when they'd lured Duane to the end of the jetty. Every detail of that week was accessible to him. But for some reason he rarely thought about senior year of high school, the year he'd talked James Pursall into shooting Madison Brown at school and then killing himself. When he thought about it now the memories were filled with blank spaces, in the same way that his childhood was now largely composed of just a few vivid, unforgettable moments unmoored by any context.

The best memories of senior year had been his meetings with Joan in the Middleham town library. They'd met seven times, always an hour before closing time, and together they'd talk about what Joan sometimes called the Madison Brown problem, and how James Pursall was the perfect person to solve it. She was the one who first thought that Richard could talk James into shooting Madison. This was after Richard had told Joan that James had two semiautomatic weapons that he'd purchased at a gun show with a false ID, and that James talked a lot about going on a shooting spree and then killing himself. It was a persistent fantasy, and Richard had told him that it was his fantasy, too. Not that it was, but Richard couldn't tell him that he'd already killed someone, his own cousin, and how that had felt.

"Could you get him to kill Madison Brown and then himself?"

"I don't know," Richard had said. And at the time, although he'd mostly forgotten this, there was a part of him that thought: *Am I a murderer?* Pushing Duane into the ocean was one thing, but Joan was talking about guns. And then he let it go, because if it was okay with Joan it was okay with him, as well.

"You could make a pact with him. He has two guns. You could form a plan, that the two of you would use them at the same time in different rooms at school. You wouldn't kill anyone, but he wouldn't know that."

"So you think I should just say to him that I have a plan. He needs to kill Madison and then himself, at the same time as . . ."

"No, no, no, no. This is what you say. You say you had this really cool thought. That you'd sneak guns into the school. That you'd both go on a hunt. He'd pick a target for you and you'd pick a target for him, and that you'd need to shoot and kill this person at the exact same time, and then kill yourselves. Don't talk about it like it's a real plan, just talk about how cool it would be in theory. Two targeted school shootings with no survivors left. Don't ever suggest doing it for real. Let him do that."

"What if he doesn't?"

"Then we'll find another way to fix the Madison Brown problem."

Richard had done exactly as Joan had suggested. James was over at Richard's house. They were both in the basement playing *Violence,* but mostly just listening to their current favorite band, As I Lay Dying. Richard had made the suggestion, not surprised when James reacted exactly as Joan had said he would. He'd loved the idea, excited to pick the person who Richard would need to kill.

He kept changing his mind, finally narrowing it down to between another senior, Danny Eaton, and a particularly horrible science teacher named Mr. Barber. "Who would you want me to shoot?" James had asked.

"I've thought about this a lot. I'd definitely want you to shoot Madison Brown."

"Oh, wow," James had said. "Oh, yeah. She's a fucking bitch. You know I'm in a class with her. Honors English. It would be easy." James had pointed his finger and cocked his thumb, making imaginary shooting gestures.

Meeting with Joan in the library on a cold night in January, at the beginning of their final half year in high school, Richard had said, "There's just so many ways it could go wrong. It's not like what we did with Duane."

"I know," Joan said. They were in the alcove where they always had their conversations, up on the balcony level. Only once in their meetings had someone else come upstairs, a wheezing old man, and by the time he had walked past their spot, Joan had ducked down another aisle. Besides, the man had never even looked at Richard sitting in his chair. It was possible, of course, that a librarian might have noticed the same two high school students had been in the library at the same late hour on more than one occasion. But Richard doubted it.

"So let's just list the ways it can go wrong," Joan said.

"He could chicken out. He could tell someone about our plan. He could kill Madison but not himself, then tell everyone I told him to do it."

"Okay," Joan said. "Those are all bad, but they aren't the end of the world. It would be your word against his. All you'd have to say was that you used to talk to him about fantasies, but you never in a million years thought he was serious."

"But I'd have a gun on me," Richard said.

"No, you wouldn't. You're not going to shoot anyone, so don't bring a gun into school. In fact, take the gun you have and hide it somewhere it won't be found. And then you not having a gun will back up your story about not taking it seriously. I mean, they might not believe you, but they couldn't prove anything, right?"

"No, you're right."

"I'm always right, Richard, when are you going to realize that about me?" There was her smile, and her hand on his leg, the intensity in her blue-gray eyes that he loved to see.

"I thought of a bigger problem. A much bigger problem."

"What's that?"

"What if James decides to shoot up the whole classroom and not just shoot Madison and then himself? You know he wants to do it during your class?"

"Yeah, I thought about that. I mean, I could skip that class, I suppose, but then . . ."

Joan was thinking, looking past Richard at the dark, frost-lined window behind him. "But then what?" Richard said.

"But then I'd miss it," Joan said. Her mouth was slightly open, and Richard thought she looked tentative, or maybe even a little embarrassed, worried about what he might think. It was not an expression he was used to seeing on her face.

"I guess it would be a risk," he said. "I could find out what James thinks about you, just to be sure."

"No, don't do that. Don't ever mention my name to him. Remember that no one knows we are even aware of one another. This is what you should do. James likes rules, right? He's a gamer like you. Just make sure that you guys have rules for what you are doing and that you can't break them. You each kill one person and then yourself. That's the game."

In the end, it had actually worked just as Joan said it would. Throughout that late winter and early spring Richard and James talked about nothing else but their plan for a coordinated attack on the school. James had settled on having Richard kill Danny Eaton, mostly because Danny was one of the worst kids at the school, a nasty bully popular enough that he got away with everything, and who was currently hooking up with Ashley Finley, one of the more beautiful students, a girl who deserved a better fate than Danny Eaton. But James had also settled on Danny because Richard had art class with Danny at the same time that James had English class with Madison. It made things easier. They picked a time, exactly 1:35 p.m. on a Friday. They would both pull out their guns, shoot their prey, and then themselves. Richard kept waiting for James to show signs he didn't want to do it, that he'd gotten cold feet, but the opposite had happened. James was acting almost manic, like a little kid on Christmas Eve, waiting for the day to arrive. On the Sunday before the week they'd planned the killings, James and Richard drove to an abandoned quarry on Cape Ann and practiced shooting at cans with their semiautomatics. It was the only time that Richard actually felt like he might want to go through with shooting Danny for real. The sensation of the gun firing, the can jumping, James's enthusiasm, all made Richard want to experience that moment of pulling a gun out of his backpack in Ms. Bryant's art class, the fear and surprise on the other students' faces, him holding all their lives in his hand. But Richard had bigger plans than being a school shooter. And, most importantly, he had Joan. Now that she was back in his life, he wasn't willing to lose her. Not yet, anyway.

On the evening before the shooting, Richard and James had met one last time, sitting in the stands of the high school's empty football field, and going over the details, synchronizing their watches.

"Is there anyone else in that classroom you want me to ice?" James said, and Richard tried to conceal his alarm. James had never talked about going off script in the past. Before he could answer, James said, "All I'm saying is there are a lot of assholes and phonies in that room."

Richard tried to sound calm as he said, "Let's stick to the plan. The most important thing is the symmetry. You kill Madison Brown and then yourself at the exact same moment that I kill Danny and then myself. It won't be sloppy or random. Everyone will spend the rest of their lives wondering about us. The kids in those classes will realize how powerless they were for that one moment. They think they're important, now, but tomorrow they'll find out how small they are."

"Yeah, okay," James said, and Richard worried he'd come across as desperate in his attempts to make sure James didn't shoot anyone else in that room. It was Joan he was worried about, of course. If Joan wound up dead that would be worse than James getting caught alive and pointing the finger at him.

He didn't sleep that night, his mind feverishly going over all the variables. The only thing that would relax him was Joan's voice in his head, her laugh, her words that everything was going to be fine. *We've done this before,* her voice said, *and no one suspected a thing. Together, we are invincible. Invisible and invincible.*

It was a beautiful spring day that Friday, the sky a hard blue and the air balmy. The trees had just begun to blossom. Richard got up early, putting the Browning semiautomatic into his backpack, then driving to the trailhead that was a quarter mile from the high school. There was no one else in the parking lot, and Richard walked about three hundred yards down the main trail, finally spotting a medium-sized rock that was identifiable by a vein of pure white quartz. He pried one end up, revealing a network of worms and beetles in the soft damp earth, then he wiped the pistol clean and buried it slightly in the soil, putting the rock back down on top of it. He didn't love the way the rock now looked, as though it had been disturbed, so he spent a little time rearranging the rotten leaves and vegetation so that it looked natural. Satisfied, he went back to his car, then drove and parked in the student lot at the high school.

He only saw James once that day; he was leaving the cafeteria, his large backpack slung over one shoulder. Richard thought he looked normal, or as normal as James Pursall ever looked.

At 1:35 p.m. Richard was in art class, where they were learning how to make monoprints. Richard's body felt as though it were full of bees, his skin electric, his vision jittery. Ms. Bryant, a nervous, tattooed teacher who was not a whole lot older than her students, had looked thoughtfully at Richard's abstract shapes. "Is it a beach?" she said.

"No, just shapes. How do you see a beach?"

She pointed out the large circle she said looked like a sun, and the blue rectangle she thought was the sea.

When Richard heard the first shot, a muffled pop that could have been almost anything, most of the kids in the classroom continued to work on their prints. But Ms. Bryant, after two more gunshots sounded, had perked up, her face angled toward the ceiling as though it helped her hear better. Richard thought she looked like a meerkat, sensing danger on the horizon.

Then the speaker system kicked in, the principal's voice telling all teachers to shelter in place, and all the students stopped what they were doing, one girl dropping to the floor and starting to moan. Richard waited to hear more gunshots, but none came, and he knew they had done it again. Joan and Richard. Why had he ever doubted her?

CHAPTER 24

KIMBALL

I could find nothing online about Richard Seddon, nothing beyond that one mention in the *Southern Forecaster* that he'd been staying with Duane Wozniak and his family when Duane had gone swimming off the Kennewick jetty and drowned. There were multiple Richard Seddons in the world, of course, but none of them seemed like a match for the one I was looking for. The only promising lead I dug up was an address for a Donald and Julie Seddon who had lived in Middleham, Massachusetts. And I found an obituary for a Julie Seddon from a few years earlier, although no surviving family members were listed. It wasn't much, but it was something.

The following day I drove out on Route 2 toward Middleham, the route familiar from my stint as a teacher all those years ago. To get to the address I'd found online, I had to pass the high school in Dartford, a single-story brick structure up a sloping hill from the road. A three-story structure was being built next to the old school and I remembered reading somewhere that a new high school was being built, and that it was going to cost somewhere around $200 million. When I crossed the town line from Dartford to Middleham the road condition changed, becoming bumpier, peppered with un-fixed potholes. There was more open land, as well, remnants from when Middleham had been primarily a farming community. I found Adams Street after passing through Middleham's small, quaint center. It was a winding, tree-lined street of mostly modest houses. I pulled into the short driveway of number twenty-nine, a ranch house, its exterior painted a light blue. I pulled in next to a parked PT Cruiser and got out of my car. A woman with a rake in her hand came around from the back of the house and peered at me through cat's-eye glasses. I walked toward her, trying to look unthreatening, and when we were talking-distance apart, I told her I was looking for Donald Seddon.

She frowned, and said, "He hasn't lived here for ten years. We bought the house from him and his wife."

"Oh, yeah?" I'd removed my wallet and was holding one of my cards that identified me as a fully licensed private investigator. The woman propped her rake against the side of a cherry tree and stepped forward to take my card. "I'm looking for their son, for Richard Seddon."

Again, the woman frowned. She wore lime-green capri pants and a vintage-y sweater with a shiny collar. I'd thought, from a distance, that she was unintentionally retro, but up close I could tell that her outfit, even for raking, had been carefully curated. While she looked at my card, I spotted a teapot tattoo on her left ankle. "I don't think I can help you," she said. "I'm not sure I ever met the Seddons."

"Do you remember where they went after leaving this house?"

I expected her to tell me she had no idea, but she thought about it for a moment, then raised a finger, and said, "You know, maybe I do. I remember we kept getting mail for them and the real estate agent gave me an address to forward it. I think I wrote it down in my address book."

"That would be incredibly helpful," I said.

"Why do you need to find the son?" she said. The sun was low in the sky and she held her hand over her eyes.

"Believe it or not," I said, "he's owed some money from a distant relative. Crazy, right? And they can't locate him."

"Lucky him," the woman said, and went inside the house to look for the address book. I stood and waited, getting into a staring contest with a brown poodle through one of the floor-to-ceiling windows of the house. When the woman came out, she was holding an old spiral-bound address book, folded over to a specific page.

"Don and Julie Seddon," she said. "I knew there was a reason I never threw this book out."

She showed me the entry, and I took a photograph of the address—42 Wagoner Road in Fairview, Massachusetts—then thanked the woman.

"Is it a lot of money?" she said as I was getting back into my car.

"They don't tell me," I said. "I'm just the messenger."

Fairview was about four towns away, west and a little north of Middleham. I'd never actually been there but had seen its name on exit signs. I crossed over into Fairview on a minor road that ran along a river past a defunct paper mill. The houses I'd seen so far seemed just a step up from shacks, and I'd spotted several larger buildings that looked like they'd once been boardinghouses for the mill workers. I passed through an old town center, a cluster of commercial buildings in the shadow of a large congregational church with a white steeple. There was a beautiful, red-brick structure that turned out to be the local library, and there was a gas station that advertised itself as "full service."

I picked up Wagoner Road about half a mile from the town center. One side was a pine forest and the other comprised old farm-land, parceled off by stone walls. I drove past forty-two and had to double back, parking across the street from what looked like an abandoned farmhouse, its windows shuttered, and half the roof caved in. What was strange was that there was a new car parked in the overgrown driveway, a white sedan that looked like a Chevrolet. I sat in my car for a moment, feeling conspicuous, trying to figure out what to do. Maybe Donald Seddon still lived there, or maybe it was even Richard Seddon. I hadn't actually decided how to approach Richard yet if I managed to find him.

As I was sitting there thinking, idly keeping an eye on the old house, a figure emerged from around the back, a tall, dark-haired man wearing jeans and an untucked flannel shirt. I popped the hood, then got out of the car, stepping around to the front, opening the hood all the way, and staring into the engine. The man from the farmhouse got into his white car and pulled down the short drive-way. I fully expected him to swing over and see if he could help, but he turned out of his driveway and sped away in the direction I'd come from, toward the center of Fairview. I watched the car retreat and memorized the license plate number.

I thought of following him but decided against it. If that was Richard—and the age had seemed correct—then I'd done what I had set out to do. I'd found him. I shut the hood of my car, then, on a whim, walked briskly down the driveway and around the house. It looked as though there had once been a backyard that separated the property from the encroaching woods, but it was completely choked now with a thick tangle of bushes, all covered with bittersweet vine. On the back side of the house there was a rusty metal bulkhead, plus a backdoor reachable by three wooden steps. I went up them and peered through one of the panes of glass, but a piece of fabric had been hung on the inside of the window, and all I saw was my own reflection. The door was locked.

I checked the bulkhead and it was locked, as well. I looked around for a place where the mail might be delivered but didn't see anything. That didn't mean no one lived here. If someone *was* living here, despite its appearance, then that inhabitant could get their mail from a post office box. I returned down the driveway and to my car, sitting for a moment, trying to decide what to do next. It seemed likely that I'd found Richard Seddon, but I needed to confirm it.

I drove back the way I'd come, passing through the town center again. I pulled into the driveway of the library, parking toward the rear, then took out my cell phone and called my old partner Roberta James, who was still working for the Boston Police Department.

"Henry," she said.

"Hey, James. How are you?"

There was a slight pause, and I could hear her muffled voice saying something to someone else. "I'm good."

"Is this an okay time?" I said.

"It is, definitely. I've been meaning to call you, because your name came up in that murder-suicide in Bingham."

"Oh, you saw that?"

"Uh-huh. I also saw that you found the bodies."

"I did."

"Jesus, what a mess. They've closed the case, haven't they?"

"That's what I heard, but I haven't confirmed it. It was pretty obvious what had happened." I had decided not to tell James about my suspicions, not that I wouldn't at some point, but it just didn't make sense to get her involved unless I had to.

"So you're not calling me with some wild story about what really happened," she said, reading me, and I could picture the half smile on her face. It turned out I missed Roberta James a lot more than I missed being a Boston police detective.

"I'm saving that for later," I said. "But I do have a favor to ask."

"Okay."

"I have a license number and I have an address, and I'm hoping you can confirm the name attached to both of them."

"These are public records, Kimball. Don't you have—"

"I'm in my car and I'm being lazy. Sorry. Should I not have called?"

"No. Just give them to me, and I'll call you right back."

While I waited for Roberta to call back, I stepped outside of my car and took a short walk back through the small town. The houses were prettier here than along the river. A landscape company van was parked in front of a gabled Victorian, and one of the employees was taking a break, leaning up against the truck, smoking a cigarette. I could smell the tobacco on the air even from across the street, and I had one of my periodic pangs when I missed cigarettes. I think it was the crisp fall weather, the clean-tasting air, that made me want to blow some smoke into it.

On the way back to my car my phone buzzed.

"Car is registered to a Richard Boyars Seddon, and the house is listed as belonging to a Donald Kizer Seddon. Is that helpful?"

"It is," I said.

"And just because I wanted to save time I ran both names to see if they had records."

"Ah, thank you."

"Donald Kizer Seddon was charged with assault and battery of a coworker back in Holyoke, Massachusetts, in 1972. And there is nothing on a Richard Boyars Seddon."

"Thank you, thank you. I owe you."

"It's not a problem."

"Still, a bottle of scotch," I said.

"Anytime," Roberta said.

I drove back to Cambridge thinking about Richard Seddon. His cousin had drowned while both of them were on vacation together, back in 2000 at the Windward Resort. And there was a possibility that Joan Grieve had been there too, although that needed to be confirmed. And then Richard Seddon's friend James Pursall had shot and killed Madison Brown and then himself. Joan Grieve had been in the same room, and Joan, if I remembered correctly, was in a fight with Madison Brown. It wasn't much, I realized, but it was something.

I was thinking about the case, and not thinking about where I was driving, and realized suddenly that I was working my way toward West Concord in order to get back onto Route 2. I would pass the Taste of Hong Kong, and just the thought of that restaurant brought up two contradictory feelings. The horror of what had happened to Pam O'Neil and the taste of Pete Liu's mai tai cocktails. When I reached the restaurant, I drove straight past, trying not to think about either of those things.

CHAPTER 25

RICHARD

All during his shift at the hardware store, Richard kept thinking about the car that had been parked out on the street in front of his apartment, that man looking under the hood. Had that man, in his dark jeans and tweed jacket, looked vaguely familiar? Was Richard being watched, and, if so, by whom? Then he told himself he was being paranoid, and that paranoia was a sign of weakness. He also told himself that if he saw the man one more time then something was probably up. It wasn't the worst feeling because that would mean he would have to contact Joan, find her and let her know that they should meet in the library. Then they'd deal with the problem together.

It was a slow day in the store, and Richard kept waiting for George to tell him he could leave early if he wanted. He always said it the same way, ambling up to Richard with his hands tucked into the overalls he wore because he was too fat in the stomach for regular jeans. "Oh, hey there, Rich," he'd say. "It's a tad slow today, so if you want to punch out and go do something more fun, then it would be fine with me. We'll manage without you, I think." Then he'd laugh like a donkey and show his mossy-looking teeth. It was just his way to try to save some money, of course, because being a cheap bastard was his prime directive. It was one of Richard's theories that everyone had a prime directive that ruled their life. George's son's prime directive was to lust after every woman who came into the store, staring at them and making them uncomfortable. Richard's prime directive was to one day reveal himself to the world.

After lunch Richard returned to his station at the register and allowed his mind to wander a little. It wasn't something he did too often at work because sometimes he'd be so caught up in his own thoughts he wouldn't realize someone was talking to him. But today was slow and he let himself imagine the book that would be written about him in the future. He wondered how much of the book would be devoted to the killings he'd done with Joan Grieve. Would they even know about them? They'd know about the big events, of course, the ones that were still to come. Collapsing the roof of the Winslow Oaks Convention Center on top of an entire class of seniors celebrating their prom. That was going to be his masterpiece. But he often wondered if he should do something else first, maybe a trial run. He'd successfully rigged a homemade bomb that he could blow up using a wireless trigger from about one hundred yards away. It was the same technology used in car locks, and it had been so easy to devise that he wondered why people weren't doing it all the time. His dream was to test it out at that Chevrolet dealership in Athol on one of the days that Danny Eaton was working. It had been such a shock two years earlier when he'd gone there to look for a car and seen Danny, one of the biggest pricks from Dartford-Middleham Hellschool, lording his way around the showroom. Danny had come right up to Richard, asking him if he needed help, and it was clear that he didn't remember who he was, despite the fact that they'd had at least three classes together. Richard had told him he was just looking and watched as Danny ran his eyes up from Richard's shoes, as though he was analyzing what kind of person Richard was from the way he was dressed. "Take your time, buddy," Danny said. "Then come find me when you're ready to make a deal."

Richard had thought about that encounter multiple times since it had happened. Danny had been the kid that Richard had agreed to murder on the same day that James Pursall shot Madison Brown. Of course, Richard hadn't done it—had never planned on doing it—but he could have, and Danny had zero fucking idea that his customer was an old member of his high school class, let alone someone who could have sprayed his brains all across the art room.

On a few occasions Richard had driven back to the dealership around closing time and watched Danny Eaton leave and get into his C6 Corvette parked out front. He followed him a few times, once when Danny went straight home to his town house condo, and once when he drove to a sports bar called Fair Ball in a strip mall off Route 23. Richard's plan was to drive to the dealership before closing time and slide one of his bombs right below the passenger-side door of Danny's Corvette. Then he'd park next door in front of the sushi place and activate the trigger just as Danny reached for his door handle. The only thing stopping him was the possibility of getting caught before he had a chance to do something truly momentous. Danny Eaton's death, like his life, was small potatoes.

"Hi, Richard," came a familiar woman's voice, and Richard swam back up from his thoughts, found himself face to face with Karen Virgilio, her eyes wide and nervous.

"Hey, Karen," Richard said, surprised that his voice sounded almost normal in his own head. He hadn't seen Karen in over a year, and hadn't expected to ever see her again, to be honest.

"Sorry to bother you at work, but I think your number changed, maybe."

"Oh, yeah," Richard said. He remembered that Karen used to call him on his landline, the one he'd disconnected.

"You can say no, if you want, Richard," she said, and she was doing that thing with her earlobe, where she twisted it between her thumb and finger, "but I was hoping we could talk, maybe get a drink or a meal or something."

"Um," Richard said, not knowing what to say but sure that he didn't want to talk with Karen, not now, not ever. He was briefly saved by George, waddling across the linoleum, spotting Karen and saying, "Oh, hey you," clearly not remembering her name.

"Hi, Mr. Koestler," she said.

"Look at your new hair color," George said, too loudly. "Last time I saw you I think it was a hot pink."

Karen touched her hair, and Richard realized that she *had* dyed it a different color, this time a kind of frosty blue. Richard also remembered that when Karen had been an employee at the hardware store, just over a year ago, George had mentioned her hair just about every time he spoke to her. Richard sometimes thought that the comments were the reason she quit abruptly after working at the store for less than six months, but he knew the real reason she'd quit was because of what had happened with him.

"Oh, yeah," Karen said. "It used to be pink."

George stood smiling for a moment, trying to think up something else to say, then wandered off, nodding to himself.

Karen turned back to Richard just as he started to say, "I just don't think—"

But Karen was saying, "I know you don't want to talk but maybe you'd do it as a favor to me. I promise I don't expect anything from you, besides a conversation."

They met that night at the Papa Gino's that was only a half mile from the store, each getting a large soda, then sitting in one of the booths that still had one of those individual jukeboxes attached to the wall, although it was highly doubtful it worked.

"Thanks for meeting me," Karen said. She was wearing the same outfit she'd worn when she'd ambushed him at the store, a baggy flannel shirt and a pair of high-waisted faded jeans. Her outfits stayed the same even if her hair didn't. She'd been a cutter in high school and both of her forearms were lined with thin white scars, whiter even than her pale skin. He was picturing her naked now, that time, the only time, she'd come back to his place when they'd been dating. She was skinny, her body creased with red marks where her bra and underwear had been after she took them off. She'd shaved her pubic hair and it had left behind angry red spots, like a razor rash. She'd stretched out on his futon bed, and she must have seen something in the way he looked at her, because she said, "I don't care what we do or anything, but it would be nice if you joined me on the bed."

This was after three dates, all initiated by Karen. On the first they'd gone for dinner at the Papa Gino's they were at now, but on their second and third dates they'd driven to the Fine Arts theater in Maynard to see *The Shape of Water* and then a film with Kristen Stewart called *Personal Shopper*. During the second film they'd held hands in the theater, Richard telling himself that Karen would be a good person to have sex with, since it was still something he'd never actually done.

He'd joined her on his bed that night, stripping down first, but not all the way, just to his boxer shorts. "I suck at this," Karen said, and laughed.

Richard was about to tell her he hadn't done it before but stopped himself. His heart felt strange, as though it had slipped out of place in his chest cavity, but he did have an erection, pressing up against the fabric of his boxers.

"You okay?" Karen asked.

"Sure," Richard said. "It's just been a while."

Karen moved his hand down between her legs, and Richard closed his eyes while he touched her, trying not to think about all the sounds he used to hear coming from his mother's bedroom after she'd married Don.

"Let's put this over us, okay?" Karen said, and while they moved their bodies to get underneath the sheet—Richard trying to remember the last time he'd cleaned it—he wound up on top of her, and Karen took a hold of him and guided him inside of her. He immediately came, his head burrowed into her neck, keeping quiet so she wouldn't know it just happened. She started to move and make noises and Richard froze, not knowing what to do. When she stopped and asked him if everything was okay, he told her he had finished, and she laughed and said she was happy.

They'd gone to one more movie after that night, something called *Lady Macbeth,* although it had nothing to do with the Shakespeare play, and afterward Richard told Karen that it wasn't a good time for him to be in a relationship. A month later she'd quit the hardware store.

"Hey, Richard, I'm sorry if this is uncomfortable for you. Trust me, it's uncomfortable for me, too." Karen looked extra pale in the harsh light of the pizza restaurant. She had a nose ring that looked like it had been put in recently, the skin around the piercing bright red.

"It's fine," Richard said.

"Look, I'm going through a thing. I don't know how to describe it exactly, but I just need to know what happened with us. I know we just hung out for a short period of time, and that it was no big deal, but I keep going over it and over it in my mind, and I want to know why you didn't want to see me anymore."

Richard spun his coke on the tabletop and didn't immediately say anything.

"There are absolutely no wrong answers, Richard. Like if you found me repulsive then please just tell me that. Or if you were bored, or you're gay, or I was terrible at sex, or you hated the movies I made you go to. Just . . . I guess I want to know because it bothers me that I don't. I want to know the truth."

Richard pressed his lips together and looked up from his soda. "I mean," he said, "it was nothing to do with you. Not really. It was—"

"Please just tell me," Karen said, rising a little in her seat. "Sorry to interrupt, but it's never entirely just about one person, is it? I mean, if I was your perfect match in the whole universe, you'd have tried to make it work, right? There must have been something about me that you didn't like."

Richard was now shaking his head, and for one terrible moment he felt an ache in his throat and thought that he might cry. Words were running through his mind, as though maybe he could just tell her about everything, just let her inside. But as soon as he had that thought it went away. There was too much to tell, for one thing, and too many things to tell that would scare her away. She wouldn't begin to understand who he really was.

Sometimes, in hard or awkward moments, Richard would think to himself: *What would Joan do?* She understood the world, the social world, in a way he never would. So he thought about it now, and he said to Karen, who was rubbing at an earlobe, "I'm into someone else, actually. She's someone I knew back in high school and now we've reconnected, and . . . the truth is, I guess . . . the truth is that I'm in love with her and I can't really be with anyone else."

Karen was nodding, and he realized he'd said something that was helpful. "Was she . . . were you two together when we were together?"

"Oh, no," Richard said, before he could stop himself. "I was thinking about her, though. She got married to someone else, but that's over now. No. We're not together, it's just that . . ."

"She's the one for you," Karen said, and spun her own soda around, taking a big sip through the straw.

Later, that night while he was in bed, Richard went over the rest of the conversation with Karen, and how he'd told her a little bit about his relationship with Joan. Most was made up, but not all of it. And for whatever reason he was now thinking about Karen again instead of Joan, imagining a scenario where he would tell her even more than he'd already told her, maybe even tell her that the only time he'd had sex was with her. He imagined them doing it again, only this time Richard would last and last, Karen begging him for more.

He was still thinking about Karen at the hardware store the next day while he was restocking the plumbing aisle. Maybe she'd come back to see him again, but he doubted it. When they'd said good night, she'd seemed happy, as though she'd gotten what she'd come for.

Richard was crouched over a box when he felt a tap on his shoulder, a man's voice saying, "Excuse me."

CHAPTER 26

KIMBALL

On the Emerson College website there was a phone number for Elizabeth Grieve, and also a listing of her office hours. I figured that if I called her directly on her line during her office hours there was a good chance she might pick up.

I still hadn't decided what to say yet. All I really wanted to establish was that she'd been at the Windward Resort, with her sister Joan, at the time that Duane Wozniak had drowned. If she confirmed that, then that would be one too many coincidences that linked Joan Grieve and Richard Seddon.

I did think about calling her up and telling her that I was doing a deep analysis of her poem, "Tides," from her chapbook *Sea Oat Soup,* then asking if I could interview her about it. That was a stretch, though. Even if Elizabeth Grieve had illusions of grandeur there was no way she'd buy some critical theorist calling up out of the blue to dissect a poem she'd published in a book that had a print run of two hundred copies.

So I tried to come up with other ways to ask her. While thinking about it, I read through her poems again. It seemed clear to me that during a trip to Maine (and Kennewick was mentioned twice) she'd discovered that she was a lesbian. There were actually two mentions of her sister in the book, the one that referred to her as being "the tender age of murderers" and that she'd gone swimming with a boy who hadn't come back. The other mention was vaguer. It was in a poem called "Moonsnail," and the line went, "my sister has broken out in scales / and they look ravishing on her." But that was a throwaway line in a poem that seemed devoted to the character of "you," the sporty girl she'd met on that vacation. I got distracted and wrote a limerick on the back inside cover of *Sea Oat Soup*.

> *There once was a poet named Grieve,*
> *Whose poems would have you believe*
> *That at a summer resort*
> *She met a girl in a skort*
> *And lost the one thing she couldn't retrieve.*

Ten minutes after her office hours started, I dialed her number.

"Professor Grieve here," she said, her voice throaty and deep, not at all like Joan's.

"Oh, hi Professor. You don't know me but I'm a private investigator, and I was wondering if you had five minutes to answer a couple of questions for me."

"Okay," she said, drawing out the word.

"Oh, great, great. Sorry to bother you during your office hours, but I thought I'd take a chance. As I said, I'm a private investigator and we've been hired to look into an event that occurred back in 2000 at the . . ." I paused a little as though I was looking it up. ". . . at the Windward Resort in Kennewick, Maine."

"Oh, that," she said.

"So you were there?"

"Is this about the kid who drowned?"

"Actually, it is. Duane Wozniak. According to the resort's records you were a guest at the time of the accident."

"Yeah, I was there with my family. But I think maybe you want to talk with my sister, Joan."

"Because she knew Duane," I said, hoping I sounded like I knew what I was talking about.

"Yeah, right. What is this about, anyway? I'm confused. Is someone suggesting that it wasn't an accident?"

"Not really," I said. "I'm not authorized, of course, to divulge my client's name, but we were tasked to just look into the events that led to his death. I don't think there's any suggestion that there was any wrongdoing on anyone's part."

"Well, like I said. I didn't know him, and I don't know anything about what happened except for what my sister told me, so I suggest you talk with her."

"I will, Elizabeth. So you never met him while you were at the resort?"

"I remember seeing him, I guess, but my sister and I, both then and now, are not particularly close. I was doing my own thing there, and she was doing hers. He talked her into going out on that jetty on the beach at night, and he was showing off and slipped into the water."

I knew I was beginning to push it, but I asked her, "So you had no interactions with Duane Wozniak or Richard Seddon?"

"Who's Richard Seddon?"

"Oh, he was Duane's cousin. They were sharing a room together."

"No, I didn't. Like I said, you're talking with the wrong sister."

"Okay, thanks," I said. "You've been helpful. It's really just a matter of crossing you off a list of people I'm supposed to talk with."

"Well, I'm glad you were able to cross me off that list." Maybe she thought that sounded harsh, so she laughed after she said it. "How did you find me?"

"Well, I have the guest register from the time when the event happened, and I'm contacting people from it."

"Are you contacting everyone who was staying at Windward Resort at the time?"

"Well, not everyone, of course, but anyone we think might have had some contact with Duane Wozniak."

There was a pause, then Elizabeth said, "This is a strange question, but have you contacted someone named Denise Smith?"

"The name doesn't ring a bell. I don't think she's on my list."

"Never mind. I was just wondering."

"Should she be on my list?"

"Oh, no. I was just curious, honestly. There's zero chance she had anything to do with Duane Wozniak."

After ending the phone call, I spun on my office chair and looked out at Oxford Street, bathed in sunlight even though I could see a bank of clouds moving in from the west. I wondered if I'd made a bad mistake in calling Elizabeth, if she was on the phone right now to her sister to warn her that a private investigator might call to ask about Duane Wozniak and the Windward Resort. Somehow, I didn't think so, though. As she said, they weren't that close. And even if she did contact Joan, making the phone call might have been the right move. I'd gotten crucial information. Not only had Joan Grieve been at the Windward Resort when Richard Seddon had been there, but she'd been with Richard's cousin Duane when he'd drowned.

The way I now saw it was that Joan Grieve had been personally involved in three separate instances where someone or several someones had died. The first was that she was with Duane Wozniak in the year 2000 when he drowned at night in the ocean. The second was the death of Madison Brown and James Pursall in her honors English class three years later, and now she had lost her husband in a murder-suicide. Out of those three events, Richard Seddon was tangentially involved in the first two. He was staying in the same room as Duane Wozniak, his cousin, at the Windward Resort. And he was best friends with James Pursall. It made me think he might have had something to do with the death of Richard Whalen and Pam O'Neil, as well.

What if Richard Seddon and Joan Grieve had met at Windward Resort all those years ago and plotted to murder Duane Wozniak? What if they'd been so thrilled to get away with it that they'd decided to keep planning murders? It sounded ludicrous, I realized. For one, James Pursall had pulled the trigger in my classroom, not Richard Seddon. Did I really think that somehow Richard or Joan had made it happen? Had they talked him into it?

And what about the deaths of Richard Whalen and Pam O'Neil? If Richard Seddon had been involved then how would that have worked? Would he have been waiting for them in the house? If so, where was his car?

My afternoon, like most of my afternoons, was free. I drove back out to the northwest suburbs, a drive I was getting very used to. By the time I reached the deck house in Bingham that was still for sale, the dark clouds I'd first noticed in Cambridge were smothering the sky, and light rain had begun to fall. I pulled directly into the drive-way, not worrying about anyone seeing me, then got out of the car and looked at the house. It was exactly as I remembered it, a brown deck house that blended into the woods around it. The last time I was here I'd heard the three gunshots coming from inside and forced myself to go in and look. I could remember every detail of what I'd found.

Instead of trying the front door I went around the side of the house, walking across the narrow strip of lawn that led to the back of the property, with a screened-in back porch and another narrow strip of lawn bordering the thick woods. The rain was picking up, coming in gusts, and I turned up the collar of my Harris Tweed jacket. I walked over and looked at the door that led to the porch, tried it but it was locked. The lock was a spring latch, and I considered digging out a credit card to find out how easy it was to open but decided against it. Instead, I skirted the edge of the property, spotting what looked like a seldom-used path heading into the woods. About fifty yards along the path it met up with a definite trail, the ground hard-packed soil, and the trees cut back. I turned right and walked slowly. It was dark in the woods, but the rain had either temporarily stopped or was not penetrating the thickly clustered pine trees. I passed a tree that had a blaze of yellow paint on it, so I knew I was on some sort of official trail. I walked through a clearing, disturbing a trio of crows that scattered from the ground to lower branches, cawing at one another, and probably me. Then I reached a road. A small sign nailed into a tree told me I'd been walking in the Bingham Town Forest. There was no parking lot at the trailhead but the road widened a little and there were tire ruts along the side of the road. I crouched and looked at one of them, pretending for a moment that I was the type of detective that could look at treads and know what kind of tire had made them.

I reversed course back through the woods, managing to find the path that led to the deck house. Sitting in my car, the heater running, I now knew that it was entirely possible that someone else had been in the house on the day that Richard and Pam had been shot. The killer could have parked along a parallel road and gone through the woods. I would never have seen them from the front of the house. There was no definitive proof that this had happened, but I'd learned it was a possibility.

I sat there for a while, making assumptions as I'd been doing all day.

Joan's husband was having an affair and she decided she wanted to kill him, plus the woman he was cheating with. She knew she couldn't do it herself, but she had an accomplice. He was an outcast named Richard Seddon and they'd killed together before, or at least instigated murders. So she contacted him, told him the place that her husband conducted his afternoon trysts, and Richard lay in wait, having parked on a nearby street. But even that plan wasn't good enough, so she decided to add a witness, a detective who would find the bodies, and confirm that it looked like murder followed by a suicide.

I decided that the time had come to talk with Richard Seddon. If all of what I was thinking was true—if he was the third person— then questioning him might provoke him into contacting Joan. What I really wanted to do was to talk with Lily again, or maybe it was time to talk with Roberta James. Tell her what I knew, and leave it to her. Instead, I formed a plan. Tomorrow morning I would park my car down the street from where Richard Seddon lived in Fairview, and sit and wait for him to go by. I needed to find out where he worked, and if I should approach him there or at his house. I already knew the questions I would ask him, that I would try the same ruse I'd used when talking with Elizabeth Grieve, telling him I was hired to investigate the drowning accident of Duane Wozniak. It would be just plausible enough, and also just suspicious enough that he would contact Joan. And if that happened, then I'd know for sure, and then I could hand the whole thing over to Roberta James and the Bingham Police Department. Easy peasy.

CHAPTER 27

RICHARD

Richard looked up, and there was the man with the jeans and the tweedy jacket that he'd seen outside his house the day before. "Are you Richard Seddon?" the man asked. Richard stood up too fast and immediately felt the blood rushing from his face, and for a brief moment thought he might pass out.

The man said, "Whoa, you all right?"

"Yeah, I'm fine," Richard said.

"I know you're working right now, but is there any chance we can have a quick conversation? I have a couple of questions for you. Won't take long."

"Okay, sure," Richard said, regretting the words as soon as they came out of his mouth. He was working, after all, and he could have told the guy he'd talk with him later.

But they wound up stepping outside, and walking to the picnic table on the strip of grass across the parking lot, Richard telling Mr. Koestler he was taking his break.

Once they were seated, the man slid a card over to Richard and introduced himself. Richard looked at the card even though he'd already realized that the man was Henry Kimball, the old teacher that Joan had hired to follow her husband. Richard's mind was anticipating questions, desperately trying to decide how he would answer. He was obviously going to be asked something about the murder of Richie Whalen and that woman he was with, or maybe even be asked about Joan Grieve. Should he at least say he'd heard about it? Should he acknowledge that he went to school with both Joan and Richie?

But the first thing the detective said was far more disturbing than he could have imagined. "Richard, I was hoping you could tell me a little bit about what happened with your cousin Duane Wozniak?"

"Oh," Richard said, and he could actually feel his eyes rapidly blinking. "He was my cousin who drowned. Why are you asking about him?"

The detective smiled. "Sorry. I feel like I just dragged you out of your job, and now I'm throwing crazy questions at you. Let's back up. All I can tell you is that someone was interested in taking another look at Duane's drowning death. It's sort of like a cold case situation. I can't tell you who my client is, but I need to basically interview people who were there when it happened and just corroborate that what the official police file from the time said is correct."

"I'm sure it's correct."

The detective ran his fingers through his disheveled hair, and said, "Yeah, I'm pretty sure it's correct too. But just so that I can cross this interview off my list, can you tell me what you remember from that time?"

"Um, it was a while ago. I was with my aunt and uncle and my cousin Duane, and I was sharing a room with Duane. We kind of did our own thing, though, since Duane and I weren't all that close."

"Oh, no?"

"He was older than me, and he'd made some friends at the resort so basically he was off doing his own thing."

"And one of those friends was Joan Grieve, right?" the detective said.

"I don't know, maybe," Richard said.

"She was with him the night he drowned, right? That's what the police report said at the time. And I figured that you knew Joan because you went to school with her at Dartford-Middleham, right?"

"I don't know her, actually. Didn't know her. I knew her name, but I've never talked with her or anything."

"You didn't talk with her at the Windward Resort when you realized that you knew each other from your hometown?"

Richard felt a sudden panic that this detective had already questioned Joan and that maybe she'd said they had recognized each other at the resort. He said, "I can't really remember. I mean, I re-member knowing that she was there because she'd been with Duane that night, but I can't remember if we ever talked or anything. I mean, we weren't friends."

"Right, that makes sense. So at the time you don't remember thinking there was anything strange about the way in which your cousin died?"

Richard shook his head no, then quickly added, "Well, it was a strange way to die, drowning at night. It was a shock. The thing about Duane, though, was that he was kind of reckless. I remember thinking at the time that it was the type of stupid thing he would do to impress a girl."

"So you didn't think it was out of character for him to be going out onto the jetty late at night and during a rainstorm?"

Richard shook his head. "No, not really."

"Okay," the detective said, and rolled his head on his neck like he was trying to get a kink out. Richard now remembered this guy from high school and he looked pretty much the same, one of those English-teacher types who thought they looked cool because they wore a fancy jacket but with crummy jeans. And even though he had messy hair and hadn't shaved, you could tell the guy thought he was good-looking.

"Anything else?" Richard said.

"Not unless you can think of something, honestly," he said. "Thanks for talking with me during your work hours. I appreciate it."

Richard stood up from the picnic table, holding on to it while swinging a leg over the bench. "Oh, one last question," the school-teacher said, "and then I'll let you go. Do you keep up with Joan Grieve since high school? I know she doesn't live too far from here."

Richard shook his head, and said, "How could I keep up with her if I never knew her?"

When he ended his shift, Richard almost decided to drive out to Dartford and go past Joan's house. He knew where she lived, of course, because he'd looked it up. It was the house Richie Whalen had grown up in. About a year ago he'd even driven past a couple of times just to get a look at it. The only reason he wanted to swing by this evening was on the off chance she'd be out in her yard raking leaves or something and he could catch her eye from the car. But that was ridiculous, the chances being about one in a thousand. If she had an actual workplace then he could swing by and make sure she saw him, but she worked out of her home. Maybe he could call her work line that she listed on her website, and then after she answered he could say he'd dialed the wrong number. Would that be enough for Joan to realize they needed to meet as soon as possible at the library? He didn't really know, and besides, calling her could be a huge mistake, proving that they'd had contact, breaking their one unbreakable rule.

Although he'd never given it too much thought, Richard was realizing now that it had always been Joan coming to him, and never the other way around.

And now that he badly needed to see Joan, and tell her about the private detective, that old schoolteacher Henry Kimball, and how he'd figured something out about their connection, he wasn't sure how to initiate contact.

He drove back to his house, wondering if he was being watched. He unlocked the back door, stepping into the kitchen that had belonged to his mother and stepfather. Most nights he didn't notice the smell of the house as he passed through it to the door that led to the finished basement where he lived since moving down there his sophomore year of high school, but tonight it was worse than usual, both a lingering smell from some member of the raccoon family dying in one of its walls, and something else, animal feces probably, mixed with the persistent smell of mold and mildew. But with the basement door shut behind him he entered his own domain, his heavily fortified basement that contained everything he owned in the world, all the contents of his childhood room, plus his computers, a flat-screen television, and, most importantly, his workstation, where he'd created the small, portable bombs that one day would become his signature achievements.

He'd lived in the basement so long that he never really registered it in its entirety, but maybe because of the visit from Henry Kimball and the feeling of being watched, he was now seeing it through an outsider's eyes. There were his old LEGO creations alongside the shelf containing his mother's romance novels he was somehow unable to throw away. It wasn't just his mother's books he kept down here, but he'd also brought down her old armoire, the one she'd gotten from her own mother, that was filled with her best dresses. That armoire was next to the single bed he'd slept in for most of his life, its headboard covered in Pokémon stickers. And while the basement didn't smell as bad as the house, there was water damage on two of the walls and the smell of mold had been getting worse over the years. And something was wrong with the toilet in the makeshift bathroom he used; the water that flowed into it was rusty brown and smelled like death.

Of course, he'd burn it all down when he finally made his move. It was really the only reason he'd continued to live in the house after his mother drowned in the upstairs tub and Don moved to the condo in Florida. He'd stockpiled enough gasoline to make sure that there'd be nothing left of this place by the time police detectives and journalists arrived to take a look. No, by then he'd only be known by what he'd done, and not how he'd lived. And it wasn't like he did anything creepy with his mother's dresses or her old hairbrushes, but they were all he really had left of her. Most of the time he had fond memories of his mother from the time when it was just the two of them, when she looked out for him. The time before Don.

After microwaving and eating two burritos Richard got onto his computer and looked up Henry Kimball. Ever since the interview he'd gone over and over the questions he'd been asked, and now he was convinced not only that somehow Kimball had figured out there was a connection between Joan and him, but that he'd figured it all out. He knew about Duane, and about James Pursall, and how they'd arranged Joan's husband's death. The only question now was whether there was any way Henry Kimball could prove it. Richard doubted it, because he'd been careful, and Joan had been careful. They always had been. Still, this asshole somehow knew. Had he told anyone else? Or was he just sniffing around, hoping to get more evidence? He wasn't a real cop, after all. He couldn't go back into that house in Bingham and start snooping around for DNA. But he could tell someone else to do it, couldn't he?

In bed that night he made a decision. There was a good chance that the detective was simply fishing, that he knew nothing. More importantly, he had probably not told anyone about his suspicions. Richard didn't need Joan for this. He could take care of it himself. And after he took care of the detective it was time for him to put some of his other plans into action. He'd waited too long. The world needed to know his name.

CHAPTER 28

KIMBALL

After meeting with Richard Seddon at the store, I'd returned to my office in Cambridge. I'd already installed the tracking software onto my desktop computer and I booted it up; the magnetic device that I'd attached to Richard's Altima was telling me he hadn't left the parking lot of the store yet. I settled in. There was a way to set up alerts so I'd know when he started to move, or if he drove toward Dartford, but I hadn't figured out how to do that yet. I was happy to sit and wait.

I had a copy of David Kintner's worst-reviewed novel, a slim paper-back called *July and August*. I'd never read it, even though I'd had the book for a while. But I was halfway through it, now, thoroughly enjoying the story even though I could see why the critics pounced. It was a thinly veiled account of his affair with the writer Margaret Cogswell, written in 1978. The first section, "July," was narrated by Douglas MacLeod, an alcoholic journalist who meets the sculptress Angela Hardwick on an unnamed Greek island, the two of them guests of a dying patron of the arts with the overly symbolic name of Athena. It was a pretty simple tale of reversal, Douglas seducing and controlling Angela in the first section, then Angela destroying Douglas in the section called "August." That was the section I was reading now, and even though it was told through the voice of Angela, it was blatantly obvious that it was David Kintner's voice taking revenge on a woman who betrayed him. Angela is a manipulative monster with no redeeming characteristics.

Still, I was caught up in it, and almost missed the moment that Richard Seddon left the store in his car, but the movement of the map on my screen caught my attention. He drove across Fairview to his home address, and it was there that the car stopped. I was disappointed, hoping, of course, that he would drive straight to Joan's house in Dartford, or to some meeting place. There was still time, though, so I kept watching the screen.

By eleven that night I'd finished my book, Richard's car hadn't gone anywhere, and I'd figured out a way to send myself an alert on my cell phone if there was any movement with the tracker. I went home, fed Pyewacket, then lay in bed and started Margaret Cogswell's debut novel *The Green Marriage,* the book that had put her on the map. I'd had the original Penguin paperback forever, but it was very thick and had very small print and I'd always been intimidated by it. I read the first chapter while Pyewacket settled down in his spot by my feet, purring. I apologized to him for my absence lately, and he opened his mouth to answer back but only managed a feeble, sleepy meow.

When I got back to my office the following morning at just past nine Richard Seddon's car had still not moved. I split the screen on my computer between the map of Fairview and an internet browser, then I read about what was happening in the baseball playoffs, googled Richard Seddon again to see if I'd missed anything, then read the Wikipedia entry on Margaret Cogswell. It didn't mention her affair with David Kintner, who was probably the least famous of her many famous lovers. She had died just two years earlier, three months after winning the Booker Prize for her final novel, *A Room by the Sea*. I remember that the common joke at the time was that she'd been holding off death until she finally made it off the Booker short list (she'd been there seven times) and into the winner's circle.

I was doing image searches of her when the dot on my map started to move, and I enlarged the tracking window to full screen. Richard had pulled out of the driveway of his house and was heading toward Fairview center, probably going to work. But when he hit the first major intersection he turned south instead, eventually getting onto Route 2 and heading west. He passed the exits for Littleton and Acton, then Dartford and Concord and Lincoln, getting closer to the city. It wasn't until he got off Route 2 and onto the Alewife Brook Parkway that it even occurred to me that he might be coming to see me. I was sitting rigid in my chair, watching as the dot passed through the two rotaries near Fresh Pond then got onto Concord Avenue, taking it all the way down to Chauncy Street. I felt like a man on a beach watching the water recede and amass itself into a tsunami, unable to move. From Chauncy Street he pulled onto Oxford, the car stopping about two blocks from my office.

He was definitely coming to see me.

I unlocked my file cabinet, removing the case where I kept my snub-nosed Colt Cobra, checking to make sure it was loaded, then placed the gun in the front drawer of my desk. I was nervous, but also a little excited. It was possible he had come to hurt me, but it was more likely he'd come to tell me something. My intercom buzzed, and I walked across my office to answer it.

"It's Richard Seddon," he said, and I could detect no particular emotion in the voice that hummed through the tinny speakers.

I cracked my door then went back to my chair behind the desk. The sound of his footsteps told me he was climbing the stairs quickly, and I removed the gun from the front drawer, took the safety off, and dropped my hand, with the gun in it, straight down and out of sight behind the desk.

But when Richard Seddon stepped into my office, he looked more like a befuddled college student than a killer. He wore jeans and a dark green hooded sweatshirt, and was wearing a backpack, its straps on both his shoulders. He came in tentatively, looking around my office. There was nothing in his hands.

"Hi, Richard," I said, and slid the gun into my jacket pocket.

"Hi, Mr. Kimball," he said, the address bringing me back not just to my teaching days, but to the time that Joan had called me the same thing in this very office, just a little over two weeks ago.

I stood up and gestured to the chair facing my desk. "Have a seat."

He perched on the padded wooden chair, sliding his backpack off and putting it on the floor. "I thought about calling but I guess I didn't want there to be a record for what I'm about to tell you," he said. "Not that there'd have been a record of what I'm going to say, but just that I called you in the first place. Do you understand?"

"Sure," I said.

Neither of us spoke for a moment and I tried to read his body language. He seemed resigned, his body limp in the chair. "I guess you know why I came here?" he said at last.

"I have no idea, but I suppose it has something to do with what we talked about yesterday."

"Yeah. It's about my cousin Duane. I feel like I should have told you that even though he was my cousin I thought at the time that he deserved to die."

"Okay," I said.

"He was a horrible guy, and I think that he was probably a rapist, or would be a rapist if he was given a chance."

"Do you think that's why he died that night? Do you think he'd tried to do something to Joan Grieve out on that jetty and she pushed him in the water?"

"I don't really know," Richard said quickly, "but it wouldn't surprise me."

"That's helpful to know," I said.

Richard looked around my office, as though he'd just been transported into it. "You work here all alone?"

"I do, for now. It's a new business so it's just me. I hope to hire help at some point."

He nodded, still looking around the room. "You were a teacher at DM, right? You were the teacher in the room when James killed that girl and then himself?"

"I was, actually. I was going to bring that up the other day, but it's not like it's relevant to the case of your cousin."

"Yeah, I get it," Richard said.

"You were friends with James," I said.

"I was, I guess. We weren't best friends or anything, but we knew each other. The thing about him . . . about what he did . . . was that the girl he killed, Madison Brown . . . she wasn't a good person, either. She was a bully, like a lot of people are, but she was smart, too, which made it worse, in a way, like she didn't have an excuse, really."

"I can see that. I remember her, of course, but only knew her as a student. But her being a bully doesn't make it okay that James killed her, does it? I mean, she was just a teenager."

"You think that people change that much from when they're teenagers?"

"God, I hope so," I said. "I was a pretentious shit when I was a teenager. I'm sure there were some people who wanted to kill me."

"Being pretentious is different than being a bad person," Richard said.

"I guess so." I was beginning to wish I'd recorded this conversation. It felt like a confession even though Richard hadn't actually confessed to anything yet. My phone was on my desk and all I would have had to do was press the record button on the audio app. Instead, I'd been focused on getting my gun from the locked file cabinet, a move that, I had to admit, was bringing me some comfort. Even though there was no evident weapon on Richard, if he went to open his backpack or reached toward his waistband under the large hoodie, I was ready to pull my gun.

"Anyway, all I really came to tell you was that Duane Wozniak probably deserved to die that night in Maine. I didn't have anything to do with it, but that doesn't mean that I wasn't a little bit happy."

"It's okay to be happy about something like that. It's not a crime to have a feeling."

"Right, it was just a feeling. I had nothing to do with it."

"But Joan Grieve might have had something to do with it?"

Richard was picking at what looked like a scab on the back of his hand. "I honestly have no idea. But if she did, she had a good reason. That's all I'm saying."

"Right. Just like James Pursall had a good reason for killing Madison Brown."

Richard's eyes shifted a little, and I worried I'd taken it too far. It was clear he'd come to me in order to offer up some sort of justification. I was torn between letting him walk out of the office before something bad happened or pushing him to learn more.

"Richard," I said, before he had a chance to respond. "Thank you for coming in and talking with me. I appreciate it. I'll be talking with Joan soon. Should I say hi for you?"

"That would be nice," he said, and I was surprised, expecting him to deny that he knew her, like he'd done before. "I should actually get going. I have a shift today."

"At the hardware store," I said.

"Yes." He stood up, his head almost coming as high as the ceiling fan in my office that I used during the summer months.

"So if I need to ask you some follow-up questions," I said, "and I doubt that I will, but you never know . . . Should I come to the store again, or call you, or maybe come to where you live?"

"I don't care," he said. "Or come to the store, I guess. I'm running late . . ."

He turned and walked toward the office door, stopping briefly to look at my Grantchester Meadows watercolor. "Pretty," he said, and then I watched him exit. There was something strange about the way he was moving, and it took a moment before I realized that he was moving like an amateur actor in a stage play. He looked as though he'd forgotten how to make an everyday occurrence look natural.

I stood up and saw the backpack still on the floor by the chair Richard had just vacated.

Time slowed down, and as I moved quickly around the desk and took hold of it by the looped strap near the top, the phrase *I was there* ran through my mind, and for some reason I saw Lily's face moving away from me. The bag was heavy to lift, and my heart began to thump. For one second I thought about racing to the window and hurling it out onto the street, but something stopped me. Embarrassment, maybe, that I'd be overreacting to something innocent.

Richard had just left the room so I took two long strides to the door, swung it open and saw him at the top of the stairs. His hood was up, but even so I could see how pale his face was. Had it been that pale in my office?

He had something in his hand, a small device that looked like a car remote. I realized his thumb was pressing down on it, and he was looking at the bag in my hand with fear. He backed away, his thumb drumming down on the device, his face twisted into something I didn't recognize, and I hurled the bag at him.

I stepped back into my office, pulling the door closed behind me. I was moving fast but the door was moving as well, ripping from its hinges, lifting me up. Then came a deafening sound accompanied by a whiteness, and I was in the air, flying, the whiteness turning to black.

PART 3

DIRTY WORK

CHAPTER 29

LILY

It was my mother, who never misses the six o'clock news, who told me about the explosion. She says she only watches the news for the weather, and it is true she reports the seven-day forecast to me on a nightly basis whether I am interested or not. But five days after Henry Kimball had come to visit, my mother said, "It wasn't our friend, was it, who was in that explosion I told you about?"

"What explosion?"

"Last night, darling. I was telling you about that house that blew up in Cambridge, how they thought it might have been a gas-line explosion and then it turned out it was some sort of device. It was the office of your friend . . . they just said his name."

"Henry."

"Yes, him."

I went online. It had been a relatively unimportant story when it had been deemed an accident, but now that it looked like it was an intentional act, the story was getting a lot more attention. The explosion had taken place on the second floor of a commercial property on Oxford Street, outside of Henry Kimball's office where he conducted his private investigations business. Henry Kimball was in critical condition at Boston Memorial Hospital, while Richard Seddon, a hardware store employee, and resident of Fairview, Massachusetts, had been declared dead at the scene. The only connection that linked the two had been Dartford-Middleham High School, where Henry Kimball had been an English teacher, present in the room when James Pursall killed a fellow student then himself. Richard Seddon had been a senior at the time of the incident but had not been in any of Henry Kimball's classes. Once that detail had emerged, however, the story had become even larger, the speculation being that the two incidents were somehow connected.

On Sunday the *Boston Globe* published a lengthy article about Richard Seddon entitled "An Unseen Life: What We Don't Know About the Oxford Street Bomber." It was now established that Seddon, who had been living in the basement of his empty childhood home, had created the bomb that he brought to the office building in Cambridge. He had a stepfather in Florida who had refused to answer any questions from reporters, but other than that, Richard had no living relatives. His boss and coworkers from the hardware store he worked at provided very little information, all of them saying that Seddon had kept to himself but had always been friendly and a hard worker.

I was a little surprised to see that, so far, no journalist had made any connection between Joan Grieve and Richard Seddon. Her name would have come up, of course, since Henry had so recently been involved in the deaths of her husband and his lover. And Joan Grieve had gone to Dartford-Middleham, as well. I imagined that some eager journalist, and possibly a detective, was trying to discover a relationship between the two, but they'd clearly had no luck.

I knew, though.

I knew that Richard Seddon had been the third person that Henry and I had discussed when he'd come to visit. Seddon and Joan Grieve had both been involved in the high school shooting, and Seddon had definitely been involved in the deaths of Richard Whalen and Pam O'Neil. Richard was Joan's partner in crime. Or had been, until recently. Henry had figured it out, and he'd paid the price.

On Sundays my father likes to have a roast dinner. That day, the day the *Globe* had published their profile of Richard Seddon, I was cooking a pork loin with crispy potatoes and two vegetables. My father was drinking beer instead of his usual whiskey and water, and my mother had made a salad with the last of the kale from the garden, a development that had enraged my father to no end.

"You don't eat salad with a Sunday roast," he'd repeated several times.

"I do," Sharon had said.

It was during dessert that I told them both I needed to be away for a couple of days. My mother merely looked confused, maybe wondering how there'd be any possible reason for me to go any-where, but my father looked genuinely scared, as though I'd told him I had a week to live.

"Where are you going, Lil?" he said, after we'd moved to the living room, and he'd returned to drinking whiskey.

"Just to Cambridge for a few days. I'll stay at a hotel and I'm actually going to meet someone who you'll be interested in. There's a Margaret Cogswell scholar who's spending a sabbatical at Harvard, and I'm going to talk with her about some of your archived materials."

My mother was not in the room at this point, having gone to her studio. I'd already told her, while we were doing dishes, that I was going to Cambridge to visit my old friend Sally Kull from Mather College. There was no way my mother and father would ever compare stories. I'd actually been telling them separate lies for as long as I could remember, even when they'd still been married.

"She's not from that school," my father said about the imaginary Cogswell scholar, "the one you told me about with all of Margaret's stuff, that wants mine now, too?"

"No, but I still want you to think about that offer. It was a good one."

I'd been spending the summer and the early fall going through all of my father's papers, and talking with various universities, and some private collectors, about where they might wind up after he died. The best offer so far had come from a private college in Arizona that owned the complete archives of the British novelist Margaret Cogswell, quite a bit more famous than my father, and a woman with whom he'd been involved during the 1970s. I knew that the college only really wanted to buy my father's papers because of his connection with Cogswell, and my father suspected it too. "We should take the offer," he'd said on numerous occasions, "then burn all my letters from Maggie, and then see how they like it."

"I think they're probably more interested in *The Broomfield Tomb*," I said, referencing my father's unpublished novella, one that had been written while he was still involved with a young Margaret Cogswell, and a book that was far more flattering to her than his novel *July and August*.

"We'll burn that too," my father said. "In fact, let's burn it anyway."

"I actually love *The Broomfield Tomb*," I said. "It's very romantic."

I'd expected him to say something cutting about that, but he'd frowned as though trying to remember, and finally said, "I thought all my books were romantic."

The next day I packed a small bag and drove to Cambridge. Along the way I kept asking myself if I was making a mistake, wondering if I really needed to get involved. Joan Grieve would be caught, wouldn't she? There would be some traceable connection between her and Richard Seddon. If Henry had found it—and it looked as though he had—then someone else would too. So why did I need to get involved? As I'd done in the past, I'd made a decision to live out my life as quietly as possible. People were dead because of me, and while the world was most likely better off without them, I had almost been discovered for who I really am. And that, to me, is a fate worse than death.

So I told myself I wouldn't get involved, I would just take a look around. If there was information that Joan Grieve had used Seddon to do her killing for her, then I would find a way to pass that information along to someone in authority.

But the real reason I was driving north was because I owed it to Henry. If I had a chance to help him, I would take it. He was deserving of that.

I drove through Harvard Square then, after a few wrong turns, made my way to Oxford Street. Henry's office was easy to spot, surrounded by yellow police tape, the second-floor windows blown out, the small yard still littered with blackened glass and dislodged vinyl siding. I had expected the building to look more like an office building, but it was a converted Victorian. The sign out front advertised a dentist's office, plus a massage therapist. I kept driving, making my way to Henry's apartment. I'd found the address online, as well. After crossing Massachusetts Avenue, I found Henry's tree-lined street, the buildings a mix of cheap-looking apartments and well-kept single-family homes, most with mansard roofs and tidy gardens. Henry's address was in one of the cheap apartment buildings, a utilitarian triple-decker that, based on the number of mailboxes affixed by the front entryway, had six inhabitants.

There was a small convenience store across the way and I parked in front of it, got out of my car, and went in to buy a cup of coffee and five one-dollar scratch cards. I got back inside my car, cracked the window, held one of the cards in my lap, and sat and watched Henry's building.

I didn't know exactly what I was waiting for, but it seemed wiser to watch for a little while before trying to figure out if there was a way to get inside of the apartment. It turned out to be a good move because at just around noon a Honda Civic pulled up, and I watched a woman with long, glossy black hair go up the front steps that led to the porch. She peered through one of the panes of glass that lined one side of the front door, then took out her cell phone and made a brief call. Then she sat on the top step, looking at her phone and waiting.

She was wearing jeans tucked into high brown boots, and a down-filled puffer jacket. Even from a distance I could see she resembled Henry, with a thin face and high cheekbones. I suspected she was his sister. She waited on the top step for about five minutes before a white Chrysler pulled up to the curb. A short, round man got out and the woman greeted him. Together they entered the apartment building. I got out of my car and walked slowly toward the building, climbing the front steps to look at the names on the mailboxes. The six apartments all had a number and then a letter. 1A, 1B, 2A, 2B, 3A, and 3B. Henry's apartment was 2A, so I assumed he was on the second floor, but didn't know which side he was on.

I walked down the steps and turned right, peering down the alleyway between Henry's building and the large brick apartment building immediately next door. There was just enough room for a fire escape, with a door at each level, plus a large window. The window on the second floor was cracked open about six inches at the top, but I couldn't make out any movement behind its dark facade. I walked to the other side of the apartment, where there was another fire escape, this one with more space around it. Both the door and the window on the second-floor landing were closed, and there was a venetian blind pulled down behind the window. I kept walking for a block then turned right. Two more rights brought me back to my car. I ducked back into the convenience store and bought myself a package of granola mix for my lunch, then sat in my car again.

Ten minutes later the dark-haired woman and the short man exited the building, the man getting back into the Chrysler and the woman getting back into her Civic. There was an empty child's seat strapped in behind her, which cemented my guess that she was his sister, and she had contacted the building manager to let her into his place since he was in the hospital. I knew Henry had a cat named Pyewacket, and maybe she'd fed him. I waited about twenty minutes then drove my car about two blocks away. It was mainly residential parking in this part of Cambridge, but I found a parking meter that took quarters and put in enough for two hours. Then I walked back to the building, trying to figure out what side was the B side and what side was the A. It made sense, somehow, that the A side would be on the left, and it was confirmed for me when I looked up at the window that had been open and saw that it was now closed. Henry's sister and the building manager must have closed it.

Moving as fast as I could I climbed the fire escape up to the second-floor landing, trying the door first, which was locked, then checking the window, which slid open. I straddled the windowsill, stepping into a kitchen, and closed the window behind me.

My eyes adjusted fast and I saw Henry's cat saunter into the kitchen. "Hi Pye," I said, and crouched down, putting out my fingers. The cat came over and sniffed them, then circled me, rubbing up against both of my ankles. His bowls were in the corner of the tiny kitchen, the water bowl filled to the brim, as was the food bowl. It looked as though he'd just been fed.

I made my way through the small apartment, the bedroom only large enough to contain a bed and a bureau. The largest room was the living area, and it was the only room that seemed decorated in the place. One wall was lined with bookshelves, and above a dark green sofa was a framed poster for the film *Withnail and I*. Henry's desk was in the living room, covered with paperwork that looked mostly like bills, plus a few stacks of books. There was no laptop, and I assumed that he had brought it with him to his office, and that it had been blown up in the explosion. I sat down at the desk and pulled out the top drawer. His passport was inside, along with a checkbook, about a hundred scattered paperclips, and two blank notebooks. I pulled them both out. One was completely filled, mostly with the starts of poems, and an occasional drawing or diary entry. There were a few dates, and the filled notebook seemed to have been completed more than a year ago. The other notebook was only partly filled so I started at the last completed pages and read backward. Most of it was poetry, some were fragments of original lines, and some were other people's poems that Henry had transcribed out, including a rather long poem by Anthony Hecht called "The Ghost in the Martini." The only completed poems that had been written by Henry were limericks. The last one he'd written told me everything I needed to know.

> *There once was a Joan and a Rick*
> *Who had mastered just one magic trick.*
> *Their friendship anonymous,*
> *Their victims were numerous,*
> *They murdered, and no one knew dick.*

CHAPTER 30

JOAN

Whenever she became angry, and boredom always angered her, Joan remembered the trick she'd learned when she'd been a young girl, probably no more than eight or nine. She'd had a psychiatrist then, named Brenda, and what she remembered most about those trips to Brenda's office, with its thick carpet and kiddie art on the walls, was that after the session was over Joan would be allowed to take a whole roll of Spree candies home with her. She always picked Spree because it was her sister Lizzie's favorite candy and she liked to eat them in front of her.

Brenda had been the one to suggest the anger box. She'd told Joan that feeling angry was perfectly okay, but that acting out that anger was not the best solution. She said that sometimes it was fine to simply pretend to be a different sort of child, a child that did not become angry, that wanted to please people, that wanted to be good. And the easiest way to do that was to find a place to put the bad feelings. After agreeing to try this, Brenda gave Joan a cardboard box, designed to look like a treasure chest, and told Joan that she could use this box if she wanted to. Back in her room, Joan had pushed the box under her bed, but she decided to follow Brenda's advice. From now on, she would pretend to be a good girl, not talking back to her parents, not being mean to her sister. It didn't matter what she felt; it mattered how she acted.

She liked to remember that time that her parents had lost her for a whole night, while she slept in the closet listening to Lizzie's Disc-man. She had felt so seen, and incredibly powerful the next day. All she'd had to do was look like she'd been in danger. It was then that she decided that fighting the world would not get her anywhere, but that she could always change the world in ways that no one would ever know. Not only was it better, it was easier.

She still felt anger, though. And on the day that Joan heard about the death of Richard Seddon she'd been in one of those bored, angry moods. It was a Tuesday and she'd woken late, climbing out of a succession of disturbing dreams, then found herself sitting at her kitchen island, drinking a cup of coffee, and wondering what she was going to do with the next few hours. Her sister, who she rarely saw, and her mother, who she saw way too often, were coming over later in the morning to check in. "I'll bring lunch," her mother said. "I don't want you to have to worry about anything." She'd go for a run, of course, but what she really wanted to do was to share some of the satisfaction she'd gotten from the fact that she'd arranged to have her husband and his stupid girlfriend murdered and no one seemed to suspect a thing.

Idly, not expecting anything, she'd put Richard's name into Google, knowing it was a slightly reckless thing to do but feeling safe about it. He was on her mind. They'd had no contact since immediately before the day of the murder, and she wondered how he was holding up. The first thing that came up was a news story about an explosion in Cambridge at the offices of Private Investigator Henry Kimball. The body of Richard Seddon had been found on the premises.

She forced herself to take two deep breaths, then sped through the news reports, quickly constructing a narrative of what she thought had happened.

Somehow Henry Kimball had actually figured something out and approached Richard with it. It was the only thing that made sense. Why didn't Richard get in touch with her? Frustration flared in her, and she could feel her face getting red. If he'd come to her, they could have figured it out together, as they always had. Instead, he'd decided to take matters into his own hands, and he'd gotten himself killed.

And he'd left Kimball alive.

Joan got up and paced through her house. She found herself continually drawn to the big window in the living room that looked out over her driveway. The police would be stopping by to visit, wouldn't they? Henry must have figured out that Richard was somehow involved in the death of her husband, and from there it was pretty easy to figure out that Richard and Joan had been in the same class at the same schools growing up. Still, was that enough? They'd been so careful over the years to never let anyone know they knew one another. At least she had. And she had always trusted in Richard, believing that he had been as careful as she was.

But maybe he wasn't. With him dead now, they'd be looking through his house. Maybe he kept a diary, a place where he'd written down everything they did together?

Panic was surging through her, but there was something else, as well, little stabs of grief, the realization that Richard was gone from the world, and he was the only person to whom Joan had ever revealed herself. It was an almost physical sensation, and Joan held on to the edge of her velvet love seat, doubled over as though she'd been punched in the stomach. The feeling was intense, and surprising. If she'd simply been told that she would never see Richard again it wouldn't have bothered her at all, but somehow knowing she couldn't see him even if she wanted to felt like more than she could bear. His death had erased a part of her own life she wasn't yet willing to give up.

And then the feeling passed. Richard had disappointed her, like every other stupid person on this planet. He'd clearly screwed up somewhere along the line or Henry Kimball would never have gotten that close to him. What she needed to find out was how much Henry knew, if there was anything concrete, or if it had all just been a guessing game. What if he'd written his suspicions down? Had he told one of his old police colleagues?

Joan put on jeans and a sweatshirt from Springfield College that she'd had forever, and got into Richard's BMW, speeding down her driveway so fast that she nearly hit Gretchen Summers, out power walking with her yappy dog. Joan lowered her window and Gretchen leaned in, her brow furrowed, and said, "Joan, how *are* you?"

"You know," Joan said.

"I know everyone writes the same thing, but what I said in my note I absolutely mean. *Anything,* I mean *anything* you need, just let me know, okay?"

"I appreciate that, Gretchen," Joan said. The little dog whose name she'd forgotten was emitting eardrum-splitting barks, and Joan wondered if she let the car roll a little forward during this conversation if she could crush it under one of her wheels.

"Where are you off to now? If you have errands, you know I'd be happy to do them."

Joan said, "I've gotten some more bad news, I'm afraid. As I'm sure you know I hired someone to follow Richard and he was the one who found the bodies. He was an old teacher of mine, and sort of a friend, and I just found out he's in the hospital." Joan had said the words out loud partly to hear them and judge them for herself. She knew that if she wanted to get close to Henry then she would need to create a narrative.

"Oh, no. What happened?"

"Did you read about that explosion in Cambridge?"

"Of course. Oh my God. Did that . . . Was that . . . ?" Gretchen transformed her rubbery face into a look of concern and shock, but Joan could also read the pleasure in it.

"It was Henry Kimball's office. I'm sure it had nothing to do with me or with what happened with . . . Richard, but I'm worried. I mean, I'm worried about Henry, and I want to find out what happened."

"Of course you do. Of course you do. That makes total sense."

"So I should . . ."

"Of course." Gretchen straightened up. "Cinnamon, stop barking at Mommy."

Joan drove away, weirdly happy she'd been able to talk with one of her neighbors. It had helped to clarify in her mind her next steps. It made total sense that she'd be rushing off to the hospital to find out how Henry Kimball was, and that she'd want to talk with police detectives. She'd been through a major trauma. Her husband had not only been cheating on her, but he'd turned out to be a murderer. She'd be frazzled and nervous and wondering if the explosion had anything to do with her. And if she was asked if there was some connection between her and Richard Seddon she'd simply deny it. There wouldn't be any proof. Even if Richard somehow wrote about it, she could just claim he'd been obsessed with her since high school, that she'd never even thought about him until she heard his name in the newspaper story about the explosion.

She was going to be fine.

And not only that, she wasn't bored anymore. She'd discovered she was happiest when the world was concerned about her. That period right after she and Richard had drowned Duane Wozniak, when she'd been repeatedly interviewed by the police about what had happened on the jetty, had been one of the happiest nights of her adolescence. All those adults, all those concerned faces, and it was like she was conducting them with every word she said, every tear that spilled down her cheek. She had felt more power in the immediate aftermath of Duane's death than she'd ever felt before, more power than she felt in gymnastics, knowing she was the best in her school.

The feeling had been almost as good in the aftermath of the classroom shooting when she'd arranged to have Madison killed. There had been attention, then, as well, everyone worried about PTSD and how she'd process the trauma of what had happened along with the tragedy of losing such a close friend. The problem then had been that she had to share the spotlight with all the other kids who'd been in that classroom, and some of the kids, like Missy Robertson, had totally fallen apart at the time. That girl had actually wound up hospitalized, which had probably all been bullshit because she was fine now, on one of the local news stations as a weatherperson, and the rumor was that she was writing a book about what it was like to survive a school shooting. No surprise there.

Sometimes Joan fantasized about what it would have been like if she'd talked Richard into convincing his psychotic friend James to kill everybody in that classroom except for her. It would have been easy for James. No one in that class was going to suddenly become a hero. Certainly not Mr. Kimball, who had frozen like a mannequin in a store window. She could picture it now. James shooting every kid, and then Mr. Kimball, and then leaving her alive while he put a bullet into his chest. She'd have been famous, of course. Nationally famous. The girl who lived.

So now she was a widow, and not just an average widow, but one whose husband was also a murderer. She had enjoyed it for a while, getting the stupid cards and the texts from friends with emojis of hearts, none of them even suspecting she'd had anything to do with all the tragedies that had peppered her life. She could only imagine what they said about her to one another, wondering how one person could withstand so much violence in her life. It felt good, but it also left her with a feeling of emptiness, that it was just so easy to fool the world. That was why Richard's death hurt so much. It wasn't just that he was her partner, it was that he was the only one who knew how smart she really was.

Without really remembering how she'd gotten there, she was suddenly on Storrow Drive, heading toward Boston Memorial Hospital. There were crew boats on the Charles River, and heavy winds were stripping trees of leaves. For a moment she thought about leaving Dartford, maybe moving to Boston now that she had the freedom. But she also knew that she'd established herself in her little corner of the world, doing just enough home decorating to feel as though it was a career. And the other truth, the one she knew down deep, was that she didn't want to live anonymously in a city, that she wanted the notoriety of small-town life. She was the talented gymnast whose life had been full of tragedy. That was not an identity she wanted to give up.

She found a metered spot two blocks from the hospital and bought two hours' worth of time. She had no idea what to expect when she asked after Henry at the front desk. If he was still in the ICU, she doubted very much that she would be allowed to see him. Still, she had to try. And maybe she'd be able to get crucial information about whether he was going to live or die.

She made her way through the revolving door, making sure not to touch either the glass or the metal push bars. She passed a patient in a wheelchair, a skull-like head bent over so that all Joan could see was sparse white hair and old mottled skin. She hated hospitals with a fervor that was almost a phobia. The thought of being so old that you couldn't take care of yourself was horrifying to her, and always had been. At the age of six she'd refused to visit her mother's dying father, screaming so hard that she was eventually allowed to wait in the car with her father while her mother and sister went inside to say their goodbyes.

At the front desk she told the receptionist that she was here to see Henry Kimball, if that was possible.

"Are you a family member?" the heavy, frowning woman said.

"I'm a very close friend. If I can't see him, that's okay. But I'd love to talk with someone about his condition."

"Hold on one moment, okay?" she said, picking up a phone, then before dialing, asked, "What's your name?"

"It's Joan Whalen."

"Uh-huh." The woman got through to someone and spoke quietly enough that Joan couldn't hear the words above the ambient noise of the busy hospital lobby. When she put the phone back down in its cradle, she looked at Joan, and said, "Someone will be right down."

She thanked her and stepped back a few steps to wait. Two young women, both in hospital scrubs, jogged through the lobby, presumably to get to some emergency that was happening nearby. Joan walked over to a wall filled with pastel abstract art but kept her eye on the entryway behind the reception desk. She didn't know what to expect. Was a doctor coming down to give her a report on Mr. Kimball's condition? It seemed odd since she wasn't a relative. It was more likely he'd died already, and someone was coming down to tell her that.

About five minutes after being told to wait a tall Black woman pushed her way through the double doors, her eyes hunting around the lobby. Joan floated forward a little toward the front desk, and the woman spotted her, smiled, and made her way over.

"Are you Joan Whalen?" she said.

"I am."

"Oh, good. I'm Detective Roberta James of the Boston Police Department." She showed Joan a badge clipped onto the belt of her pantsuit. "Do you have a few minutes to talk?"

CHAPTER 31

LILY

I'd been in Henry's apartment for an hour, when it occurred to me that I could stay there. Searching through his desk for anything else he might have written down about Joan Whalen, I found a spare set of apartment keys. There was nothing stopping me from coming and going now. If a neighbor questioned me, I'd tell them I was watching his cat. And if I was in the apartment when someone came up, I could either hide in a closet or slip out the kitchen window and go down the fire escape. It was a risk, of course, but preferable to checking into a hotel. I didn't want to leave any traceable evidence that I'd come to this area if I didn't have to.

At dusk I left the apartment building through the front door and went out to the street to retrieve my car. I drove to a nearby seafood restaurant called Summer Shack, parked in their big lot, then entered the restaurant and sat at the bar. I got a glass of pinot grigio and the fish chowder. As I ate, I thought about what I was doing here, and if I was making a big mistake. My place was in Connecticut, at Monk's House, looking after my mother and father. At times, I thought that that property, with its crooked farmhouse, and the encroaching woods, was my true and proper home, where I was destined to live out the remainder of my life. Where I was destined to die.

I didn't find such thoughts uncomforting. I'd learned a long time ago that, for whatever reason, I didn't mix well with the world of humans. I'd gone to college, and fallen in love, and that experience had led to nothing but tragedy. I didn't feel bad about what I'd done to Eric Washburn, who, before I killed him, was destined to spend the entirety of his life making other people miserable, but I realized that ending his life had caused reverberations that had left me vulnerable to the world. Henry Kimball, when he was a police detective, had seen me for what I am, had come after me, and I'd made the biggest mistake of my life, trying to protect myself. He hadn't been deserving of that.

After dinner I left my car in the lot that was shared by the restaurant and several nearby businesses and walked back with my small bag that contained my toiletries and clothes to Henry's building. The windows to his apartment were dark, so I entered the building and climbed the single set of stairs and let myself inside. I tried hard to be quiet without trying to seem like I was being quiet. I didn't know anything about the other tenants but hoped that none of them were the type to call the police if they heard a strange noise.

Pye came and greeted me as I stepped inside the dark apartment. I let my eyes adjust then walked toward the bedroom, the cat following me and meowing, and then I shut the bedroom door behind us. The curtains were already pulled, so I flipped on Henry's bedside lamp. This was a slight risk, but the bedroom's windows were all to the back of the building, and with the curtains shut tight I didn't think anyone would notice. Besides, this was the city, not exactly the type of place where neighbors paid close attention to everyone else's comings and goings.

Henry had an alarm clock by his bed, and I set it to six in the morning. I needed to be up early just in case someone was planning on showing up the next day, maybe to feed Pye. I changed into leggings and a sweatshirt and lay down on the top of the bed. There was a stack of four books on the bedside table, including *The Green Marriage* by Margaret Cogswell. The other books were a Faber edition of Louis MacNeice's *Autumn Journal,* Kingsley Amis's *Lucky Jim,* and a falling-apart copy of Dorothy Hughes's *In a Lonely Place.* The Cogswell was the only one with a bookmark in it and I picked it up and opened it to where Henry had left off. I'd read *The Green Marriage* in college; it had actually been an assignment in a contemporary British fiction class, and I'd even written a paper on the main character of Muriel Pollock, never mentioning to my professor that I'd actually met the author on at least one occasion, and that my father had been one of her lovers.

I flipped to the beginning of the book and started to read. Pyewacket got onto the bed and meowed a little more, then turned twice and settled onto a furry patch of the quilted bedcover. I read two chapters then managed to fall asleep.

The next morning I hid my overnight bag beneath the living room sofa, then left the apartment shortly after dawn. It was cold outside, and the sidewalks were wet. I walked to Massachusetts Avenue, then headed east, stopping into the first coffee shop that was open. I lingered there until nine a.m., reading the free *Boston Globe,* and wishing I had *The Green Marriage* with me, even though bringing Henry's copy would probably have been a mistake. I walked into Harvard Square, where I found a barbershop that was open, and asked if they were taking walk-ins.

"It's all we take," the nicely dressed man said, and indicated a leather barber chair for me to sit in. "We don't do too many women's haircuts, but I'll be happy to give you a trim."

"I was hoping for a buzz cut," I said.

He looked a little surprised, but simply said, "All one length?"

"Uh-huh."

"And do you know what number?"

"Surprise me," I said.

I left twenty minutes later, having left my long red hair behind. I'd had the same haircut since high school and walking away from the barbershop I ran my hands over my head, liking the way the short hairs ruffled under my fingers. After stopping for another coffee at an empty café on Bow Street, I went and found a salon on the other side of Harvard Square and asked if they had time to dye my hair. The youngest stylist in the shop said she could squeeze me in, and I asked her to dye my new haircut blond. "Did you buzz this yourself?" she said, running her fingers over my scalp.

"I did," I said. "What do you think?"

"You did a nice job. What kind of blond are you thinking? Natural or platinum?"

"What do you think?" I said.

I ate lunch at a pizza place in a dark inside shopping area, sitting in a chair that faced a mirrored wall. I kept catching glimpses of myself and thought that the platinum hair had totally transformed me, but that my clothes no longer went with my new look. After lunch I found a used clothing store and bought several new items. A plaid skirt held together with safety pins. Two sweaters, one fuzzy and white, and the other a man's orange cardigan. I bought fishnet stockings, plus a pair of fake leather pants, and I found a genuine black leather jacket that had once upon a time been bedazzled on the back with an image that might have been a coiled snake, or maybe a beehive. I sold the clothes I was wearing to the unimpressed salesgirl and left the store in one of my new outfits, going up one set of stairs and finding a place where they pierced my nose septum with a silver hoop. The last place I went was Newbury Comics, where I bought some high-end temporary tattoos that I wasn't sure I needed, but thought I'd get just in case.

Walking back down Mass Avenue in my new clothes, teetering in my high-heel boots, I felt like myself again. Not because I liked the clothes, or even felt comfortable in them, but because I felt invisible, camouflaged. I suspected that if my mother walked past me on the sidewalk she wouldn't give me a second look. I still didn't have an exact plan for what I was going to do next, but it felt important that I was essentially in a disguise. I hoped to find a way to meet Joan Whalen, and if she had done her research on Henry Kimball—and I imagined she had—then she'd know about me, maybe even seen a picture of me attached to one of the news stories. But unless she really paid attention to what my face looked like, then I thought my new look would probably fool her.

I passed a library and went inside, finding a free computer and opening up an internet browser. I hadn't found out too much from my search through Henry's apartment the night before, but I'd found a little more than the limerick. There had been a stack of books on Henry's desk, including the 2003 yearbook from Dartford-Middleham High School. I'd found pictures of both Joan Whalen, then called Joan Grieve, and Richard Seddon. Two other books on his desk interested me; they were both volumes of poetry by Elizabeth Grieve, who I guessed was Joan Grieve's sister. In the slimmer of the two volumes, a book called *Sea Oat Soup,* Henry had left a pencil marking a poem called "Tides." Its subtitle was "Kennewick, 1999," and Henry had faintly underlined the word *Kennewick* with the pencil. At first, I wondered if he'd done that because of our connection to Kennewick. It was the town where Ted and Miranda Severson (rest in peace to both of them) had been building their dream house. But Henry had also underlined the word *sister* and the word *drowned* in the poem, and I'd made a mental note to investigate it later when I could get on an anonymous computer.

It took a while but I eventually found what I was looking for. There had been a drowning off the jetty in Kennewick in the year 2000. A teenager named Duane Wozniak who had been accompanied by an unnamed girl also staying at the Windward Resort. There was very little information but in one of the articles I found it mentioned that a Richard Seddon, Duane's cousin, had also been staying with the Wozniaks at the resort. It all fell into place. I'd learned what Henry had learned, maybe not all he learned but enough. Richard and Joan had been involved in at least three incidents that had resulted in death. The first was the drowning of Duane Wozniak in Kennewick in 2000. The second was the school shooting three years later in Dartford, and the third was the death of Joan's husband and Joan's husband's girlfriend. Actually, there were four incidents, because now Richard Seddon was dead in an explosion at the offices of the private investigator who'd been hired by Joan.

Before logging off, I did a quick check to see if there had been any updates on the story of the explosion. There was nothing new, not since yesterday, which made me think that at least Henry hadn't died. That would surely make the news.

After leaving the library I walked to a busy Irish pub in Davis Square and got a table to myself. I ordered a Guinness plus the veggie burger and scrolled through my phone so I would look like everyone else who was alone in the place. A young guy wearing a flannel shirt and black jeans sitting at the bar caught my eye and I gave him my flattest, coldest look, hoping he'd stay away. For the last two years, since I'd been living at Monk's House, I'd forgotten what it was like to be out in the world. Now that I was back in it, all I saw around me were flawed animals who didn't really know they were animals. Sad, horny men. Drunk, flirty women. That sounds judgmental, but I don't mean it to be. It's who I am too, an animal just trying to survive, trying to understand my impulses. And maybe being here, away from the simplicity of my real life, was a huge mistake.

I could go back to Henry's apartment, sleep until dawn, then drive back to Connecticut. My parents would be surprised by my new appearance but that wouldn't last long. I could go back to sorting through my father's materials, to taking long walks in the surrounding woods, to rereading my Agatha Christie collection at night.

The burger came and was better than it should have been. When I'd finished it, and paid my bill, I stood up to go. The burly guy at the bar stared at me a little more as I left through the swinging doors.

I'd decided to not go home just yet. I wanted to meet Joan Grieve first.

CHAPTER 32

JOAN

"It's good that you're here," Detective James said. "I was planning on reaching out to you anyway."

"Oh, yeah?" Joan said. They were sitting on either side of a hard couch in the waiting area of the hospital. Even with Joan sitting up as straight as she could, the detective was looking down at her, the expression on her face unreadable.

"First of all, I'm sorry for your loss, and for the circumstances around it. That must have been quite a shock."

"It was."

"How are you doing now?"

"I mean, I'm still in shock, I think. I'm grieving, but I'm also trying to come to grips with what Richard, with what my husband, did. It's like I didn't even know him."

"I can imagine," the detective said, and crossed one leg over the other, like they were settling in for a long chat.

"I was so shocked when I heard about what happened to Henry Kimball," Joan said. "He'd been . . . he was always kind to me, and I already felt bad about what he had to see . . . to discover . . . when he was investigating my husband. I know it doesn't make sense for me to come here to check on him, but I can't stand being alone in my house, and then I was so worried, so here I am." Joan held both palms of her hands up in a gesture that immediately felt unnatural to her. Why had she just said all those things to this woman? She made a decision to stop babbling and just answer questions.

"Totally understandable," the detective said. "So I take it from what you're telling me that you don't think there's any connection between Henry Kimball's involvement in the case of your husband and the attack on him in his office?"

Joan shook her head. "No. I mean, that's not why I'm here."

"Right."

"Is there a connection?"

"That's what I was hoping you'd be able to tell me." The detective smiled, her lips moving fractionally.

Joan pretended to think for a moment. "You mean, besides the fact that Richard Seddon went to the same high school I went to?"

"Well, let's start there. If that's a coincidence, then it's quite a coincidence. Did you know Richard Seddon?"

"No, I didn't. I didn't even recognize his name, but then I read the article that said he'd gone to Dartford-Middleham and I remembered him."

"You grew up in Middleham?"

"I did."

"And so did Richard Seddon?"

"I guess so, yes. I mean, he went to the high school, so—"

"I'm sorry," the detective said, "I'm not making myself entirely clear. It's a regional high school, right? It includes all the kids from Dartford, which is a fairly large town, and from Middleham, which is a lot smaller, right? And you and Richard were both from Middleham, so you would have gone through elementary and middle school together, as well, right?"

"We did. I do remember him, but honestly, I hadn't thought of him for years. We didn't know each other at all. I mean, it's possible we've never actually spoken."

"What do you remember about him?"

"Hardly anything. He was super quiet and kind of nerdy. I mean, I do remember that he was friends with James Pursall. I think they were gaming friends, or something like that."

Detective James was nodding along. "Yes, they were friends."

"Do you think that's why he was targeting Mr. Kimball?"

The detective pushed her bottom lip, and said, "We don't really know. That's why I wanted to talk with you."

"I wish I knew more."

The detective nodded again but didn't immediately say anything. Joan said, "So how is he? How's Mr. Kimball?"

"He was your teacher, right?"

"Uh-huh."

"I'm asking because you call him Mr. Kimball."

"Oh, yes. Old habits, I guess."

"I get it. And last I heard he's out of immediate danger, but he's still unresponsive. He had a subdural hemorrhage that they seem to have dealt with, and he has a lot of abrasions, but strangely enough, no broken bones. We're all just waiting for him to open his eyes and tell us what happened."

"You think he'll be able to do that?"

"Well, hopefully, he can at least fill us in on his connection with Richard Seddon. Oh, that was what I was going to ask you: Your husband went to Dartford-Middleham too, right?"

"He did. I didn't particularly know him, then, though. He was the class above me, and he grew up in Dartford."

"Uh-huh. And did your husband know Richard Seddon?"

"I don't think so. I mean, if he did, he never told me about it."

"What about James Pursall?"

"No, I don't think so. I mean, we all *know* James Pursall, I guess you'd say, or know *of* him, because of what he did. But I'm pretty sure that Richie didn't actually ever talk to him, or anything."

"Richie was what you called your husband?"

"Richie was what my husband was called in high school. I guess sometimes I still think of him that way, even though he hated it, and wanted to be called Richard now."

Joan heard the detective's cell phone buzz and saw her light gray jacket pocket light up briefly, but she didn't check it. "So I think I know the answer already, but I just want to make sure. Your husband never took a class with Henry Kimball, when he'd been a teacher at Dartford, right?"

"I doubt it. No, I'm sure he didn't. He was only there a year, you know. Mr. Kimball. He came in as a student teacher for my honors English class and then he stayed on."

"What kind of teacher was he?"

"Oh," Joan said. "He was kind of like the cliché of an English teacher, if you know what I mean. He was really into it, especially poetry, and he wore ties sometimes, and you'd always see him smoking in the parking lot. It's weird because he was probably only a few years older than me back then, but he seemed older, you know, because he was a teacher."

"So what made you pick him when you were looking for someone to investigate your husband?"

"I wanted a detective to confirm what I knew about my husband, so I googled local ones. I saw Mr. Kimball's name and it made me wonder if it was the same Henry Kimball who'd been my teacher. So I looked him up, and it seemed like it was him. He'd become a police officer, right, after leaving teaching?"

"He was my partner for a while, yes."

"And there was some kind of controversy. He was suspended."

The detective said, "Something like that."

"So yeah. I realized I probably knew him. I wasn't a hundred percent sure, but I booked an appointment, and it was him, and he agreed to do the job. Obviously, I feel a little bit bad about it because of what he walked in on, but, honestly, I had no idea."

"No, I'm sure you didn't." The detective pulled her phone out of her jacket pocket and checked it.

Joan said, "Is there a chance I can see him?"

"Not now there isn't. Like I said, he's not responsive, and it's only really family who have been in."

"No, I understand. It's good that I got a chance to talk with you. I don't know what it was but when I heard the news I needed to come here."

The detective nodded, put the phone back in her jacket, then reached into another pocket to pull out a card. "You'll call me if you think of anything else, any other connection there might be between Richard Seddon and Mr. Kimball. Even if it seems unimportant."

"Of course. But I don't think I'll think of something. I honestly haven't heard his name in years."

The detective stood up, and so did Joan. They shook hands, the detective's dry and warm. "One more thing, Mrs. Whalen," she said. "You were in the classroom during the shooting, right?"

"Uh-huh."

"How did Mr. Kimball react?"

"Oh," Joan said. "He was pretty amazing. He stood his ground and tried to talk that kid into giving up his gun. I mean, it didn't work, but he tried. Everyone else in the room—all the other kids—we just cowered on the floor."

"Okay," Detective James said, and walked back across the lobby floor.

Joan left the hospital, breathing deeply once she was through the rotating doors. There was mist in the air, and the tops of all the buildings were hidden by low clouds.

She returned to her car, feeling good about her visit. She'd gotten a lot of information, and while it had been unnerving to be interviewed by that police detective, it was obvious she knew absolutely nothing. She was curious, of course, about the connection between her and Henry Kimball and Richard Seddon. That made total sense, since all three of them had been associated with DM High School at the same time. But the detective hadn't asked anything about Kennewick, hadn't asked anything about the Fairview library. It was pretty clear there was no evidence that she and Richard were connected, at all. Her only fear was that Mr. Kimball had figured something out, and that if he recovered consciousness, he'd tell what he knew. But what could that even be?

Joan got off Memorial Drive in Cambridge, then got stuck in bad traffic through Harvard Square. At a red light she punched "Henry Kimball" and "address" into her phone and was given lots of listings with the Oxford Street address, but one with another address in Cambridge. She put that one in her GPS and wound up outside a run-down apartment building, where she sat in her car for a while. Would the police have searched Henry Kimball's apartment? She doubted it. They'd have searched Richard Seddon's house, of course, since he was the apparent perpetrator of the bombing, but Henry was just the victim. Joan wondered if it made sense for her to try to get in there, just on the off chance Henry had written something down. It was a huge risk, though. It was one thing for her to show up at the hospital, but another thing entirely for her to break into his apartment. Besides, she didn't know how to break into apartments.

She drove back to Dartford, and it wasn't until she was pulling onto her street that she remembered her mother and her sister were coming over around lunchtime. As soon as she had that thought her phone buzzed, and she looked down to see that a message from her mother had just popped up on her screen. She turned into her driveway. Her sister, Lizzie, was peering through the cut-out window of the front door, and her mother was pacing in the driveway, looking at her phone.

"I'm here, I'm here," Joan said, getting out of her car.

Her mother came over and hugged her. "Sweetheart, we were so worried. Where did you go?"

Deciding she didn't want to get into it, Joan said, "I went to a client's house, just to do an estimate."

"Seriously, Joan, do they even know what you've been through? You need to take some time away from all that."

Lizzie came over, holding a large casserole dish, and Joan was relieved that it meant they wouldn't have to hug. "Mom made four pounds of chicken and rice. Please open the front door so I can put this down."

They ate at the island in the kitchen. The casserole had been something Joan's mother used to make years ago, and Joan discovered she was famished, eating two heaping portions.

For dessert Joan's mother found a quart of coffee ice cream in the freezer that had a layer of frost on it, but was otherwise fine. "What I've read, Joan," her mother said, "was that it will really take two whole years for you to get back to a normal life. It's a whole process, you know."

"What's the process when your husband is a murderer?" Joan said.

"Oh, Joan," her mother said and stretched out to put her hand flat against the island's tiled top in Joan's direction.

Joan looked at her sister and thought that Lizzie looked strangely concerned. She said, "It's probably going to be longer, you know, Joan. I think you must still be in shock."

"Are you planning on writing a poem about it?" Joan said.

Lizzie shook her head slightly, a half smile on her lips. Joan thought she looked closer to their mother's age than she did to her own. It wasn't just the gray hair or the lack of makeup. It was also just the resignation in her body. "Probably not."

"I don't care, Lizzie. Feel free to write as many dead brother-in-law poems as you'd like."

"Oh, that reminds me, Joan," Lizzie said. "Did you hear from that private detective, the one that's looking into the boy who drowned in Kennewick?"

"What are you talking about?"

"I got a call. It was from . . . I don't remember his name . . . some guy who said he'd been hired to relook at that drowning case. I told him I didn't know anything about it, that he should probably talk to you."

"When was this?"

"He called me during my office hours, so it must have been Thursday. We talked for about three minutes, and I told him I didn't know anything about it. I thought he'd call you next."

"What was his name?"

"Honestly, actually, I'm not sure he gave me one. He just said he'd been asked to take another look at the incident. Why are you so upset?"

Joan's mother said, "She's upset because you're upsetting her, Lizzie."

"That's a tautology, Mom," Lizzie said.

"I'm not upset," Joan said, "I'm just curious. I hadn't thought of that trip in years."

"Well, don't think about it now, sweetheart," her mother said. "Let's all go for a walk, why don't we?"

Joan didn't want to go for a walk, but she didn't want to sit inside the house with her family either. "Let's take a quick walk, and then I think I'll take a nap," she said, and her mother and sister agreed. They all left the house and did the shortest loop through the neighborhood she could think of.

When she was finally back in her house, alone, Joan allowed herself time to think about what she'd learned from Lizzie. The call must have come from Mr. Kimball. He'd figured out that both she and Richard Seddon had been in Kennewick at the same time that Duane Wozniak had died. He'd probably even read that stupid poem that Lizzie had written, called "Sea Tide," or something like that. She went to the bookshelf in the living room and found *Sea Oat Soup,* a cheap stapled book that wasn't a whole lot bigger than some STD pamphlet you'd get in a doctor's office. She found the poem, the one where Lizzie said that her sister had gone swimming with a boy who didn't come back, and she imagined Mr. Kimball reading it. He'd have eaten it up, of course, because it was poetry, and because it was a clue, probably his two favorite things. She thought that it would be a very good thing if Mr. Kimball never woke up from his injuries.

CHAPTER 33

LILY

I left Henry's apartment the next day at seven in the morning, and as I was walking down the residential street where he lived a familiar car passed by me and double-parked in front of the apartment building. I looked over my shoulder and watched the same dark-haired woman, the one I'd assumed was Henry's sister, dart out of the car and go through the front door. I wondered if she'd notice that Pye wasn't particularly hungry.

I kept walking, stopping to get a cup of coffee and a breakfast crepe at a place near the subway entrance and thought about the best way to meet Joan Grieve Whalen. I didn't particularly want to just go up to her front door and knock on it, but I couldn't think of a better alternative. It seemed clear from her website as an interior decorator that she didn't have an office. I also doubted she was going out to bars and restaurants so soon after her husband had died. It's not that I thought she was grieving him—she'd most likely killed him, after all—it was just that it would look unseemly.

I did know that if I wanted to establish any kind of relationship with her we'd need something in common. And I'd already decided what that was.

After eating I walked to Porter Square, finding a chain store that sold cheap prepaid cell phones. I paid for one with cash, then went to another coffee shop where there was a place for me to charge it while I drank another coffee. At around eleven o'clock I found a bench in a small, quiet park on the outskirts of Harvard Square and called Joan's work number with my new phone.

"Hello?"

"Oh, hi," I said, stammering a little.

"Who's this?"

"Sorry. My name's Addie Logan. You don't know me."

"Okay." Joan sounded annoyed.

"I was hoping that you and I could meet. It's kind of important. I could come to you . . . to your house, or we could meet somewhere else, wherever you—"

"Are you calling about your house, because I'd be happy to come to you."

"No, sorry. I didn't have a different number for you, so I'm calling your work number. But this isn't about work. It's a . . . it's a personal situation."

There was a short pause, then Joan said, "Do you want to tell me what it's about?"

"Yes," I said, "although I'd love to be able to do it in person. I just think it would be better. You and I have a mutual friend, and . . . you'll understand when we talk."

Again, there was a pause. I could sense that she was very close to just telling me to fuck off and hanging up the phone. If she did, there wasn't much I could do about it. Before she could speak, I said, "I'm sorry this sounds so mysterious. I don't mean to spook you, but it's important. Is there a place near you we could meet, maybe even a park or something? I'd come to you."

"Okay, sure. What's your name again?"

"Oh, great. Thank you, Joan. My name is Addie. Like I said, we haven't met, but it would be great to talk with you. Is there a good time?"

"I could meet you this afternoon."

"Oh, my God. That would be amazing," I said. "Just pick a place and I'll be there."

"There's a state park near me, called Endicott Farms."

"Okay, I can find it."

"It has two entrances, one that brings you to a trailhead and one that brings you to a petting zoo and a farm stand. I'll meet you at the trailhead parking lot."

"Sounds perfect. What time?"

"I could do four o'clock if that works for you. How will I recognize you?"

I laughed and told her that I'd recognize her. I could tell I was making her nervous, but I also knew that she was interested. And being interested in something usually trumps being nervous about something.

With some time to kill I walked slowly back to Henry's apartment. Along the way I called the landline at Monk's House and my father picked up.

"Everything going all right, Dad?" I said.

"Ah, Lil. When are you coming back?"

"Soon, I hope. Is Mom feeding you?"

"Mostly salads, but she made some spaghetti last night. Lil, I was looking for a book and couldn't find it."

"What book was that?"

"The one I was reading a while ago, and now I've just forgotten its name. It was by that Scottish writer, and it was in diary form . . ."

"Was it *Any Human Heart*?" I said.

"That's the one."

"Check the side table by the yellow chair in the living room, and if you don't see it there then I'd look on the coffee table on the back porch."

"Oh, here's your mother. She wants to say something."

My mother told me that the rabbits had eaten all her savoy cabbage.

"They probably need it more than we do," I said.

"I know you're joking, Lily, but rabbits will eat anything. When are you coming home? Can I have you pick some things up?"

"That's why I called. I'll be back soon but don't know exactly when. Are you two going to survive without me?"

"Your father can't find anything, but he did agree to clean the low gutters on the north side of the house."

"I'll do that when I get back. Dad shouldn't go anywhere near a ladder unless you're trying to kill him."

"Well . . . ," my mother said.

I had reached Henry's apartment building and told my mother I needed to go and that I would call them back as soon as I knew when I was coming home. On the second-floor landing of the apartment building, as I was inserting a key into the door, a middle-aged woman emerged from the other apartment, holding a miniature poodle in the crook of her free arm. "Oh," she said, when she saw me.

I smiled at her. "Sorry, I should have let you know I'd be in here. I'm Henry's girlfriend, Addie. I'm looking after Pyewacket."

"Oh," the woman said. "How is he doing?"

"He's critical, still," I said, "and unresponsive. I think we're all hopeful that he'll be okay."

"Do you know what happened to him? Not *what* happened to him, I mean, but *why* it happened to him?" The woman was short and stout, with dyed blue hair and granny glasses. Her dog stared at me with distrustful eyes.

"I know nothing, and they tell me nothing." I could hear Pye meowing on the other side of the door, so I opened it.

"If you need anything," the woman said, and I smiled at her before shutting the door.

After checking Pye's food dish I pulled my bag out from under its hiding place and picked an outfit to wear for the afternoon meeting. I put on the flannel skirt, deciding that it was warm and sunny enough outside that I didn't need to wear tights. I looked through my temporary tattoos, picking two—one a line drawing of Chucky the doll with the words *Let's play* and one of an ornate dagger, part of its blade missing so it would look like it was piercing my skin—and put them on the front of my thighs so that they'd be visible under the hem of my skirt. It was a little much, I thought, but if I was hoping to get Joan to talk with me, then it wouldn't hurt if I looked like someone unbothered by the idea of killing.

I stood in front of the mirror before leaving the apartment, looking at myself in my disguise, and had a moment of total lucidity, understanding something about illusion and reality that passed as soon as it had made itself known to me. I stepped in closer and really looked at my face. I had put on a lot of eye makeup, and I did feel transformed. I wondered why I was doing this, then remembered that it was Henry who had badly wanted to discover the truth of who Joan really was. I was just doing a favor for him. And Henry was the reason I was not spending the remainder of my life behind bars. He deserved a favor.

I arrived at Endicott Park at three thirty and parked near the farm. A group of children had been brought to see the goats and the pigs. There were blue skies overhead and the air was cool and dry. I watched one of the little boys wander away from the pens of farm animals, crouch in front of a stump on the ground. It took me a moment to see that he was staring at a busy red squirrel a few feet away. "Justin, buddy, over here," one of the daycare workers said, and he turned and made his way back to the group.

Wandering past the farm I found a large wooden sign that had a map of multiple trails and figured out how to walk to the parking lot where I was supposed to meet Joan. I walked slowly, past a meadow bordered on three sides by crumbling stone walls, then through a brief thicket of dense woods. I got to the small parking lot a little before four. It was empty except for a Subaru Outback. The parking lot by the farm was much larger, and filled with cars.

I found a large boulder, moss blanketing one side, and leaned against it to wait. At five minutes past four a silver BMW pulled into the lot and I knew at once it had to be Joan. I felt a familiar calm come over me, my senses sharpening, then reminded myself that I was Addie Logan, and I was a nervous person.

Joan got out of the car and came around the front side, spotting me as I stepped onto the gravel parking lot. She was short but took long strides and was wearing black leggings and a dark green fleece top. Her shiny hair was pulled back into a tight ponytail, and when she spotted me I saw something soften in her, as though she'd instantly decided I didn't pose a threat.

"Addie," she said, and I nodded, taking another step forward but not reaching out my hand. Joan took a breath in through her nose, and said, "Should we take a walk? How are those shoes?"

I was wearing a used pair of Converse sneakers, and said that they were fine. Joan began down the path that led through the woods, and I caught up to her. "Thank you so much for meeting me here," I said. "I wouldn't have asked, but . . . you know, it's important."

"What did you want to talk with me about?" Joan said.

"It's about Richard Seddon. I was a close friend of his."

Joan turned her head to look at me. She had round eyes, very blue. Her skin was pale except for two splotches of red on either cheek. "You're the second person I've talked with recently who wanted to know if I knew Richard Seddon. Trust me, I didn't."

"Well, he told me he knew you," I said.

Joan stopped. "This is the Richard Seddon who just blew himself up in Cambridge, right? I'm sorry, but he was a freak who I went to school with when I was a kid. I didn't know him then, and I don't know him now. I have no idea why he went to see Henry Kimball with a bomb. Maybe it had something to do with high school and James Pursall but if it does, I don't know anything about it."

I was watching her carefully. She seemed angry, the way most people do when they've been caught in some kind of lie. I decided to say what it was that I had come here to say. "Joan, he told me he knew you, and he told me that you two killed people together."

CHAPTER 34

JOAN

The strange-looking woman stared at her with those flat green eyes, waiting for her to say something. "He told you that?" Joan said.

"He didn't tell me details, but he told me that you two had a special bond. I want to talk with you because I know that side of Richard, too."

Joan shook her head. "I'm sorry, you're wasting your time. I think Richard Seddon must have had some kind of sick fantasy about me. I have no idea why, and I have no idea why you're here, honestly. If you think Richard Seddon was some kind of murderer, you should go to the police."

"I'm not interested in going to the police. I mean, Richard's dead, right? But he was my friend, and I know that you were his friend, so I wanted to meet you."

Joan gave this freak her most condescending look, and said, "He actually wasn't my friend. That's what I'm telling you."

They were stopped now, in the dark woods, leaves falling around them. The woman, Addie Logan, was just looking at Joan, studying her. Joan's mind was racing, trying to quickly figure out the best approach to this woman that Richard Seddon had clearly confided in. Right now, her gut instinct was to deny everything, to deny she'd ever even known Richard, at all.

"Okay," Addie finally said, jutting her lower lip out a little, as though she were a disappointed child. "All I want you to know is that I'm on your side, just like I was on Richard's side. And that I wanted to meet you, that's all, and I also wanted to tell you the reason that Richard brought that bomb to that investigator's office was because he knew everything. He knew about what the two of you did to your husband and that slut he was seeing, but he also knew about other things. Richard told me that Henry Kimball knew all about Kennewick, what you two did at the Windward Resort."

The woman paused, and Joan tried to keep the surprise and fear off her face. She hadn't expected to hear anything about Maine. She took a deep breath that she hoped looked like exasperation, and said, "I'm sorry, Addie, but it's clear that Richard told you a lot of made-up stories. I'm not angry at you for believing them, but just know that I'm telling you the truth. And now I'm going to walk back to my car and go home."

Joan began to walk, but Addie stayed by her side, saying, "I knew you'd say that. I get it. I really do. But just know that I want to be your friend, that I want to help you. And I know a way I can get rid of Henry Kimball for good."

Joan spun, her jaw frozen, and finally let herself yell. "Hey, freak," she said. "Fuck off." Then she turned and kept walking, and the woman stayed where she was. When Joan was back in the parking lot she got into her car, still in a rage, and began to pull out of the lot, but then stopped in front of the green Subaru, the only other car in the lot. Was this that woman's car? It was registered in Massachusetts, and there were two bumper stickers on the back, one an OBAMA BIDEN sticker and one that said NO FARMS, NO FOOD. The car didn't exactly fit the woman that Joan had just been talking with. Addie Logan had also not emerged from the woods yet. Had she parked in the other lot? And if so, why?

Joan pulled out on the road and headed for home, her head spinning. She calmed herself by trying to think logically about the situation. What exactly had she learned? One thing was certain and that was that the woman calling herself Addie Logan must have truly known Richard Seddon, and that Richard had confided in her about what they'd done together. How else would she have known about Kennewick and the Windward Resort? For the moment Joan put aside her feelings about that, the hurt she felt that Richard had betrayed her, and concentrated on what he might have told Addie, and if any of it could be proved. Obviously, it could be proved that she and Richard were at the Windward Resort at the same time, there when Duane Wozniak had drowned. But so what? No one could prove they had met, or talked, or planned anything. And it was the same with their time in high school. Richard was friends with James Pursall, and James had killed Joan's ex-friend Madison. But, again, so what? It was all just speculation.

Joan was more worried about what would happen if the police discovered that it was Richard Seddon who had committed the murders of her husband and Pam O'Neil. Richard had no connection with either of them. No, that wasn't entirely true. He had gone to high school with her husband, and that was a connection. But he'd also gone to high school and elementary school with Joan. And then they'd figure out that they'd been at the Windward Resort together. They'd piece it together.

Back at her house, Joan paced, still wearing her quilted Burberry coat. She told herself to calm down, took the coat off, and got herself a glass of wine. Then she went to her computer and did a search for

Addie Logan, along with Addison Logan, not coming up with any-thing that seemed related to the woman she'd met. But that didn't mean that Addie Logan wasn't for real. She was clearly a weirdo, with those creepy tattoos on her thighs, and that haircut. How had she met Richard in the first place? It was probably some sort of gam-ing thing. Joan imagined that Richard was still into those types of pursuits, and Addie Logan looked like someone who would definitely be into gaming, as well, despite the fact that she was clearly in her thirties. So Richard and this woman had met and became friends, or became more than friends, and Richard told her what he'd done. And the person he'd done it with.

That was the part that was really bothering her, the part that was making her feel like she wanted to peel the skin right off her own body. She always believed that what Richard and she shared was some kind of sacred bond. And it wasn't just that it put them in danger for either of them to talk about it, it was more than that. It was only between them. And Joan knew that Richard knew that too. So why had he told this woman Addie? Because he trusted her? Because he knew she was like him?

Joan got up and was pacing again. She felt as though everything was coming down around her. First, she'd found out from her sister that someone—obviously Henry Kimball—was asking questions about Kennewick, and now this goth chick showed up out of the blue with the same information. Did Henry have actual evidence? Was that why Richard had felt the need to go to his office with a bomb? And had Richard meant to kill himself, as well? Was it a suicide attack?

There were too many questions that Joan didn't have an answer for, and she wondered if she even needed the answers. Maybe the smart thing to do was to play dumb and hope for the best. She and Richard had been careful, very careful. She told herself to stop thinking about it.

But that night, lying alone on the king-sized bed in her pitch-black bedroom, Joan kept going over the encounter in the woods. Maybe she should have been nicer to the strange woman, found out everything she knew. She did say that she wanted to be friends, that she wanted to help her. What exactly did that mean?

Joan had learned very early in life that there were exactly two types of people. The ones that were on your side, and the ones that weren't. Her sister, for example, had never been on her side, probably not from the moment that Joan had been born. Joan had taken Lizzie's specialness away from her, her position as center of her family, and Lizzie was never going to forgive Joan for that. For a while when Joan was young, her friend Madison had been on her side, someone Joan could tell anything and everything to. There was no judgment. And then, in high school, Joan had overheard some of Madison's new friends saying how Joan hadn't gotten her period yet, and knew, instantly, that Madison had betrayed her. And in that moment Joan had written Madison off. It had been coming for a while, to be honest. She knew that Madison was a backstabber, so she shouldn't have been surprised when she got stabbed herself. And after that she shifted Madison into a new category, and even though they might still talk, or share some things in common, Madison was dead to her, a member of the category of "not on her side." And by senior year she was dead to everyone else, as well.

It hurt that it turned out Richard had betrayed her. She suspected he had his reasons, but that would never change the facts. But she didn't want to think about Richard anymore. Now she was interested in Addie Logan, who'd told her she wanted to be a friend. It *was* interesting. Not that she trusted this person who had come out of nowhere, but not trusting her now didn't mean that she couldn't trust her at some point in the future. Maybe she was for real. And if she really wanted to help her out, maybe she'd be dumb to turn that down. Because Joan did have a problem, and that problem was Henry Kimball. She'd been thinking how nice it would be if he never regained consciousness, and now she was wondering if there was a way to ensure that happened, and if Addie Logan might be an asset in that particular situation.

CHAPTER 35

LILY

Before returning to Henry's apartment I parked my car in the Summer Shack lot again, then walked until I found a restaurant that seemed busy enough I wouldn't be noticed too much. It was a Cuban place on the line between Cambridge and Somerville and I sat at the bar, ordered wine and empanadas.

I wondered how Henry was doing. The last time I'd done a Google search on him nothing new had come up, which told me that he was probably still alive.

My wine arrived, delivered by a heavily tattooed bartender who had hair almost as blond as mine, although hers was down past her shoulders. "Here you go, hon," she said, and I could see myself through her eyes, how my appearance—dyed hair, nose ring, thrift-store cardigan—somehow made me more approachable than I usually was. I sipped my wine and wondered what Joan Grieve Whalen was thinking about me right now. I'd upset her, as I'd known I would, but I didn't know yet if my upsetting her was going to bring her closer to me or not. My plan was to wait a few days, to see if she tried to get in touch with me. I thought she probably would, just to find out how much I really knew, and to find out if I was serious when I'd told her I wanted to be her friend.

The question now was where I should wait for her. It was increasingly risky for me to be staying in Henry Kimball's empty apartment, although I liked spending time with Pye. But the longer I hid there the higher the chances that someone would see me. And it was possible it would be someone who would recognize me. I was thinking specifically of Detective Roberta James, Henry's ex-partner, and someone who I suspected was taking a keen interest in what had happened to Henry in recent weeks.

So I was thinking of returning home, shocking my parents with my new hair, but figuring that I could cover up the temporary tattoos with a pair of jeans. I decided to think about it tomorrow, that it would be fine to spend one more night at Henry's place.

It turned out I didn't need to make a decision about where to go next. The following morning at seven my burner phone rang while I was getting ready to leave Henry's apartment to go seek out coffee and breakfast.

"Hi," I said into the phone, finding myself naturally using the same nervy voice that I'd given Addie the day before when I'd met with Joan.

"It's Joan."

"I know," I said. "Thank you for calling me."

"I thought maybe we could continue our conversation from yesterday. I'd like to know everything Richard said about me."

"You were really important to him."

"Well . . . we can talk about that."

"Okay. Where do you want to meet? I could come to that same place again."

"No. Let's go somewhere where we can sit and talk for a while. Where do you live?"

"I live in Allston but I can meet you anywhere you want to meet," I said.

"So there's a library in Fairview."

"Uh-huh."

"Let's meet there at two this afternoon. I'll find somewhere to sit where no one can hear us talk. Just wander around until you find me."

"Okay," I said, "I'll see you then."

I sat for a moment thinking about the phone conversation then left the apartment and walked back to my car, driving west toward Fairview. I didn't know where the town library was, but it wouldn't be too hard to find. I wondered why she'd picked a library for our meeting place. I suppose she wanted someplace public but also private, a place where we could sit and talk, and other people wouldn't necessarily see us.

It was another nice fall day and as I took back roads across rural Massachusetts I thought about the years I'd spent here, as an archivist for Winslow College. I'd loved so much about that time in my life. I had a sense of purpose, and a small house of my own. When I had free time I would either read or walk in the woods. It was ideal, in a way, but thinking back on that time now it was all a blur of interchangeable days. I thought much more about the times in my life when I was changing the world around me and not just existing in it. I thought about what I'd done to that predator named Chet who had stayed at my parents' spare apartment the summer I turned fourteen. I thought about my first and only love, Eric Washburn. And I thought constantly about the events of just a few years ago when I'd met Ted Severson and agreed to help him murder his wife. Nothing good had come of it, any of it really, except for the fact that it led me to Henry Kimball, and the strange relationship that we now shared.

I passed Fruitlands, a nature preserve and the historical site of the farmhouse where Amos Bronson Alcott failed to establish a commune based on transcendentalism and the Shaker religion. It was a place I had visited often when I lived in the area and I pulled into its parking lot now. The buildings weren't open to visitors but I wandered the woods for an hour, at one point sitting in the hollow base of a twisted apple tree, and just watching the natural world. A family of turkeys wandered by, and chipmunks rustled through the fallen leaves. On my way back I passed a hay meadow that had been recently mown, and saw a dark fox that looked as though it had found a nest of mice. He spotted me too, and we stared at one another for a while before he decided I was not a threat and continued digging in his meadow.

On the way back to my car I passed the farmhouse, remembering a tour I'd taken years ago and how everyone in our group had laughed when the tour guide said that the Shaker religion forbade procreation. A man had laughed and said, "I wonder why that religion's not around anymore?" as though he'd been the first person to ever say that. And I remembered thinking at the time that I could get behind a religion that would eventually lead to the end of the human race, the world returned to birds and animals.

I arrived at the library exactly at two in the afternoon, after spending the intervening hours at a diner in the next town over. The library was a hundred-year-old structure of brick and slate roof, with a large addition that looked as though it had been added sometime in the 1970s. I pushed my way through the front doors into the familiar smell that was a combination of well-preserved books and the acidity of newsprint. It was quiet in the library on a weekday afternoon, a few mothers with small children in the annex to the left of the front desk. I turned right and headed into the high-ceilinged main room, an open balcony running along three of its sides. I cut down one of the aisles between shelves and found a small seating area but no one was there. I wandered the entire first floor, only spotting an elderly man, asleep with that day's *Boston Globe* across his lap. I climbed a spiral staircase to the balcony level, lined with shorter shelves, and found Joan in one corner, seated on a wooden chair that was up-holstered in sturdy green fabric. She held a hardcover book, *Full Dark, No Stars,* by Stephen King. I sat down across from her.

"Tell me everything Richard said about me," she said, "and keep your voice low."

I expected this. I knew she wouldn't admit to anything unless she had total trust in me, and I wasn't sure I was ever going to get that. But I had to try.

I said, "He wasn't specific, at all. He said that he wasn't supposed to tell anyone, and he only told me some things because I begged him to. The thing is, the way we met . . . and I'm telling you this in total confidence . . . was from a message board on a website. It's not there anymore, but it was an anonymous place where you could talk about how you'd gotten away with murder. We met there, and eventually we shared our real emails, and then eventually we met—"

"So you're telling me you killed someone?"

I looked at her, while chewing on the inside of my cheek in a way I knew was visible. "You're not wearing a wire or anything, are you?"

She made a face like I'd just told her the dumbest thing she'd ever heard. I imagined briefly the succession of girls in Joan's past who had seen that very face: the elementary school friend who still believed in Santa Claus; the girl in middle school who'd never kissed a boy; a series of mildly bullied friends and enemies.

"Well, are you?" I said.

She stood up and spread her arms out wide. She was wearing a light gray cashmere sweater, tight white jeans, and black boots. I knew she wasn't wearing a wire, of course, but stood and ran my hands down her sides, feeling a crackle of static electricity. I took off my leather jacket and she did the same for me, checking the pockets.

"I'm only telling you because I know that Richard trusted you," I said, "so I suppose I trust you too. When I was in high school, I found out that my best friend was seeing this much older guy, a professor at a nearby university. He'd been invited to give a reading to our English class and that's how she met him. She told me everything about him, how he was getting her involved in all this creepy sex stuff, and how he'd started to hurt her. I knew the guy, as well, because the three of us had hung out, and he'd hit on me a bunch of times. So one night I went over and told him I wanted to talk with him but in his car. We sat in his back seat, and I made him close his eyes, which was really easy because he thought it was a sex thing. And I slit his throat with a kitchen knife."

Joan was watching me, and I could tell she wasn't sure whether to believe me or not. "It wasn't easy," I said. "And I knew that if his body was ever found I would get caught. So I made sure to hide that car, and his body in it, in a place that no one would *ever* find. And they never did. He's a missing person's case, now, and that's all he'll ever be."

"Wow," Joan said. I still didn't know if she believed me. The story wasn't true. The part about my friend and the creepy older professor was, however. And I had definitely formed a plan to kill that man and hide him in his car. I had even begun to dig a hole in some nearby woods, but I had never gone forward with it. My friend had stopped seeing the professor, and I hadn't completed the hole, and I let it go. But sometimes I remember it as something that actually happened, just like occasionally I pretend things that have happened actually didn't.

"So you told Richard all that?"

"I told him on the message board. Well, I told everyone on the message board because it was anonymous. But then he and I started sending private messages back and forth and eventually we told each other our real names. And then, eventually, we met."

"And what did he tell you?"

"He was really vague, at first. He said he'd been involved in two incidents he could talk about. The first was when his cousin drowned in Maine when he was just fifteen. And the second was a school shooting. He didn't go into specifics, but he said that he had help from the same person in both circumstances."

"And he said that person was me," Joan said.

"He didn't, actually. Not at first. He said it was a girl, and that he would never tell me your name, even though he trusted me. He wouldn't have, either. But then that detective showed up, and he really freaked out." I lowered my voice, and leaned in. "We met, the two of us, at the place we always meet. It's this divey bar in Waltham, and he told me how he was involved with the murder-suicide that had happened in Bingham. I knew all about it, because it was big news, and I was just interested, I guess. I'd read about it, and I read how both the dead man and his wife had gone to the same high school. To Dartford-Middleham. And I read your name, and I knew. I mean, I knew even before I googled you and found out that you had been one of the survivors of the school shooting. I told Richard, our Richard, about it, saying your name, and he tried to deny it but he couldn't. I saw it in his eyes, and eventually he told me that you were the one. He didn't want to tell me, but he knew he was caught out.

"The other thing you need to know is that at this point he wasn't worried about my knowing who you were, he was worried about the detective. That detective had tracked him down, and asked him all these questions, and Richard knew that it was just a matter of time. The last thing he told me was that he was going to take care of it."

Joan was thinking. I had tried to keep things vague enough, to make it look as though I only had the most general picture of what had happened, so that I wouldn't screw up a detail. I knew that she wanted to trust me.

When she finally spoke, she said, "Do you know if Richard meant to kill himself at the same time as Henry Kimball, or was it an accident?"

I leaned back in my chair, realizing just how tense my body had been. "I don't know," I said.

Joan turned her head slightly, her eyes on a tall painting on the wall, a full-body portrait of some long-dead library patron, holding a leather-bound book in one hand. She was deciding whether she could trust me or not, and I honestly didn't know which way she would go. But when she turned her eyes back to me I knew somehow before she spoke that I had hooked her.

"You think if Henry Kimball lives, he'll be able to prove that Richard killed my husband?" she said.

We stayed in the library for another hour. As far as we knew no one had even come up to the balcony level all afternoon. I left first, walking briskly to my car that I had parked along the street instead of in the lot. I'd been stupid to not change the license plates and if she'd left first, then there would have been a possibility of her seeing me get in a car with Connecticut plates. Driving back to Cambridge I told myself that I needed to be even more careful moving forward, especially now that I knew what I had to do.

I was sick of eating out, so I bought a sandwich at a sub shop in Huron Village, and took it back to the apartment. It had just gotten dark, and there were no lights on in any of Henry's windows. I went upstairs and pushed open the door, stepping inside, and heard the sound of Pye jumping from the bed to the floor, then bounding toward me. I looked him in the eye to see if he was disappointed it was me returning to the apartment and not Henry. I couldn't tell. Maybe he was simply hungry.

After eating I got into bed and continued to read *The Green Marriage,* but only managed a chapter before putting it back on the bedside table. I turned off the light and went over the entirety of the conversation with Joan Whalen. The more we had talked the more I had sensed in her the excitement she felt at what we were planning to do. I don't think I generally understand people, but I had understood Joan that afternoon. She and Richard had taken lives together, and once you've done that and gotten away with it, everything else in life pales a little. And now she'd found me—not me, exactly, but Addie Logan—and her life was exciting again. It wasn't meaning she was after, but the thrill of transgression.

"How are you planning on killing him?" she'd asked me.

"I'm going to smother him with a pillow. It shouldn't be too hard."

"I have a better way," she said, her voice just a whisper. "Get a piece of piano wire and sharpen one end, bending it slightly. It just needs to be about five inches long. You push the sharp end through the inside corner of one of his eyes, straight into the brain, then twist it around. Do it a couple of times, and if you do it right, there won't be any external sign of damage. It will just look like he had a brain hemorrhage. They'll never even know it was a murder."

I'd widened my eyes, and said, "How do you know all this? Did you do it?"

I saw her contemplate lying, but instead she said, "No, but I read about it. It's just a suggestion. I trust you."

"Okay," I said, and reached out and touched her leg, and saw something else in her eyes. I thought at first it was superiority, but then I recognized it as happiness.

CHAPTER 36

JOAN

After getting home Joan stared into her refrigerator for a while, but she was too amped up to even think about cooking dinner. She went and changed instead, got back into her car, and drove three towns over to a trendy farm-to-table bistro called Glasshouses. She'd been once with just her husband, and once with a group of friends, mainly real estate people that Richard had known.

She entered the restaurant and told the hostess she was looking for a bar seat, then made her way to the long, elegant bar constructed from refurbished barn wood. She took a seat near the far end of the bar, and only after her water was poured did she swivel on her stool to survey the other patrons at the bar and in the dining room. It didn't look as though there was anyone she knew. She turned back to the bartender, young enough to be sporting what was probably an ironic mustache, and ordered a glass of cabernet and the beef tartare.

It wouldn't be the end of the world if there was anyone she knew in the restaurant—widows needed to eat, after all—but she was glad that so far no one had recognized her. Something about her conversation with Addie Logan had made her want to celebrate, to be alone in a place full of people. She felt good. Not as good as she'd felt all those years ago when she'd met Richard Seddon for the first time at the Windward Resort and she realized there were other people like her in the world, but meeting Addie made her feel pretty darn good, especially the fact that they had concocted a plan, one they were putting into action tomorrow. Who knew what would happen next? Maybe Addie was a total flake, but, then again, maybe she wasn't.

The bartender gave her a taste of the wine, and it tasted thin to her. She must have shown it on her face because he cracked open another bottle almost immediately—a Spanish wine—and splashed it into a new glass. It tasted unfinished somehow, raw and funky, and she nodded at him. When the beef tartare arrived, she mixed the raw egg into the meat, adding a little bit of onion, then devoured all of it, asking for more toast at some point. She hadn't remembered being this hungry in years, and if she had been a little less self-conscious, she would have ordered a second plate. Instead, she ordered the duck breast and another glass of the same wine.

When the food was gone and she'd said no to the dessert menu, a man who seemed vaguely familiar to her tapped her on the shoulder.

"Joan Whalen, right?"

"Uh-huh," she said.

"You won't remember me, but I actually went to your wedding. I was a plus-one. Olivia Waring's date."

She actually did remember him, very vaguely. Olivia was one of Richard's college friends, one of those fake-nice people that was always complimenting everyone, and the only reason she remembered this guy—Olivia's date—was because he'd worn a white linen suit and Richard had mentioned it, saying he thought it was pretentious.

"Sure," Joan said. "You wore a white suit."

"Ha," he said. "I did. Olivia made a joke about it, said I was up-staging the bride."

"Yes, I'm still livid."

"I'm sure you are."

"Are you still with Olivia?"

"God, no," he said, and looked back toward the dining area. Joan followed his eyes, looking for this man's wife or some new girlfriend anxiously waiting for him. Instead, a group of three men were getting up from a table, nodding and waving in this man's direction.

"Are those your friends?" Joan said.

"Those are the men I just had dinner with. But they're leaving now, and I have my own car."

"Tell me your name again."

"You remembered my suit but not my name?"

"I did."

"It's George Mayer. Nice to see you again."

"Nice to see you, too." They shook hands, and a few more memories of this man came back to her. He'd actually been stunning in his suit, which was why Richard had made the comment, and he was fairly stunning now in a dark blue woolen shirt and gray jeans.

"I heard about what happened with Richard," he said, "with all of it, and I was totally shocked." Joan just nodded. "And I'm so sorry for what you must be going through," he continued. "I can't even imagine."

It was the conversation she'd been hoping to avoid when she'd decided to go to a restaurant, but she put her hand on his arm and said, "Thank you."

"Hey, you look as though you're leaving but I'd love to buy you a drink if you have the time. No pressure." He was leaning up against a stool, ready to slide on top of it.

"Do you live around here?" Joan said.

"I don't. I'm here for work. That dinner was a client dinner."

"Oh. Where are you staying?"

"Wadsworth Inn. About ten minutes away. You know it?"

"Yeah, of course. Why don't we just go directly there," Joan said, sliding off her own stool, suddenly feeling short next to George Mayer, who had at least a foot on her.

"Okay, sure," he said, and Joan led him out of the restaurant.

She got back to her house at five the next morning. At the inn, she'd managed to extricate herself from the tangle of sheets, and then the room itself, without waking George.

After making coffee she sat on the back deck, watching the early morning mist burn off, wondering why she didn't get up early more often. She felt as good as she'd felt in a long while. It was cold, but she'd changed, after getting home, into jeans and a thick sweater, and the coffee mug was keeping her warm for the moment. Why was it that when you swam in icy water in the summer your body acclimated to the cold, but in cold air you just kept getting colder? When her coffee was gone, she went back inside the house. On the island in the kitchen was her purse. She pulled out the burner phone that she'd gotten the day before from Addie Logan and looked at it. It was a flip phone with a small digital screen and didn't do a whole lot more than make phone calls. Her instructions for later that morning were pretty simple. Call the Boston Police Department and tell them there was a bomb placed in the oncology wing of the Boston Memorial Hospital, the same hospital where Henry Kimball was currently recovering. She knew they'd try to keep her on the line, and she'd been wondering if it made sense to say more, maybe that her husband had died of cancer and she was getting her revenge. But there was no real reason for her to do that. The call was only a slight diversion, and maybe not even necessary. Addie Logan had told her that she worked for seven years in a hospital as a receptionist, and she said that bomb threats were not uncommon, but all personnel were immediately notified and it put the staff on edge. It would make it a little easier for her to walk into Henry's hospital room and take care of him the way they'd discussed.

Joan wondered if it really made a difference calling in the bomb threat, but she also thought it was Addie's way of making sure Joan was at least somewhat involved with the plot to kill Henry Kimball. It would also potentially connect Joan with what happened to Henry if they could prove she was the one who made the call, and for that reason, Joan was considering not making it. She just wasn't sure yet. Maybe it *would* help Addie, and if Addie was able to get rid of Henry, Joan's life got safer, in return. She decided to make a game-time decision.

When it was ten thirty Joan went to her car and removed the transponder, leaving it in the garage as she drove two towns over to the busy lot of one of the farm stands that sold pumpkins and apple cider doughnuts during the fall season. She had the flip phone with her but had left her own phone at home. She wasn't sure it was going to make any difference that she wasn't near her house if she made the call but decided it couldn't hurt. She sat in her car, the engine turned off, the window cracked. It was a weekday but there were a lot of cars in the lot, city couples hunting through the pumpkin piles for perfectly round specimens, taking pictures of one another for their Instagram accounts. She decided to make the call. She trusted Addie, actually, or at least she trusted that she hadn't suggested the bomb threat as a way to implicate her in the crime.

At exactly eleven she dialed the number for the Boston Police Department, then holding her mouth open the way she'd practiced at home, she said, "I'm calling to report that there is a bomb in the oncology wing of the Boston Memorial Hospital." The words sounded garbled in her own ears, but the woman on the other end of the line calmly said, "Can I have your name and where you're calling from?"

"The bomb will go off in ten minutes. I don't want to hurt anybody, but I want to destroy the building. You've been warned."

She hung up, skin buzzing. She put the phone in her pocket and got out of the car, wandering through the displays of pumpkins to the large market building. Outside were pallets covered with fall produce, apples, squash, brussels sprouts still on the stalk, plus piles of decorative gourds and ornamental corn. She skirted around the building, passing a parking lot that was for employees only, and found a half-filled dumpster. She pulled the SIM card from the phone, snapped it in half, then threw the pieces, along with the disabled phone, into the dumpster.

Instead of going straight home, she wandered through the market, picking up a half gallon of apple cider and a frozen chicken potpie. Driving home she listened to NPR, curious if there'd be anything about an evacuation at Boston Memorial, but there was nothing, of course. And there was nothing on the news that night, after she'd eaten half the chicken pie, while flipping through news channels and drinking wine. Of course, if everything had gone according to plan there would be nothing on the news. All that would have happened was a fake bomb threat, and a patient in critical condition suffering an entirely predictable brain hemorrhage. Neither event would be remotely newsworthy.

She was starting to fall asleep on the sofa in front of a *Real Housewives* marathon, so she forced herself up the stairs, stripped out of her clothes, and slid under the bedcovers. Her bones were heavy, and she realized she hadn't really properly slept in two days. Twenty-four hours ago she'd been in bed with the man in the white linen suit. His name suddenly escaped her. Even though she was exhausted she went through the routine she used every night to fall asleep, closing her eyes and imagining herself tipped back on the surface of the sea, sun baking her skin, the cool water keeping her afloat, and the sky impossibly blue.

CHAPTER 37

LILY

That morning I cleared all my possessions from Henry's apartment, gave Pye enough food to last two days, and was outside in the cold dawn before most of the world had woken up.

I walked to my car, wondering what I was going to do with my day. There were a few errands, of course, but not enough to fill the long stretch of hours ahead. I drove into Boston, filling up already with commuter traffic, and parked near Copley Square. I spent most of that day in the Boston Public Library, finding and finishing *The Green Marriage*, then finding a biography of Margaret Cogswell, and reading the sections that talked about my father and their affair. I knew the story, of course. My father was a young, up-and-coming writer, married to Clarissa Pavlow, his first wife, and Margaret was engaged to Robert Rutherford, the painter. The two couples had met on the island of Crete, where my father and Margaret had been invited to a Marxist literary conference. The affair did not begin in Greece but back in London over the winter months, my father and Margaret meeting in secret at a friend's flat in Maida Vale. Reading the account, it occurred to me that all the players in that particular farce were now dead. Margaret, of course, and Clarissa, my father's first wife. The painter Robert Rutherford had been dead now for thirty years, and so was the owner of the love nest in north London. It was only my father who was left to remember the true specifics of what had happened that winter.

I left the library in the early afternoon, then bought some supplies and drove one last time out west. It was another pretty fall day but there were puddles on the road and it was clear it had rained at some point during the night. I spotted the muddy parking lot for a state-run conservation area and pulled in. I was the only car there and spun through a deep puddle a couple of times to splash mud onto my car. Then I got out and plastered mud onto my license plate, obscuring enough of it so that it would be impossible to read. I didn't know if it was necessary, but I knew it wouldn't hurt.

I left my car at a glorified convenience store in Dartford center, the type of place that sold local trail mix and organic wine along with lottery cards and potato chips. There was a gas station next to the convenience store and in the restroom I changed into the hiking pants and the fleece hoodie I'd bought in Boston. I also took out my nose ring, depositing it down the drain, and scrubbed my face of makeup. At the convenience store I bought bottled water and ham-and-cheese croissants, plus a map that showed the trails that crossed through Dartford. I didn't think I'd need the map—I'd spent part of the day memorizing the multiple ways to get to Joan's house—but, again, I figured it wouldn't hurt.

Most of the public trails in Dartford were essentially dirt sidewalks along the roads, separated from the sparse traffic by a single line of trees. But every once in a while, a trail would divert from the road and cut across old farm fields or through pine forests. Joan's house was only two miles from the center of town as the crow flew, but it took me over an hour to reach it through the adjacent woods, settling in the shadow of a large boulder where I had a view of the narrow backyard, and the screened-in deck. I watched the house for twenty minutes or so, and when I had detected no movement inside, I snuck around to the front driveway. The silver BMW was gone. Maybe it was possible someone else had the BMW and Joan was in the house, but I doubted it. I checked the front door, which was locked, then worked my way back around to the deck. The screen door was open but the sliding glass doors that led to the interior of the house were locked. I'd brought tools to deal with a locked door but decided to check the windows first, and I found one that slid open. I dropped into the dark room and shut the window behind me.

After waiting for a minute in order to listen to the house, I made my way to the kitchen. Inside the refrigerator there were two bottles of chardonnay, one opened, with about a half bottle left, and one still sealed. There was also a large plastic bottle of vitaminwater.

Before Joan returned, I was able to look at the rest of the house. It was a strange mix of dated furniture and high-end new pieces. The walls were all painted the same beige, and the kitchen had been remodeled at some recent point, the floor a dark slate, the back-splashes subway tiles. Both Joan Grieve and her departed husband, Richard Whalen, had grown up in the area and this was clearly one of their parents' houses. There were four bedrooms upstairs, the master plus three small rooms, one of which had been converted into a storage area, filled with boxes and old furniture. That was the room I waited in, creating a comfortable nook between the far wall and an unused bookshelf.

I didn't hear the car in the driveway, but I did hear the front door slam. It was midafternoon, and I settled in to wait.

She came upstairs once in the afternoon, probably to change, and then went back downstairs. I wasn't nervous. There was absolutely no reason to think she'd decide to pop into this particular room. Even if she did, I was ready.

Sometime around seven I could hear the distant sounds of the television. After three hours I decided she had most likely passed out in the television room but told myself to wait another twenty minutes just to be sure. With five minutes to spare, I heard the television turn off then listened to Joan's heavy footsteps on the stairs. She went down the hallway, away from the room I was hiding in, toward the master bedroom. The light in the hallway went out. I waited another hour.

It was midnight when I stood above her in her bedroom. She'd left the light on in the adjoining bathroom and the door cracked so I could easily see her. She was on her back, one hand pressed against a cheek. It looked as though she'd spun around at one point, the sheets twisted diagonally across her chest like a toga, her left breast exposed.

After removing the stun gun from my bag, a weapon I absolutely did not want to use, I said her name, softly at first, then loudly. She didn't move. Then I tapped gently at her face. Her eyes squinted a little but that was it. I held her by her shoulders and shook her. Again, nothing. I had spiked the half-filled bottle of wine and the vitaminwater with enough chloral hydrate to drop a football player. She'd clearly had either the wine or the water or both. I was amazed she'd made it up the stairs and into her bed. She was a fighter, I could see that, and for a moment I almost felt bad for her. But then I reminded myself that she'd always gotten someone else to do her dirty work for her.

I put the stun gun on the bedcovers within easy reach, just in case. Then I reached back into my backpack and removed the five-inch length of piano wire, its end sharpened and bent.

CHAPTER 38

JOAN AND RICHARD

Twenty-four hours after they had pushed Duane Wozniak off the Kennewick jetty and into the ocean, Joan and Richard had met at Uncle Murray's Book Nook at the Windward Resort. It hadn't been planned but neither was surprised that the other was there. They'd talked rapidly about what they'd done, and when they'd decided that they each needed to get back to their rooms they'd stood facing one another.

Joan blinked rapidly, smiling and showing all of her small, perfect teeth. "This is amazing," she said. "I feel so close to you." They hugged. "I can't believe we did what we did."

"I believe it," Richard said.

She was nodding. "This is going to sound like a strange thing to say, but it's almost like we're married. Secretly married. And instead of some stupid ceremony we did something so much more amazing. Does that sound weird?"

"No, I know what you mean. I feel the same way. Let's just say that we're married."

"Okay," Joan said, and he could see all the different strands of color in her eyes. It was a whole world in there. "We're married now, in a way that is more important than a real marriage. And only you and I will ever know about it."

Richard nodded.

"Let's kiss," Joan said. "Do you want to? Otherwise the last person I kissed will have been Duane."

"Okay," Richard said, but didn't immediately move his head. Joan stared up at him. She really did want to kiss him in a way she'd never wanted to kiss someone before. Kissing boys was usually about wanting to feel power, wanting to feel someone else's desire. But with Richard, at that moment, she wanted to kiss him purely for the physical sensation, to get closer to his body and his face. She stepped up onto his feet and pulled his head down to hers and pressed her lips to his. He was surprised by how warm her mouth was, how soft her lower lip felt against his. Richard thought a lot about that kiss in the ensuing years, and how it had actually felt like a wedding kiss, one that had sealed them together forever.

When they stopped kissing, they both laughed, and Joan said, her voice a little hoarse, "You're good at kissing."

"I've never done it before."

"Really?"

"Really."

"What do you think?"

"It's nice, but strange."

"That's what *I* think. I liked how it felt with you but most of the time I think how strange it is that humans want to put their mouths together."

"Very strange," Richard said. His eyes suddenly moved because there was a distant sound, like a door shutting somewhere in the hotel.

"We should go before anyone comes in here," Joan said.

Richard nodded.

Before she left, she looked at him and said, "My secret husband. I think I like that."

Richard nodded again, and Joan said, "Do you take me as your lawfully wedded wife, your secret wife?"

Richard, smiling, said, "I do."

"Ask *me* now."

"Okay. Do you take me as your lawfully wedded secret husband? Through sickness and in health? Until death do us part?"

"Oh, fancy," Joan said.

Richard shrugged.

Joan said, "I do."

CHAPTER 39

LILY

Four days after I'd returned to Monk's House I read that Joan Whalen Grieve had been found dead in her house, and that the cause of death appeared to be natural. I took a long afternoon walk through the woods to a small pond I liked, one that I'd named McElligot's Pond when I'd been young, after the Dr. Seuss book. It had been a particularly dry summer and my pond was now more of a swamp, but I sat quietly at its edge and thought about Joan and wondered if there would be more to the story, and if I would ever know about it. I was amazed to think she might be buried with no one knowing she'd been murdered in her bed. If so, she had devised her own death, and she had done so flawlessly.

It was cold now, almost every day, but I sat for as long as I could, my hands and feet growing numb. I recited a list of names to myself—Chet, Eric Washburn, Miranda Severson, Brad Daggett, Joan Grieve Whalen—then thought about Henry and how close he came to being on that list.

I have no regrets in my life even though I've killed people. I've always had a reason—a good reason—for what I've done. But I do think that if Henry had died on that cemetery on a hill that I would have regretted what I'd done. I hoped I wasn't just telling myself lies to make myself feel better, but who knows.

A week later a small item on the *Boston Globe*'s website said that Henry Kimball had been discharged from the hospital. I wondered how much he remembered about what had happened to him. And I wondered what he had thought when he heard that Joan was dead.

I still had the buzz cut but I'd let my hair grow out a little before going to another barber, this time in Connecticut, and my hair was now back to my natural color, a pale red.

When I had first returned from Cambridge my mother had been utterly baffled by my blond hair, and finally I told her I was dating a man who had suggested it, and that I wasn't dating him anymore.

I don't know if she believed me, but it made her forget about the haircut and start speculating about the man instead.

My father, who had not initially noticed the new hair, spotted it after we were playing a game of backgammon one night, when I was taking a long time on a move.

"Look at your hair, Lil," he said.

"Oh, you noticed."

"I knew you looked different when you came back from your trip, but I was so glad to see you that I barely paid attention."

"I thought novelists were meant to be observant."

He smirked. "God, no. No, that's not true. I actually have a theory about this."

"Oh, yeah," I said, pretty sure I'd heard it before, but willing to listen again.

"There are two kinds of writers," he said, "observers and imaginers. Even though my books are supposed to be realism, I'm basically an imaginer, with a little bit of observer dashed in. There's a lot of writers out there like me. And a few writers who are purely good observers. Updike's one of those. Incredible observation. Terrible imagination."

"You've given this some thought," I said.

"A little bit."

"Isn't there a William Faulkner quote about this?"

"I don't know. Is there?"

It was ringing a bell so I looked it up on my phone, no doubt irritating my father. "Yes," I said. "He said that authors need observation, imagination, and experience. And he said that any two of which or sometimes even one of which can supply the lack of the others."

My father frowned, then said, "Well, that second part is true. But the thing about experience is that it's overrated. If we're alive we have experience. You don't have to go on a fucking African safari to be a good writer. Barbara Pym never went anywhere. Philip Larkin never went anywhere."

"Didn't Barbara Pym go to—"

"No, writers just need either imagination or observation. That's all."

"So tell me an author who is purely imagination, besides fantasy writers?"

"I suspect that not all fantasy writers are bad observers, but maybe most of them are. Let me think of a good example. Oh, here's one and you won't like it, but your favorite author, Lil, Agatha Christie. All imagination and a terrible observer."

"You think so?"

"Oh, yeah. She cares about getting her plots right and doesn't care about getting the world right. Nothing wrong with it."

"Hmm," I said.

"Trust me, she was probably the same in real life. If you met Agatha Christie on a walk, she'd have no idea where she was. She'd just be dreaming up murder plots. We are who we are."

"Okay," I said.

"Don't get tetchy. It doesn't make her a bad writer, just a lousy observer. But the best writers, of course, are equal parts imagination and observation."

"Who are those?"

"Oh, you know, the biggies. Charles Dickens, Jane Austen. Shakespeare, of course."

"But not you?"

"Good lord, no. My novels are basically wish fulfillment, and I was lucky enough to be able to craft a decent sentence. But, honestly, I have zero idea how this world actually works."

I'd made my move and was waiting for my father to roll his dice. "I feel the same way as you do. About the world, I mean," I said, as he rolled a four and a five and groaned about it.

In early December, Henry came to visit. As usual, he didn't call ahead or send a letter. He just appeared on a cold and beautiful Saturday afternoon.

"This a good time?" he said as I came out onto the front stoop to see him. He had gotten out of his car and was leaning against it.

"It is," I said.

"What about for your parents?"

"I'll just tell them you were expected, and that they'd forgotten about it. They'll never know. And they'll be glad to see you."

He had brought a small overnight bag, so I showed him upstairs to the room he usually slept in. On the way we passed my mother in the kitchen prepping green beans for that night's dinner, and she got up and came over and gave Henry a hug, saying, "Oh, I'm so glad you're here," as though she really had been expecting him.

"Does your mother think I'm your boyfriend?" Henry said, after putting his bag down on the single bed in the guest room. I was standing in the doorway. He looked thin, which wasn't a surprise, and I had noticed a slight limp as he'd gone up the stairs.

"Probably," I said. "How are you feeling?"

"Physically I'm okay. Emotionally I'm a little shaky, like I'm living in a strange new world. It's not a good feeling when you wake up in the hospital and don't know why you're there."

"Is that what happened?"

"They told me that a bomb had gone off outside of my office and that it was brought there by Richard Seddon, but I don't remember that."

"Do you remember who Richard Seddon was?"

"A little bit. I know that he was friends with James Pursall, and I know that he was somehow connected with Joan Grieve, but it's fuzzy."

"You remember Joan?"

"Yes, I remember the case, and I remember finding her husband's body, and Pam's body. That's the last completely clear memory I have. The rest is . . . incomplete."

"Do you remember coming here?"

"When? After I'd found the bodies?"

"Yes," I said.

"I kind of remember that. No, I do remember. I wanted to talk with you about what had happened."

"You thought that there was a third person involved, someone Joan knew who had killed her husband and his girlfriend, and you wanted help figuring out who that person was."

Henry was nodding his head, his eyes on the ceiling, trying hard to remember. He sat down on the edge of the bed, and I moved into the bedroom, turning the desk chair so that it faced him and sitting down. "I told you all that?" he said.

"You did. And I think that you figured out that Richard Seddon was the third person, and he knew that you knew, and that was why he tried to kill you."

"And kill himself?"

"Maybe," I said. "I don't know. He brought a bomb to your office. Maybe he was going to leave it there or maybe he was going to blow both of you up."

"The police told me that I was on the other side of my office door when the bomb exploded, otherwise I wouldn't be here right now."

"That makes sense. You look pretty good, considering."

He pushed a lock of hair off his forehead and revealed a faded triangular scar. "My souvenir."

"Looks good."

"Your hair is different."

I reached up and touched it. I was wearing a headband that served no practical purpose except to cover up the awkward length of my hair. I hadn't decided whether I was going to tell Henry what had happened while he was in the hospital, recovering. If he specifically asked, I'd tell him, but he was clearly catching up with his own memories, and the thought that I had lived in his apartment for a time, and that I'd met Joan, might be too much for him.

"I'm growing it back out," I said.

"It looks good short, too."

He seemed tired, so I stood up, and told him to get settled, and that he should come down and join us at six, when my father would officially declare that cocktail hour had begun.

He did come down, only a little bit late, and he seemed much more like himself than he had that afternoon, maybe because he wasn't being asked to think about the time and the memories he'd lost. My father was thrilled to see him, of course, and I told him to tell

Henry his theory about novelists being either observers or imaginers, and the three of us spent an hour categorizing all the writers we could think of. My mother came in, and even joined the conversation, saying, "My friend, Martha Grausman, you know the one who got that one-person show for what are basically collages . . . I guess she's got imagination because I actually think she might be color-blind."

I went to bed early that night, before either Henry or my father, and lay in my childhood bedroom, listening to the sounds of the house, listening to the people who were still up and about, something I'd been doing for as long as I could remember. Listening to people I loved, for better or worse.

About fifteen minutes after I heard my father gallop recklessly up the back stairwell to his room, I listened as Henry walked slowly past my door, making his way down the second-floor hallway, then taking the old attic stairs to his guest room. And then the house was quiet.

After breakfast the following morning Henry and I took a long walk, skirting the meadow, then picking up the trail that connected with the conservation area where my favorite pond was located. Along the walk, he said, "Do you remember the first time we met?"

It was a game we had played before, reconstructing the way we had gotten to know each other. It was something I'd done maybe once or twice with Eric Washburn, the only serious boyfriend I'd ever had, and I recognized it as something lovers do. Construct a narrative. Tell it to each other. Ours, of course, was a warped version of that particular game. I said, "When you came to my house in Winslow to ask me about Ted Severson."

"And I knew that you were lying to me," Henry said.

"And I knew that you knew."

"So I came back to ask you why you lied to me."

"And then you started following me."

"Yes, I started to follow you."

"And then I tricked you into going to an empty cemetery, and I stuck a knife in you."

Henry had stopped, breathing a little bit heavily. We were at the top of a ridge and because most of the leaves were now off the trees there was a view down the slope of a hill, across a wooded area, all the way to the edges of McElligot's Pond, and he was looking at the view before turning to me.

"Do you remember what you said when you did it?"

"Of course, I do. I told you that I was sorry."

We started walking again, continuing our story. "When did you decide to forgive me for that?" I said.

"You think I've forgiven you? How do you know I'm not just waiting to get my revenge?"

"You have a pretty good opportunity right now. You have a weapon on you?"

"Nah, it's not the right time. Your parents know we went on this walk together. I'd have to walk back and kill them, as well."

"No, really. When did you decide to forgive me?"

He was quiet for a moment. Although we'd played this game before we didn't usually give one another too many details.

"I think it was the third time I came to visit you, when you were in the lockdown unit. After I'd lost my job. Do you remember? You told me that you'd done bad things, but that you did them for good reasons. And you told me that you were pretty sure that you were going to get caught, that there was a construction project next to your house, and that a well was going to be uncovered, and that was where you put all your secrets."

"I did tell you all that, didn't I?"

"You did."

"It felt good. Like I was taking it out of my hands, giving you all this information that you could have used against me. Why didn't you tell anyone?"

"I don't know, honestly. Some of it was that I was no longer a police detective, that they'd fired me and I didn't owe them anything, but maybe most of it was that I was a little bit in love with you. I guess I wanted to save you, because, even though you'd clearly done some bad things, you needed saving. I'm getting embarrassed so I'm going to change the subject. You heard that Joan Grieve is dead?"

"I did hear that. How did she die?"

"She had a massive brain hemorrhage. That's what I heard."

"Are you glad about it?"

"I am glad. I don't think she was a good person, exactly . . ."

"Not someone worth saving," I said.

"Right. Not someone worth saving."

We were at the pond now, a pair of crows on the other side talking to one another in strangled caws, and Henry was leaning against a tree, still breathing a little hard from the walk.

"Do you remember what I asked you when it looked like you were going to be released without a trial?"

"I do," I said. "You asked me if I was ever going to kill again."

"And you said?"

"I said that I would make every effort to never hurt another living soul."

"Uh-huh," Henry said. "It just seems amazing to me that Joan, after suffering the tragedy of what happened to her husband, would suddenly die from a brain hemorrhage."

"She was a rotten apple, Henry. To the core."

"I know she was."

"And maybe if she were still alive that would mean that your life was in danger."

"I've thought of that, as well. I did know things about her."

We walked back, quiet at first, but when we reached the meadow, Henry said, "Did you know that I came down here, when you were still in the hospital, back when they were digging up this meadow?"

"I thought you might have, but you never told me for sure."

"I came here on a weekend, and I found the meadow. There were bulldozers and diggers but nobody was working so I walked all around, looking for that well."

"You didn't find it?"

"Actually, I did. It had caved in a little, but I dropped a rock down and it seemed as though it was about twenty feet deep. I stood there for about half an hour trying to decide what to do." He was quiet and we kept walking. Eventually he said, "There was a pile of dirt near the well and I found a shovel and pushed some of that dirt over to cover it up. It was a very strange experience."

"Strange because you'd made a strange decision," I said.

"That's right. I don't suppose you want to tell me what I covered up that day."

I thought for about thirty seconds and then said, "There were two bodies in there. One was a man who came and stayed at this house when I was fourteen years old. He was a predator. The other was the man who murdered Ted and Miranda Severson."

"Thanks for telling me that much," Henry said.

"They're just skeletons now," I said, "but they're my skeletons."

Henry laughed dryly. "Why didn't you tell anyone?" I said.

"I don't know, exactly."

Henry left that night, a little before dinner. My parents were both bitterly disappointed, especially my father. But they said their good-byes, and I walked Henry to his car in the early dusk.

"My father is desolate. You'll come back, I hope."

"I don't know if I will."

"I'd understand that, too."

"Remember that game we played last night, authors who can see the world and authors who can only imagine it?"

"Uh-huh."

"It's the same with love, I think. Some people fall in love because they are excellent observers and they can see what is in front of them. And some people fall in love because they only imagine what is in front of them. They construct something that isn't there."

"You're probably right about that."

"I'm not trying to be as cryptic as I sound," Henry said. "Just thinking out loud. And maybe I'm trying to tell you why I won't come back."

"I get it. Do you want to know what I think about love?"

"Maybe," he said, and smiled.

"I think that romantic love, not family love, is the most destructive force on earth. It's the only thing that makes otherwise good people hurt one another."

"It doesn't have to."

"It does, actually. I'm not talking about what people will *do* for love. I'm talking about what people do *to* the ones they love. They break each other's hearts."

"There are probably some couples who don't do that to one another."

"Sure," I said. "But very few. And even with the happiest couples, one of them will die first at the end. We all eventually wind up in a tragedy."

We stood for a moment in silence, both of us starting to shiver a little, and Henry said, "So, it's a good thing that you're not in love with me."

"Yes, I suppose it is," I said.

Henry smirked at me. "I actually appreciate your honesty. I've thought about this a lot, about me loving you and you not loving me back. I think it's fine. I actually think it's greedy that humans expect the ones they love to love them back. They don't expect it from books, or from movies, or from nature. Why do we expect it of people? Maybe my love is better because you don't love me in return?

"And now I can tell from the expression on your face that it is time for me to leave."

I laughed, while stepping into his arms for a hug. Then we looked at one another, his face tinged purple, and deeply shadowed, in the dusk. He touched his forehead to mine and brought a hand to the side of my neck. I kissed him lightly on the lips.

After his car had disappeared down the driveway I stood in the cold for a moment, thinking about what he'd just said. That the best kind of love was one-sided, so long as there were no expectations about it going both ways. I did worry that Henry might hope that there was some kind of future for us, despite the fact he said that he didn't. But I'd already decided to trust him, for better or worse.

I turned back to my parents' house, walking slowly toward it, my father in the downstairs living room window, watching for my return.

ACKNOWLEDGMENTS

Angus Cargill, Mireya Chiriboga, Caspian Dennis, Isabelle Fang, Emily Fisher, Bianca Flores, Kaitlin Harri, David Highfill, Evan Hunter, Sophia Ihlefeld, Tessa James, Lyssa Keusch, Jennifer Gunter King (anything right about archival library work is due to her, and anything wrong is due to me), John D. MacDonald, Libby Marshall, Sophie Portas, Barbara Pym, Josh Smith, Nat Sobel, Virginia Stanley, John Updike, Sandy Violette, Judith Weber, Phoebe Williams, Adia Wright, and Charlene Sawyer.